Coroskirr

The ache in Kate's heart has brought her home to Coroskirr, that lonely place on the lovely west coast of Scotland, where dreaming islands shadow the horizon. Here, others too are drawn—by the spell of its peace and beauty, and by their own needs. Ninian, the musician and new laird of Coroskirr. Alastair, twisted by early tragedy. Jimmy McCann, on the run . . .

From the meeting of these lives the story is born—a story of love, gentle and tender, of past and present, of hurt and healing, of desperation and of hope.

JENNY ROBERTSON, herself a Scot, draws on family roots for the setting of *Coroskirr*. At present she lives in Edinburgh, spending part of the year in St Petersburg, where she and her husband are working. Jenny has written numerous novels and has also published several volumes of poetry.

*To Sylvia, with many
thanks*

COROSKIRR

Jenny Robertson

A LION PAPERBACK
Oxford · Batavia · Sydney

Copyright © 1992 Jenny Robertson

The author asserts the moral right
to be identified as the author of this work

Published by
Lion Publishing plc
Sandy Lane West, Oxford, England
ISBN 0 7459 2074 8
Albatross Books Pty Ltd
PO Box 320, Sutherland, NSW 2232, Australia
ISBN 0 7324 0608 0

First edition 1992

A catalogue record of this book is available
from the British Library

Printed and bound in Great Britain by
Cox and Wyman Ltd, Reading

Oh, I do believe
Dust will turn the seed
Home

Recovery by Runrig

1

'Do you mind if I join you?'

Kate looked up from the guidebook she was scanning—and, waist level, glimpsed a belt of some sort of shiny material buckled with polished bone.

'Of course not. I'll move my things. I've almost finished,' she said pleasantly, piling crockery together to make room for the stranger who squashed himself and a plate of salad into her corner of a crowded food bar just off Princes Street.

Seated, the owner of the belt gave her a smile. He was in his mid-thirties she guessed, from the vantage point of her twenty-eight years, with dark wavy hair and surprisingly dark blue eyes.

'What a fantastic belt!' she observed. 'I couldn't help noticing—right at eye level. That brilliant sheen . . . mouth watering!'

'Just bits of salmon skin . . .' he said, with easy nonchalance.

'I thought so,' Kate returned, adding, 'I hope you don't mind my remarking—but it's so unusual.'

'Aye—I fell for it at once,' he smiled, and there was a directness in his manner now which put Kate at ease. 'There are some on display at a craft fair in the Assembly Rooms, not too far from here, as a matter of fact. I guess you're visiting Edinburgh?' He nodded towards her book.

Kate shook her head, lifting a slim hand in a dismissive gesture. 'No, not visiting, just travelling through. I wouldn't mind coming back for a proper visit some time. It's a wonderful city—though I suppose you get hacked off with tourists,' she added sympathetically.

'Depends on the tourist,' he said with a smile which made Kate feel she was one of the all-right ones. 'I must say, I like variety,' he went on. 'The world in a nutshell.'

'That's it,' Kate agreed. 'The global village. I like it too.'

Or did once, she thought, remembering student days, friendships and encounters. *Once bitten*... she reminded herself, ruefully. And now was on a quest, away from people, into her family's unknown past...

'You say you're not staying long?' he asked, breaking into her thoughts. His was a singing voice, warm, lilting. It appealed to Kate.

'I'm heading west,' she told him firmly, tilting her chin. Someone with a journey she has to make.

'The further west the better,' he smiled, pausing, his fork poised. A ring slipped on his fourth finger. A wedding ring? Or was that some sort of heraldic device?

Careful, Kate, she found herself thinking, as he scooped up salad. *Can you ever be sure?* She warmed to his easy manner, nevertheless: self-assured, yet open and friendly.

'I'm going to a place called Coroskirr... is that far enough west?'

She saw his face change, although he replied casually enough, between mouthfuls, 'One step more and you're set for America.'

'You've been to Coroskirr, then?' she queried, and her attention went back to those sensitive hands as he pulled his bowl of fruit salad towards him with fingers which seemed both pliant and controlled.

'Just once—wide shores and a rainswept sky.'

'Sepia,' she said—explaining—'There was an old framed photograph in my grandmother's house.'

'Your folks were from Coroskirr?' he asked, earnestly.

'My grandfather, but he never went back. His sister, my great-aunt Morag who's a lot younger, has always wanted us to come for a holiday; but my parents preferred the south. Nothing to do in Coroskirr. Too far away, too cold and wet.'

'But you're going just the same?'

'I like far places,' Kate told him, with that determined lift of her chin.

He smiled. 'You're going to the right place, then. Beauty and peace. But it's almost deserted.'

'I suppose everyone left for fame and fortune like my MacDonald grandfather,' Kate hazarded, and was surprised to hear him say, 'Forced away by landlords who preferred the profits from sheep.' Then he smiled again. 'Sorry. Here you are, setting off for the land your grandfather left. I'll toast you in apple juice for want of *uisghe-bha—* whisky.' He raised his glass. 'Blessings upon your pilgrimage.'

Kate looked startled. Her eyes held his. 'Pilgrimage!' she exclaimed. 'That's exactly it.'

This is amazing, she thought. *How could he know?*

'Tell me more,' he invited. 'How about something to drink? Coffee?'

Kate glanced at her watch. 'That would be nice,' she agreed. 'My train's at one. Almost an hour left.'

'That's fine,' he said and held out his hand in a gesture both polished and intimate. 'By the way, I'm Ninian. And you are?'

She smiled up at him. 'I'm Kate.'

She watched him in the queue, the salmon-skin belt gleaming round his waist, the rest of him quietly crumpled in natural fibres. *Is he on his own? He must be. I love his style, his easy courtesy* . . .

'You've made me feel very welcome,' she said as he returned to the table with their coffee cups.

He smiled. 'To aid a pilgrim is to share the grace.'

'Grace?' she repeated, and again that sense of surprise . . . 'Ninian, you're uncanny!' she said impulsively. 'Fey. Are

9

you sure that's *just* salmon skin round your middle?' she teased. 'I'm beginning to think you can read my thoughts! Grace is what it's all about—ever since last year . . . I went to Greece with friends.'

She gave her attention to the froth round her cup. *To help me get over the loss. Help me forget.*

'My business is music,' she heard him say. 'Do I detect a change of key?'

Kate looked up. 'You are uncanny. Yes, you're right. There is.' She sipped her coffee. 'It happened on the last day of the holiday. I went for a walk in the hills behind the place we were staying.'

'Parched earth, wild thyme,' he prompted.

'Goats,' she nodded across at him. 'Their bells sounded like a waterfall. Anyhow, I found a well with a broken marble edge. The sun was hot—like a blanket—you know the way it is? But the water in the well was cold.'

Half unconsciously she stretched out her hand. It brushed against his, and his fingers caught and held hers for a moment. 'So you put your hands in the wishing well?' he smiled.

'Not a wishing well, exactly.' She paused. 'I made a promise, though. I swirled water into bubbles, and, oh, I don't know . . . You know how a well like that—it was obviously very old—might have been considered sacred?'

'Hung with apples for the garlanded maid or youth led as an offering to the gods. Do you know those hazel eyes of yours are a total giveaway? I can see how much all this means to you. So you made a promise?'

She hesitated. *Apples . . . yes, he's right: I thought of apples green as grace for each drowned Ophelia afloat with wreaths of rue. Rue for sorrow; apples bringing healing after loss. Arthur's Isle of Apples, Avalon . . . Would there ever be such apples of grace for me?*

Aloud, she said, lightly. 'You really do seem like a sort of guardian angel—a guide to help me chart my pilgrimage. The promise? That's an easy one. I decided to take up my great-

10

aunt's invitation and come to Coroskirr. Not just as a tourist, though, as you so immediately understood. Wasn't Arthur's Isle of Apples in the west? Tir-nan-Og—all that sort of thing... Though you mustn't think I'm naive enough to suppose there'll be a well with healing waters in Coroskirr,' she added with her usual directness.

'You never know your luck,' he countered. 'The ancient Celts believed in the hazels of wisdom and the salmon of knowledge—and they didn't go to Greece to find them. Haven't you heard the story of the Well at the World's End? I tell you, I've been to Coroskirr. A holy spring may very likely be found on those thyme-covered hills within sight of the Hebrides... Let me give you my phone number. Perhaps you'd like to get in touch when you get back. I'll be interested to hear about your pilgrimage to Coroskirr.'

Kate got out her diary and turned to a blank page. He reached for it and wrote his number—a personal touch, she thought, liking him for it.

'Ninian Bruce,' she read. 'Now I've got you in black and white in your own handwriting.'

She picked up her rucksack. 'I'd better get going.'

'Let me help you with that pack,' Ninian offered. 'The station's on my way... One o'clock,' he repeated as they paused to cross Princes Street. 'Change at Glasgow,' he went on, negotiating the crowded pavement. 'You should be in Oban by five.'

'Yes, then a ferry across to Mull. I'm looking forward to that—then I get a bus across the island and there's another ferry crossing after that.'

Ninian nodded as they headed down into the station. 'It'll be platform fourteen.' He indicated the way with those long, sensitive fingers. 'Perhaps there's too much of the global village now...' A note of irritation sharpened his voice as he tried to make himself heard above the noise of loudspeakers, the clamour of the station.

'Please don't feel you have to wait,' Kate assured him. 'It looks as if the train's in.'

He lifted her rucksack onto the train. 'I wish you God-speed,' he said. She felt the pressure of his fingers on hers, smiled into those blue eyes and waved from the door as his tall figure disappeared into the crowds.

Would she contact him again? Once she would have rushed into an encounter, loving the intimacy which comes from sharing ideas, the otherness in another; and Ninian appealed to her enormously. But too much had happened over these last two years and, as the train pulled away from under the Castle, Kate was content to sit back and immerse herself in a landscape which her forebears had once called their own.

At Oban, Kate crossed the station concourse packed with tartan paraphernalia out to the pier where she boarded the Mull ferry.

As the boat turned into the open sea and islands she couldn't name swung into view on every horizon, Ninian's words echoed in her mind: *Blessings upon your pilgrimage*.

Pilgrimage, and perhaps a homecoming too? This un-known man who had toasted her with apple juice had understood this.

It was a year ago exactly, she thought, leaning over the rail, watching a grey sea and an overcast sky. Dead at birth, my twin daughters who never were. A year ago.

There were few passengers, and Kate was the only person travelling alone. She was glad of solitude, and stayed on the upper deck, well wrapped against the wind; glad too of the warmth of the bus which ground through Mull's deserted glens where rowans flowered in roofless crofts.

A smaller ferry took her back to the mainland, and this time Kate was the only passenger. The evening sun struggled through the clouds. A ruined castle took the light. *A land of ruin and loss,* she thought, this homeland she sought. But Achnacrois pier was bright with the evening sunlight. A tall white-haired woman in old-fashioned tweeds waved. There was no mistaking Aunt Morag, until then known to Kate only as a voice on the telephone, a figure in family photographs. Sailors helped Kate ashore and Morag MacDonald drew her great-niece to her.

'Kate, my dear, how good to see you at last! Welcome to the land of your fathers! I know you'll be very happy here.'

*

The weather was chilly, this May day, but during the afternoon the sun appeared and Donald Cameron moved away from his seat beside the fire.

Shaky, but with characteristic purpose, Donald made his way across to the window and looked out at the shore of Achnacrois.

The Island of Mull lay opposite, its glens deep in shadow. To the right, twisting across bare moorland like a length of knotted rope, ran the road which led seven miles across the hills to Coroskirr.

Coroskirr, Donald's birthplace, and the place of his childhood: a steep brae and then the sweep of blue—sea, islands and sky, merging together, slipping apart with the drift of cloud and light.

Ah yes, thought Donald, who often recalled the scene—but never let himself think long of the furthest bay along Coroskirr shore: Port-na-Tuinne, the Bay of the Wave. The new laird was to live there, it was said, but Dougal's mind veered from that place as hastily as the large seagull opposite, startled by children freed from school and careering across the rocky shore made bright by the sudden appearance of the sun.

The lassie Kate will have a bit of sun after all, thought Donald, pleased, wanting Morag's kinswoman to see Coroskirr at its best. And what was it Morag had said, which Donald hadn't caught and couldn't quite mind, but it had to do with an ache, a sorrow?

She will have been in love, thought Donald, alone himself after forty-five years of marriage . . .

Mothers called children in for their tea. Donald made his own: scrambled egg on toast. And, having eaten and listened

13

to the six o'clock news, he sat beside the fire, his thoughts wandering back into the past he had shared with Margaret. Forty-five years—and they'd known each other longer than that... It was a long, long road for a body to wander. He missed Margaret sorely, and knew with each nightfall that his night too was near; but, he was sure, the onrush of all-engulfing dark would be an awakening to something sweeter than youth and more wholesome than strength. He would see Margaret again, and that other dear dead one too, the drowned son...

Busy in the past, Donald forgot to switch on the electric kettle in readiness for the visitor from England—and there was the old grandmother clock chiming quarter to the hour. A quarter to eight! It was time for Morag to be calling by with her great-niece Kate, just off the last ferry.

2

'It's yourself, lassie. Come away in, you're very welcome. Come in, Morag, and how are you today?'

'Fine, Donald. Have you the tea made? I'm sure Kate's ready for a cup.'

'The tea will be ready as soon as the kettle boils,' promised Donald. 'I meant to have it on for you, but I've been away in a *dwam*—a daydream,' he added for Kate's benefit. 'Come and get a wee heat at the fire. Let me help you off with that. Yon's a heavy pack. It puts me in mind of the days when women carried creels,' he added, helping Kate, while Morag was warming the teapot.

'How are you, after your long journey?' Donald went on.

'Fine. I like travelling,' Kate assured him.

'It's good of you to call in here. I'm sure you'd rather have gone straight to Coroskirr, but your grandfather Iain and I were at the school together. I couldn't let his kinswoman pass my door. And how are all your family?'

'They're fine, thanks. My parents are off on holiday themselves,' Kate said, ' . . . to the Far East.' And as she spoke she was conscious of the contrast between her parents' life and the simplicity of Donald's front room—though no doubt he thought it very modern with its night storage heaters. Suddenly aware of what she might seem to be taking for granted, Kate turned to Morag, who was clothing the

15

teapot in a knitted cosy. 'It's kind of you to have me. I hope I won't be any trouble.'

'Trouble? Our own kith and kin? No, no, we're delighted you've come. Except—I'm a wee bit worried you'll be lonely: there's only one person in Coroskirr just now beside ourselves.'

'My son Alastair's up for a week,' said Donald, and exchanged a worried glance with Morag.

'He knows Coroskirr like the back of his hand,' said Morag. 'He's a great one for fishing. I'm sure he'd take you out in the boat, if you fancied a trip.'

'A boat? Of course, the sea.'

'Yes,' said Donald. 'Alastair loves the sea.'

Kate looked across at her host. His lean face had the high cheekbones and close-set eyes of the Celt. There was wisdom in those faded eyes, Kate thought, and a rueful humour. *I'm glad I called in,* she thought, and couldn't know that Donald, thinking about his son, was feeling again the pang that Alastair had chosen to stay in the old family cottage at Coroskirr, rather than here with him.

I'm being selfish, he told himself reproachfully. *Alastair has his own problems. He'll likely invite me out for a meal in the hotel with Morag, and of course I won't go, which will annoy him.*

Annoy him, and increase his sense of guilt. Donald sighed. These uneasy feelings between Alastair and himself had lasted more than half a lifetime, ever since the breaking waves of Port-na-Tuinne had drowned the elder brother. A sense of duty had forced Alastair to follow his dead brother's chosen profession—in an act of self-renunciation not unlike many marriages of an earlier time, entered upon to legitimize the unacceptable. And his mother had been too fond, his father too grief-stricken, to realise what their second son was really doing with his life.

Out of the whirlpool of these thoughts, which nowadays often interrupted his sleep, Donald said to Kate (his pleasant blue eyes now shuttered): 'Alastair is my younger son. Our eldest boy, Kenneth, was drowned.'

'Drowned . . .' Kate cradled cold fingers around her china teacup. Loss, yes, she knew only too well; and, oh, waters of birth, waters of death, the separation is for ever. 'You lost your wife recently too,' she said, with what she feared was clumsy sympathy.

Donald sighed, then his face relaxed. 'Margaret is at peace, and my greatest comfort is that she is with our son again. Perhaps I'll be closing my own eyes soon, and finding those I hold most dear. When Kenneth was lost, for many years I longed for there to be no God, no hereafter. Sometimes nothingness is more to be desired than being. Ah, forgive me! But there *is* a hereafter, a great and splendid brightness. It presses all about me and I know Margaret is there.' He smiled.

Liking his sincerity, Kate smiled back. *He's a dear,* she thought, *a poet in his own way. There's a dignity about him too*.

'I'm glad I didn't go straight to Coroskirr,' she said, conscious of the need to speak slowly at his pace. 'You're different—in touch. Perhaps it's being so close to the sea,' she added thoughtfully, holding out her hands to the fire. 'No one at home seems in focus.'

'We see that from the television,' Donald agreed. 'Certainly Glasgow seemed a busy place when I first went away to study there.'

'When was that?' asked Kate.

'Way back,' said Donald. 'Folk were all moving away. The War began it, the First War, you know.'

'There was no work here, you see,' said Morag from her seat beside the table.

'Only hard toil, for men and women—especially the women,' Donald recalled. 'The young ones started to drift away. The men went to sea, like your grandfather, and the women went into service in the big houses and hotels.'

'Or nursing, like me,' said Morag. 'There was more Gaelic than English spoken in the Nurses' Home at times.'

'Do you both speak Gaelic?' asked Kate.

Her new friends laughed. 'Yes, we do,' Aunt Morag said.

'Now, I'll just wash those cups and we'll away, or you'll be thinking you'll never get to Coroskirr today.'

'Leave the cups,' Donald said. 'It will be a fine evening on Coroskirr shore.'

'Won't you come with us?' asked Kate impulsively. Donald shook his head, and Morag sighed, for those shutters were firmly in place, and he hid solitary behind them.

'May I come and visit you here?' asked Kate.

'Now, that would be a great pleasure for me,' he returned with a smile.

Then they were off, waving from the car, and Donald, turning back into his room, told himself that he was being stubborn—selfish too: for he had not asked the lassie a thing about herself. Margaret would have done better, he knew. He could almost feel her at his elbow, reproving him for failing to understand unspoken thoughts she so often perceived— though never those of her own younger son.

Donald sighed, and went outside for a breath of evening air. It was a bonny evening, right enough, that lifted his heart as he sat on a bench overlooking the sea. Words from the Scripture in Gaelic and in English came to him. His mind sang psalms as he sat. He was greatly comforted. Having been for a long time in the dark, Donald knew how to hold on to these moments of comfort. The thread which bound him to the white-feathered Spirit dove was fragile indeed, the comfort tenuous, but it was life to hold, and, well he knew, death to lose.

The same evening sun lit Morag and Kate on their way to Coroskirr. The narrow road which lurched giddily across peat bog and barren rock seemed to Kate desolate beyond words, but her great-aunt obviously took this dearth of human comfort as much for granted as a southern motorist takes a crowded motorway, or a street kid takes the smell of chips.

A final brae, a last steep bend, and . . .

'That's us.' Morag stopped the car to let Kate look at the view.

'So that's Coroskirr! You know, Aunt Morag, I've seen this bay in sepia ever since I was a child.'

'So your grandfather had a photograph?' his younger sister asked, looking carefully ahead as she talked.

'In the spare bedroom. I used to lie and look at it night and morning, but I never guessed it would be as beautiful as this. I've never seen beaches like these—so white and empty.'

'Empty indeed,' agreed Morag, starting the engine again. 'I'm pleased to hear that your grandfather didn't forget about Coroskirr altogether...'

'No, he didn't forget,' Kate assured her. 'He told us stories about it too. I remember he said schoolchildren had to take a piece of peat with them for the fire.' She saw her aunt smile at this. 'His stories seemed as if they came from another world, but I remember thinking: this is my life too, this is where I belong.'

'And so you've come at last—and I'm very glad,' said Morag, taking the car slowly downhill.

'I am too,' Kate assured her.

'The new generation,' her great-aunt smiled. 'Your mother keeps me up to date with the news. You must tell her how much I appreciate it,' she added. 'It's so easy for families to lose touch...' She paused to point out of the window. 'Our family had the cottage over yonder.'

'The one that's been burnt? What a mess! What happened to it?'

'It *is* a mess,' Morag agreed, turning the car up a bumpy track towards her own house. 'It could have been an electrical fault—though I have my doubts.'

'You mean, someone might have set fire to it deliberately?'

'The timing made me just a wee bit suspicious. It happened last autumn, when the last of the holiday makers were away. I'm left here on my own then, Kate.'

'All winter? It must be desperately lonely!' Kate said.

She'd spoken in her usual quick, impulsive way, and Morag's face lit in real appreciation as she nodded, 'It is indeed. If I didn't have the car, I'd have to move. The car, and, of course, Donald,' she added briskly. 'I retired here to be near him and Margaret. Anyway, the cottage. It's changed hands several times since your parents sold it. I didn't want it. I'd been left the house that's ahead of us now . . . There was talk that the new owners were planning a salmon farm.'

'Wouldn't that be a good thing—bring jobs to the area?'

'Aye, but there are some who don't like it,' Morag said, switching off the engine.

Kate eased herself out of the car. Silence: the swish of the wind, larksong, a cuckoo calling. 'It's too sad to think of trouble happening here,' she said, remembering what Ninian had said about beauty and peace at that chance encounter in Edinburgh. 'It's another world,' she added. 'Only the road—and that phone box to keep you from being quite cut off. Nothing else—except sea and sand and sky and islands on every horizon.'

Morag named them for her: Tiree and Coll, Muck, Rhum and Eigg and a glimpse of the cliffs of Canna.

'Names like a song. Thank you so much for inviting me. I'm so glad I've come.'

Morag smiled and led Kate into a cottage with a living-room and a kitchen downstairs, a bathroom and two small bedrooms under the eaves.

Hills rose steeply behind the cottage. Seabirds called. The wind sang, inviting Kate outside; and, after they had eaten in Morag's quiet kitchen, filled with the westering sun, Kate went out to explore her new surroundings. She kicked off her sandals and walked barefoot, her insteps whipped by sharp marram grass. Rabbits scurried into burrows. Sheep, their lambs at their sides, were everywhere. A fishing-boat passed on the horizon and a yacht dipped by. Kate jumped from the dunes into a sandy bay where waves broke with their own wild music.

A pilgrim, making a ritual out of small gestures, Kate walked into the foaming water—and hopped on chilled feet back up the sand.

Perfection has its drawbacks . . .

Smoke from Aunt Morag's fire rose into the air, but no life stirred in the white cottages dotted around the shore. Their windows stared blankly at the sea, and those burnt-out roof joists stood like a sinister question mark among the rest.

How sad, Kate thought again, *that trouble could happen here*. But she pushed that thought away and gave all her attention to the wonder of this western sea.

Perched on a rock, Kate watched—made small at first by the immensity; then magnified by stillness. She was chilly now, and her bare feet were very cold, but she kept her eyes fixed on the sea. The waves were herself. The water swirled in her being: water of child-birth, water of drowning; wet-eyed mother watching the water; hazel-eyed lass, pregnant, swelling, watching the waves for the boat that went seaward, never returning. Would watching bring wisdom? Was God all that emptiness, dwarfing humanity, offering sustenance, energy, drowning? The question tugged at Kate's heart, and she knew that she was right to come to this empty place, to the kinswoman who made her feel so much at home.

Time passed, as she sat chilled and stiff. Stillness intensified, and now all sorrows were sea-sorrow, all inexplicables sea-sounds and all darkness this northern never-dark. The hills behind her, flushed pink now in the late evening light, isolated this shore from cities and commerce. Ahead dreamed and floated deep-shadowed islands. Beyond were countries undiscovered, a no-land, a dream. Hugging her updrawn knees, Kate watched the waves lift and splinter with light, watched a small boat return to the shore, its steersman beach it high on the sand; and now lights twinkled in a line of cottage windows on the headland across the bay, and Kate returned homewards to her great-aunt's coal fire.

Practical as ever, Morag had hot chocolate ready. 'This will warm you. I've milk today, there was some in the shop for a change.

'The shop's a disaster,' she went on, as Kate curled up beside the fire. 'A couple took it over last year, and they're not making a go of it at all ... You'll not have seen our loveliest bay, Port-na-Tuinne?' she went on, obviously longing to share Coroskirr with her great niece. 'It's over the cliff road yonder. The ground's too rough for me, and it's a place of sorrow too,' she added. 'It was there, we suppose, that Kenneth Cameron was drowned, as you were hearing.'

'I see,' Kate said slowly, and thought: *that old tragedy again*. Aloud she asked, 'How old was he when it happened?'

'Seventeen—a fine boy, and he loved Coroskirr. His great ambition was to become a minister. Yes, he was a fine lad, but a wee jealous streak came out in his feelings for Alastair.' Morag paused, interrupting herself to explain. 'I want you to know the story, Kate. You were so kind to Donald. But, you know, I want this to be a real holiday for you. You are able to drive, I suppose? Use my car as much as you like. Well, now, where was I?'

'A jealous streak,' Kate prompted.

'Ah yes—he shouldn't have been jealous, for he was quicker than Alastair at almost everything, and, besides, his father loved him. Yes,' said Morag, her eyes on the fire, 'his father loved him, but his mother had that wee bit extra feeling for Alastair. There were sometimes bad feelings between the boys, though they seldom came to blows. I don't think Margaret would have allowed it. She was a fine, understanding woman, but she was often blind where her own were concerned. So they wounded each other with words. So it was this time...' Firelight played across Morag's face—a face full of character and kindliness. She had been a red-head once, Kate thought, from her fair complexion. How old was she? In her mid-sixties, probably, and wearing her years well; about fifteen years younger than grandfather Iain, the last of a large family. The others had all died or gone to Canada; and Kate half smiled into the fire, remembering how, when she had been small and hearing tales of faraway Scotland, 'died' and 'gone to Canada' had seemed one and the same thing.

'Alastair was always the one for the water,' Morag continued, her native Gaelic giving her English a music all its own. 'He could handle a boat like an experienced man. You'll maybe have seen him out in the bay this evening?'

'I saw someone bring a boat in just now.'

'That would have been Alastair. Well, there was a quarrel, and Kenneth launched his canoe into the sea. It was a bad summer, no weather for a boat. Alastair, his face stricken as a fourteen-year-old's should never be, told me afterwards that he had shouted to his brother to come back, but the wind took the words away—and anger has a way of shutting ears too, and maybe not quite making voices carry. The last he saw of Kenneth was him paddling the canoe through those rough seas. The canoe was found later, and Donald stood all night in the bay yonder, Port-na-Tuinne, the Bay of the Wave. All night and all the next day—the doctor made him go to bed after that. The next day he was down there again, but there was nothing, nothing at all.'

'That's terrible.'

'A tragedy indeed, and Donald has never got over it; but to my mind what happened to Alastair was tragic too, and neither parent saw it.'

'What did happen?'

'He became a minister instead of his brother . . .' Kate must have looked puzzled, for Morag explained, 'That's our Scots name for a clergyman. A minister—no, it was more like a cloak for his guilt and grief. He married, and has a wee daughter—that's her photo you see on the stair. But things have broken down. Alastair took up teaching to ease the strain on his marriage, but they divorced last year, and he's come here on his own.'

'I see . . . You're obviously very close to Donald and Alastair . . .'

'Aye, we're friends from way back. And of course, coming from Coroskirr, we've stuck together all these years. There's so few of us left,' she sighed. 'Now, there's the fire nearly out . . . It's late, and you're a good listener, Kate. But this is your holiday. We can't have you thirled to an old woman and her tales. You must do your own thing, as they say . . . No, lassie I mean it. It means a lot to have you here.'

Touched by her aunt's words, Kate lent forward and let her hand rest on Morag's knee. Roughness of tweed, baggy, for Morag MacDonald would never hitch her skirt up those extra inches to keep it from becoming kneed... A good homespun feeling, like Morag herself. 'You said I'd be happy,' Kate reminded her aunt. 'I know I shall.'

On that note they went to bed. Tired, but still not feeling like sleep, Kate turned on the radio. Music drifted into her room: notes green as jade, clear as the sea which bounded this shore. Then the announcer's voice: 'The Scottish Chamber Orchestra played *A Song for Jane* by Ninian Bruce...'

Ninian Bruce! She recalled his long fingers with the ring on the left hand as he took her diary, wrote his name. *He said his business was music—and what music. For* Jane. *Forget him, Kate.*

Kate turned off the radio. Sea sounds filled the room as she drifted to sleep.

3

Early May sunlight dappled the polished floor of Ninian Bruce's Marchmont flat. Edinburgh looked its best at this time of year. The severe old lady became a bride, whose blossom softened the classical rectitude of Georgian squares and blew like confetti across the Meadows.

From the cobbled street below piped the shrill voices of nursery school children borne off to begin a decade and a half of socialization and learning. 'Learning should be fun,' the Head Teacher of the school opposite had once said to Ninian, trying to persuade him to run a music workshop. *What a fallacy,* thought Ninian. *Learning is sweat. Like breaking open new soil. They've engineered this myth that learning is child's play because too many young minds have fallen by the wayside. But it is only by the sweat of his brow that Adam earns his bread, and the reward is simply this: to see the long furrow shine.*

'Sheer plod makes plough down sillion shine.' The truth of that one line was set gem-like in its music, Ninian reflected, for the poet had made every syllable bright. Still, he had other things to think about today. There was the much-acclaimed young Danish composer, for a start, who was providing a symphony of Nordic austerity on Ninian's music centre; but Ninian, who had promised himself that he would study this latest music, gave the piercing woodwind and lonely strings little attention. The new laird of Achnacrois (with Coroskirr) had to sort through his papers.

And what a mixture they were: pencilled notes, title deeds, ancient parchments in handwriting he could barely decipher—these would have to be placed in archives, thought Ninian. Yellowing newspapers, two centuries old, reported the health of the monarch, George III:

The King, we are assured, is much better. He has been perfectly recollected for *seven hours*.

And again:

The King was so well on Saturday last as to play piquet with the Queen, with as much recollection as at any former period of his life.

Did douce Edinburgh citizens rejoice at the news of their sovereign's tranquillity? Scarce half a century before, they had flocked after the rival claimant to the Crown, the Bonnie Prince; and windswept wynds had skirled with Jacobite strains.

Ninian himself had set some of those Jacobite airs into a tapestry of sound which had won him considerable acclaim at the last Edinburgh Festival. He should be working on a new piece now, but, against all his principles suddenly made owner of bog and rock, Ninian set himself to the job in hand: he was never one for paperwork unless music could be made out of it.

Those reports on King George III's health had a melody rich in irony as well as pity. Ninian returned to them. *Perfectly recollected*. A rocking movement in a major key... He switched off his radio and went across to the piano, trying out sounds with skilful, questing hands. *For seven hours*. One discordant note now, perhaps from the brass. He tried it in the bass clef—not quite right—tried again. A lull in the storm of distress, a brief flowering hope. A lighter note then, to be taken by the flutes—none of the Nordic chill of that Scandinavian virtuoso, whose work seemed to Ninian to lack feeling.

Feeling. It was all important. And yet (he thought of Jane)—it caused hurt.

He turned back to the piano, but the impetus had gone. He surveyed his notes, hummed. There was something here, something for later. He must round it off with the same rocking melody, but in a minor key.

The phone rang.

'0020.'

'Ninian . . .'

'Jane! How are you?'

He pictured her: thick brown hair waving back from her face, troubled blue eyes, a singing mouth. Slender and tense, she came up to his shoulders. Impeccably educated, she had grown increasingly to feel that her mezzo-soprano voice for which he had composed some of his best songs, was only an echo—that her true creativity lay elsewhere, and that their relationship, far from leading to marriage as they had once hoped, was damaging her.

She would be wearing jade, cool on her lovely neck, each bead rounded like the notes of an oboe. Ninian had wanted to buy emeralds, but jade echoed her name, and among its virtues—he had read somewhere—was kindness. Jade can never be twisted—and had he not hoped this for their love?

'Are you busy?'

He thought of his papers, the new music about this sick King. 'Fairly . . .'

She must have heard his uncertainty. Her voice came to him crisply. 'How about fitting in a lunch-break? I've just bought a rather nice French cheese.'

Lunch with Jane—it was several months since he'd been in her New Town flat. 'Okay,' he heard himself agree. 'Thanks, Jane.'

He returned to his papers. It was hard to concentrate now. Here was a survey of the estate by its Victorian owner, Sir John Murray of Achnacrois. Ninian riffled through yellowed parchments. It was obviously a bad deal, the land which was now his, for he read:

The most part of arable land, wrought only by the spade, is exposed to sea blasts and oppressed by too many tenants. It is best suited for Cheviot sheep. It would seem proper to reduce the number of tenants, which will occasion the removal of a number of the poor.

Sir John Murray, an innovative landlord from the Borders, was quick to carry out his evictions, for a page from an incomplete diary noted:

The year of the removals began bitterly cold. There is much suffering among the people. Sir John purchased 500 bolls of meal, but it is all gone. If there is any truth in the old adage 'as the day lengthens so the cold strengthens' we may expect to see distress increase.

Yet Sir John's efforts proved vain and the heirs of his inheritance wrote in despair: 'Land in abundance, but no one bids a farthing for it.'

A ruined land, then, was Ninian's heritage, whose roads had been cut by paupers, the women knitting as they bore creels of stones, the children, barefoot and starving, hewing hard rock—for only the industrious could receive the meagre relief.

And now the estate consisted of two dozen folk living along the shore of Achnacrois; the pier and a single shop; a hotel and the parish church; while Coroskirr was occupied almost entirely by 'white settlers' who holidayed there. Odd how yesterday in Brewster's Bar he'd met that girl, Kate. What had drawn him to her? She was tall and vivid, if not actually beautiful: a tawny woman, brown hair with a hint of gold threaded through that shoulder-length mass of curls; a scattering of freckles across her cheekbones; those hazel eyes, an expressive mouth. A pilgrim he'd called her, and it turned out he'd been right. Indeed there seemed something other-worldly about her, even a hint of the Gael, despite her southern accent. She was on her way to her forebears' past and an elderly aunt. Well, that was all she would find in Coroskirr; little else but seals, and rare butterflies, ruins and driftwood. Was it, then, what one built of these poor off-scourings of tide and storm that counted? Was this the reason why, against every inclination, he had not refused the title deeds of the distant headland, encircled by islands and bounded on three sides by the Atlantic?

And what could he build except music? *Biggings* of sound, thought the laird of Coroskirr, adrift among his papers.

The sun rescued him. Ninian went out for a walk across the Meadows before he made himself coffee and set off to have lunch with Jane.

*

Sunlight woke Kate, and with it the thought of the wide wild shore beyond her window. She sprang out of bed and pulled the curtains back. Not a soul in sight (though from the kitchen she could hear the sounds of Aunt Morag singing a hymn tune). Waves lifted white crests on an indigo sea. Morning cloud drifted across the peaks of the highest island, and Kate raced into action: a splash of Coroskirr's soft, peaty water, a rummage in her rucksack for something to wear—no need for shoes. Just a quick brush of her thick hair which the wind would soon ruffle, and she ran downstairs to greet her aunt.

'Hi, Aunt Morag. Have you been up for ages? What a fantastic day! Do you mind if I go out straight away?'

'Of course not, Kate. But will you not have a quick bite of breakfast?' Morag began—but seeing Kate's eagerness, her aunt, who never missed meals unless in direst necessity, smiled and waved her away. Kate headed over the dunes

* Biggings = buildings

and clambered down to the shore. Bird tracks criss-crossed the bay. The only footprints were her own.

A small bird darted in front of her, piping shrill agitation, and on a bank of blown sand was a nest with three spotted eggs, so well camouflaged that Kate might easily have trodden on it.

She changed direction and headed towards rocks which jutted out to sea. This barren shore was quick with new life, and Kate had no wish to destroy any small fledgling.

Somewhere she'd read that the poet of the Gulag, Solzhenitsyn, once held in hands all too familiar with the paralysis of imprisonment a newly hatched duckling, and, knowing that he could crush it, felt instead such a respect for each atom of creation that the fluttering chick became an icon which brought him to faith.

Hurt had led the poet to glimpse the holy—Donald Cameron, whom she'd met yesterday, had allowed bereavement to deepen his sense of the eternal. 'There is a hereafter,' she heard his soft Highland voice affirm—above the shrilling seabirds, the wind whipping around her and the sound of the tide—'a great and splendid brightness. It presses all about me . . .'

Like the sea and the Hebrides, rising shadowy as dreams on the horizon. There should be music here, liquid as Ninian Bruce's lyrical piece she had heard last night—*A Song for Jane*—only blue, thought Kate, not green, blue as the islands; and she found herself humming the over-popularized *Road to the Isles*, written 'for the lads in France during the Great War'—lads whose loss, she was learning, left shores like these underpopulated. 'It's the blue islands that are pulling me away . . . wi' heather honey taste upon each name.'

Waves swirled around the rocks. The sand gleamed like pale honey; 'heather honey taste upon each name'. Yes, there was honey here among the clouds and islands. *Tir-nan-Og*. Kate recalled her conversation with Ninian: the sunlit isles of eternal youth lay in the West. Avalon also, she had told him. And Ninian had said—only yesterday, but it seemed an age away—that a holy spring might be found in Coroskirr, bringing healing for loss.

For I've known the loss of my nestlings, tiny still babies: waxen faces and swirling dark curls. Yes, Donald, like you I know what it is to lose the fruit of my body . . .

Tears pricked her eyes. Brain-damaged, Kate reminded herself. 'Better that they hadn't lived,' the midwife had reasoned in an effort to console her.

She hadn't cried; nor even wanted to touch those two little strangers who had been part of her, nor given them names . . .

A shadow fell across the rocks. A man stopped beside her. 'Hi! It's a fine day. You must be Kate. Morag sent me to find you. I'm Alastair Cameron.'

'Nice to meet you,' Kate smiled, holding out her hand.

'I've been hearing you made a big hit with my father,' Alastair said, returning her handshake. 'But you're cold . . . Here, have this.' He swung his quilted jacket round Kate's shoulders. She huddled gratefully into its warmth. 'I've coffee here,' Alastair was saying. 'Morag made you a flask.'

'I'm beginning to discover that's typical of her.' Kate unscrewed the flask. 'How about you, Alastair? Will you have some?'

He hesitated.

'I'm sure there's enough.'

He relaxed. 'Aye, go on then. That'll be lovely, thanks.'

Kate passed him the cup. 'How did you find me?' she asked, looking into eyes which were the same pale blue as his father's. He was medium height and lean, wearing climbing breeches, a chunky sweater, and knitted socks— Aunt Morag's handiwork? The wind tugged at his greying hair. *This is his world: he looks perfectly at home here,* she thought, as he answered, 'Find you? Easy. I followed your footprints. Bare feet.'

'Cold feet—but I like to be barefoot when I walk across sand.'

'A woman of the elements,' he said approvingly.

They sipped the fast cooling coffee in silence, watching sunlight fracture into multitudinous splinters across the waves.

31

'I could sit hours like this, just looking,' said Kate.

'Until an overgrown St Bernard comes along with a flask,' he said, and Kate smiled, warming to the note of laughter in his voice.

'A welcome St Bernard,' she assured him; and as he stowed the flask she added impulsively, 'I know how much you like Coroskirr—Aunt Morag told me.'

'I come whenever I can—and that's never enough . . . Did Morag tell you I'm here on my own?'

Kate nodded, gazing at the sea, iridescent as the length of salmon skin worn by the man she'd met yesterday. She remembered her aunt's story, Donald's shuttered eyes. On my own . . .

How must this man feel? she wondered. *He's spent his whole life struggling with loss.*

'I'm on my own too,' she offered. His eyes were fixed on her face, though his fingers pulled at a seapink. 'I think I can understand . . .'

She saw his face change—look confused, almost shocked. Hardly aware of what he was doing, he pulled the small pink flower to shreds. Then he recovered himself. 'What I came to say . . . well, it's just that I'm available if you want anyone to show you around.'

'That's kind of you. I'd love to explore.' He offered his hand to help her to her feet. Kate grasped it gladly, chilled and cramped from sitting on the rocks. 'Thanks for the helping hand.' Her mouth puckered mischievously. 'I'm glad Morag sent her resident St Bernard,' she told him, slipping his jacket from her shoulders.

'Do you not want to hang on to it?'

'No, it's okay. I'll take the flask back, shall I?'

'Fine. Will we meet at Morag's in about half an hour?'

*

Kate was chatting to Morag, ready with camera and walking-boots, when Alastair appeared along the track.

'Now, are you sure you're warm enough? Well, have a nice time,' said Morag hugging Kate.

'Thanks,' said Kate against a cheek soft as a wrinkling apple, toned by wind and rain to a colour which could never come from a bottle. 'I'm sure I will. I *do* like Alastair.'

Morag patted Kate's shoulder and released her with a smile.

*

They scrambled up steep flat rocks, and stopped to look down on the huddle of empty white cottages, the cluster of ruined stone houses, the moorland and long level sand which was Coroskirr.

'No wonder you love it,' said Kate. 'I'm hooked too.'

Alastair smiled. Kate took a photograph. 'Debasing perfection . . . No camera can do this justice.'

'You *are* hooked, aren't you?'

'Totally.'

'Want to go on?'

'Let's wait a moment longer.' She could tell he was pleased. 'It's not just the view, is it? It's the feel of the place. So empty. Just the wind. The sun. All sorts of sounds in the silence. Listen.'

Plaintive mews shrilled from a gully behind them.

'What are they?'

'Buzzards.'

'Odd that birds of prey should sound so lost.'

A lark spun long threads of song. A cuckoo added its tremulous chorus. Lambs cried above the endless plash of burn water, pouring from some hidden source deep in the veins of the hill.

'The well at the world's end . . .' *Did Alastair, who had spent all his boyhood summers here, know of that healing spring? Could she even ask him? There was a delicacy about this man, a restraint . . . Hemmed in like the hidden spring.*

'Let's go on,' Kate said.

Their route took them over the summit. It was too steep for talking. Once or twice Alastair reached out to give Kate a helping hand, and she nodded her thanks. Down the next hillside they scooped up burn water, splashed hands and faces, drank.

'We've got a choice of routes now. Through this glen—or up the next brae, a bit of scrambling and we drop down to the road just short of Coroskirr.'

'Another climb,' Kate decided. 'More puff but better views.'

And the wide seas and sweep of islands they saw from the top more than justified Kate's choice.

'Magic . . . There's only one thing which makes me sad.'

He looked at her quizzically.

'It's too empty. No people . . .'

'Some folk might say that's what makes it magic,' Alastair suggested. He seemed to like this sort of rueful irony. 'But I know what you mean . . . That's a nice wee camera . . . Would you like me to take a photo—get you in as well as the view?'

Kate positioned herself. 'Human interest among hilltops and islands . . . Thanks.'

'Very human and a whole lot of interest,' he told her, returning her camera.

Kate shot him a glance, a bit surprised. 'Mmm! Thanks!' she returned, a smile in her hazel eyes.

They set off again, side by side over smooth slabs of rock. Their talk flowed to the rhythm of their walking.

'What does Coroskirr mean?'

'*Skirr—sgurr*—means cliff, see over there.' Alastair pointed to a sheer headland to the north of the bay.

'Gaelic?'

'Norse. Viking raiders.'

'Of course. And Achnacrois?' And to herself she thought, *There's a lovely down-to-earthness about him, like his father, nothing to make me think he's a clergyman*. Aloud she said, teasing him. 'All this talk about languages! I mustn't forget I'm with an exponent of the language of heaven.'

He looked puzzled, then he shook his head. 'No, Kate. Not an exponent. A non-speaker, I'm afraid.' His face dulled. There was a heaviness about him which Kate was quick to counter.

'I'm sure that's not true! Anyway—other languages. What about Gaelic? Do you know any?'

'Now that *is* the language of heaven!' His smile rewarded her effort on his behalf. 'Not really. A few phrases, just. I can get the gist when folk are talking . . . Morag tells me you work with languages,' he added, and she detected appreciation of her as a person with an intellectual life of her own.

'Research,' she said. 'How children from non-English speaking homes cope with two cultures. That's one reason why I find your father so interesting. Aunt Morag, too. They belong to another way of life—which my grandfather disowned.'

'A dying race, and a dying language.'

'That's defeatist,' Kate protested, 'language is the lifeblood of a people'—and felt annoyed when Alastair said, 'Then Scotland needs a complete blood transfusion. We're a lost cause . . .'

They walked in silence which Alastair broke at last. 'Sorry, Kate. That sounded negative. This is your first day . . .'

'It's just that I care about lost causes,' Kate countered.

'Some causes are more lost than others,' Alastair returned, with his usual self-mockery.

'Maybe, but you still have to believe in them.'

He smiled at that, laying his hand briefly on her arm, cool from the wind which sang about them. 'Then there's hope for us yet.'

Did he mean Scotland? Himself? Or Coroskirr? Himself, more like, Kate thought, as she asked, 'Do you see any future for Coroskirr?'

They were looking over the bay as she spoke. 'No people,' she said again. 'Not a living soul.' Forced away by landlords who preferred the profits from sheep, Ninian had said, with real vehemence. He cared. But what was he doing for a place

35

like Coroskirr?

'Future? There's no future here. We have a new laird—but the last one just used the place for holidays, like everyone else. That's all that's left for Coroskirr. It's just waiting for some tycoon to set up a marina.'

'The people who were trying to start a salmon farm got attacked,' Kate reminded him.

'Too bad it had to be the very house your family once belonged to.'

'It doesn't matter. After all, Grandad opted out. Oh, but look at the sea! How could anyone ever leave a place like this!'

'D'you know something? I think the same,' Alastair said as Kate settled herself to survey the scene.

'No future—well, what about the past? Did much happen here?' Suddenly Kate felt it was important to find out, as Alastair said, matter-of-factly, 'Not much—the land was too poor. Folk only came once they'd been driven from further inland.'

Just as Ninian had said. 'When was that?' Kate asked.

'Last century. As a matter of fact, I've made copies of the parish records. I'll look them out for you, if you like.'

'Yes, please . . . Thanks very much. By the way, where is your cottage—can we see it from here?'

'The one by the shore,' Alastair pointed.

'Is that where your father was born? Didn't he want to retire here?'

'No, Kate.'

Something in his voice made her turn her head towards him. His eyes were troubled.

'My father will never come back to Coroskirr,' he said.

'Because of your brother? Your father told me about that yesterday.'

'Is that so? Just shows what an effect you've had on him,' Alastair said, his eyes returning to the sea. 'That was our last holiday in Coroskirr. They never came back. But once I was ordained—as if I'd made my atonement, at least as far as my mother was concerned—they let me have the cottage: it had stood empty almost ten years. I even came on honeymoon here . . . That was another mistake.'

'Don't, Alastair,' she said, and put her hand on his. 'We all make mistakes.'

Yes, Kumar and I two years ago . . . We hadn't planned to be lovers, going on holiday, but those friends of ours showed us our room—a large double bed.

One solitary bed, its feather quilt plump like newly risen dough, and Kumar Mukarjee's eyes inviting so eloquently, *Be truly Asian, bed before kiss.*

Now, on a West Highland hilltop was Kate the all-wise offering counsel? She moved her hand away. 'Tell me more about Coroskirr, Alastair. There would have been songs here once; laughter and stories.'

'Sure!' he said, as glad as herself to be on this safe topic. 'Morag knows plenty of songs. The new laird's a musician, seemingly. Oh, and you were asking about the meaning of Achnacrois.'

'So I was. Does the *crois* bit mean cross?'

'Aye, and *ach* means field. There's a stone cross by the shore.'

'A castle too,' Kate put in.

'True. This place belonged to the lords of Barra.'

'Barra? Is that one of the Hebrides?'

Alastair pointed. 'Due west. Far out. Can you see?'

'Yes. No. I'm not sure. Could just be clouds.'

'It's better not to see Barra,' Alastair smiled. 'It's a sign of bad weather—how long are you staying?'

'Ten days. I can see they're going to fly. Let's get on with our walk. It looks like it's going to be steep.' They began to pick their way down, Kate going gingerly, slithering over scree, jumping over bog as they got down to the road.

'That was great.'

'The *company* was great,' he stressed.

'Thank you,' Kate smiled. 'Oh, do look, Alastair! That's the marvellous view Aunt Morag showed me last night.' She grasped his arm to attract his attention—and saw a tremor in his hand. He thrust it into his pocket.

Pretend I haven't noticed ... 'Do you think this view would come out?'

I was going to take one of him, but not if he's feeling upset, she thought, clicking her camera.

'Aunt Morag's lending me her car,' she said as they walked on.

'That's good. All I can offer is a rusty bike with no gears. And a boat.'

'The boat sounds interesting.'

'Any time, you name it.'

They dipped down towards Coroskirr. *He's nice, but there's something locked up in him, and no wonder! Well, I should know all about that, after everything I've been through* ...

Hoping she sounded casual, Kate hazarded, 'I believe you have a family—a little girl. Aunt Morag showed me her photo.'

He smiled. 'Aye, Joanne. She's almost nine.'

'Is she a Jo, or a Joey?'

'Both, but mostly a wee Joey.' His smile broadened.

'I bet she loves coming here.'

'She did when she was smaller. She's not been this last while. In fact, I've not seen her for ages,' he added sadly.

Kate took a deep breath. 'At least you've still got her. I lost twin daughters.'

He stopped suddenly, a small shower of pebbles spurting round his boots. 'But you're not ...'

'Not married. No.'

'Kate, I didn't mean ...' He tried again. 'It never occurred to me ... I just assumed that you ... When did all this happen?'

'This time last year.' Kate bit her lip. 'It's all right,' she added huskily. 'I'm getting over it. They didn't ever live. They were stillborn.'

'Stillborn?'

'It's all *right*,' she repeated, forcing a smile. 'So much for our Highland walk! By the way, I haven't told Aunt Morag yet.'

'You've hardly had time . . . But she's been a nurse. She knows what life's about . . . And she's so pleased you've come.' As they walked on slowly, Alastair added gently, 'Thanks for confiding in me, Kate.'

'Perhaps I needed to,' Kate said. 'Absolution, and all that.'

He didn't pick her up on that last statement. 'Can I ask— what was the problem?' he asked carefully.

'No movement. But they say twins don't move so much. Anyhow, I went for a check-up. There was no foetal heart beat.'

I'm hiding behind jargon . . . Maybe it makes it easier for him too.

'Did they operate?' he asked, and Kate welcomed the concern in his voice, making it easier for her to go on. 'They induced me,' she said, 'though I was fairly heavily sedated.'

'So you had to go through labour . . . Were you alone?'

'Yes. Oh, it's a long story. My boyfriend—we've lost touch. He doesn't actually know about the babies.'

'Oh, Kate . . .' His voice trailed away.

'Would you like to come in, Alastair? Knowing my aunt, there's sure to be tea on the go.'

'Dead right. But I won't, thanks. I'll be coming round again—there are always wee things needing done. And plenty work in yon garden. You'll be fed up with me before long. But the sea is there, and the boat. And I'll try to track down those papers if you're still interested. Do you have any plans for your holiday?'

'I thought I might explore a bit first, drop in on your father again. I can't believe I've barely been twenty-four hours here. It seems like for ever.'

He nodded. 'It's always like this here. Never enough time. Thank you for everything, Kate.' He held out his hand. It was broad and calloused. A working hand. She'd been glad of its support over rocks and scree. She took it, and felt his other hand enclose hers as he bent towards her, his cheek brushing hers. 'Bless you, Kate. Bless you.'

Kate was touched. 'Thank you for that, Alastair,' she said softly.

He nodded, smiled. 'Till tomorrow, then.'

Kate turned into the house, to join Aunt Morag for a mug of tea in a sheltered corner of the wilderness she vainly tried to turn into a garden. And could not know that Alastair lingered outside—and not just to enjoy the fluting call of the curlew, nor to reflect how birdsong had replaced the lost sounds of Gaelic on this far shore.

For Alastair himself was finding a new song, a new language. But he did not yet know the notation or grammar, and could not tell if this was a melody he would be allowed to sing.

*

Jimmy McCann came from the hill with a rod and three small trout for his supper. He skirted the clifftop and followed a grit track down to his squat in the laird's house overlooking Port-na-Tuinne, that bay of breaking waves which never failed to lift Jimmy's heart. Often he'd sit for hours at the window, just watching the sea.

Coroskirr had drawn him like a magnet. He'd recognized the sandy beaches as soon as he'd arrived in early spring. On the run—and then he'd bumped into those guys in the hills who said there was this place with only the one old woman living alone. And it had proved safe enough. Even if the police came, there'd be no shortage of places to hide; and although in Achnacrois everyone knew one another, here in Coroskirr the only folk who came were strangers.

Coroskirr. It was one of Jimmy's earliest memories, years back, when he was only six. He'd been to the doctor's with his big red-headed father, Rab. It was about the only time Rab McCann had taken any of his weans to the doctor's in the Glasgow housing scheme where they lived. A tatty pile of magazines lay on the table. Jimmy was bored. No comics, but

Rab, leafing through coloured photographs said, 'See that. Coroskirr. Ma granny wis frae there.'

Rab stuffed the magazine into his pocket, and when they got home he tore out the picture and hung it above the fireplace, beside the photograph of the Rangers team.

Coroskirr and his father were associated for ever in Jimmy's mind.

In his squat in the disused byre, Jimmy cooked fresh trout on a camping stove and wrote in his jotter marked *Poems*:

They took my old man away for life. Life for life.
The doors are closed. I'll break the bars.
I'll shatter glass. I'll reach the stars.

Shatter glass. Years rolled back. 1970. Jimmy was ten, standing in front of his headmaster with his brother and a pal.

'So you missed school? Perhaps you stayed out all night?'

Robert, red-headed like their dad, shifted from one foot to another. 'Sir, yes, sir.'

'You'll be put away.'

'We'll no dae it again.'

And Robert hadn't. But once his brother had gone on to secondary school Jimmy, sandy-haired and undersized, took to missing school again. He had found a warm shelter in the local library and one day he brought home a card for his father to fill in.

'So I can borrow books.'

'You stick in at your reading, son,' Rab approved, tightening his belt across his paunch.

'Is that you away now, Rab?' their mother asked sharply, and thirteen-year-old Jean looked knowingly at her parents. Jimmy stared at the black-and-white television screen, hoping there wouldn't be a row. But his father just said, 'Aye, I'm away the now,' and swung out of the house.

That night, Jimmy dreamt he was following his father up a sweep of steps which seemed to go on for ever. He wanted to shout, 'It's me, Da, wait!' But his father went inside without looking back. Glass doors banged.

The noise of glass shattering woke Jimmy. He got up. The living-room window was smashed. His father was rocking on his feet. His mother was sobbing. Her face was bleeding. A fat woman stood beside his dad, clutching her coat across her with one hand, trying to support Rab. He reeled and crashed to the floor. Jimmy fled back to bed and pulled the covers right over him.

Next morning there was no sign of his mother. Their big brother Alec pulled them all out of bed.

'Where's my Ma?' Robert demanded. Jean was red-eyed. Wee Danny clung to her, howling.

'She's away.'

The fat woman poured herself a cup of tea. 'I'm looking efter youse weans.'

Jean burst into tears.

Jimmy pulled on his sandshoes without bothering to untie the broken laces. He didn't feel like bread or jam or tea. He went out to his den, a sooty tree beside a dried-up canal next to the library. He must have fallen asleep, because the clock in the library said ten o'clock when he went inside.

'You come here a lot,' the librarian looked through her glasses at him. 'Shouldn't you be at school?'

'Ma class is on part-time education,' Jimmy told her, quoting something he'd overheard his dad repeat from the telly. He handed her his card.

'You can borrow books now,' she said, issuing three tickets.

He chose a book with pictures of trees, which is how he learnt that the tree in his den was a willow.

The fat woman was sitting on the chair by the fire drinking tea when Jimmy came in, and wee Danny, his dummy in his mouth, was asleep on the settee.

She jumped. 'Whit's wrang?'

'I wisnae feeling well. The teacher asked if I'd had my breakfast. I said "naw", and she sent me hame.'

He helped himself to bread and tea. Someone knocked at the door. The woman got to her feet. She rubbed her back.

Her shape reminded Jimmy of the way his mother had looked before Danny was born.

An attendance officer stood on the doorstep with a bundle of cards. Jimmy stayed out of sight, and as soon as it was safe he sneaked off, taking care to stay away till the school came out.

His father was waiting for him. 'Whit's this Isa tells me? You've no been gaun tae the school?'

'They marked their cairds wrang.'

'You'd better be telling the truth. I'm no peyin ony mair fines.'

There was a loud knock at the door. It was the officer who prepared court reports. Rab tried to bluster, but the evidence against Jimmy changed his denials into threats. Jimmy cowered back, whimpering. The door shut. Rab unbuckled his belt.

When it was over, Rab stormed out of the house. Thrashed and sobbing, Jimmy fell back on the settee. Through his tears he saw the white sands of Coroskirr. Perhaps those distant waves comforted him as he cried himself to sleep.

It was pitch dark when he woke up. The fire was out. He was cold and sore. Wet too. He had no other trousers either. Isa was shouting. 'Get the ambulance, Rab! Rab, waken, please!'

But Rab slept on, heavy with drink. It was Alec who went out in search of a phone that worked.

Isa's screams woke the family. Even Rab got up. They heard his voice, stupid and thick, then the yells of the newly born baby.

Alec came back at the same time as the ambulance. The men made tea and joked with the children while they waited for a nurse.

They saw themselves out next morning, leaving wee Danny clambering over the settee, his sodden nappy hanging between his legs.

Jimmy forced himself into school. He'd missed so much he hadn't a clue what was going on. When the interval came he fled to his den beside the willow tree.

And now, alone in Coroskirr, eating trout by the light of an oil lamp, Jimmy wrote in his notebook:

> *They tore out the willow tree*
> *to make a motorway.*
> *Where's left for me?*
> *I'm here to stay.*
> *They'll never send me away.*

But tourists would return—he'd seen a couple in the hills. If the laird himself turned up, Jimmy's hiding-place would be endangered, like the old willow tree.

4

'Tea,' suggested Jane. 'How about elderflower?'

The sun lit her kitchen, all tiles and pinewood, filled with plants and herbs. 'I picked these last week,' she went on, herself more fascinating than her surroundings. She wore her jade beads tucked around a scarf of shimmering silk, and moved with the ease and assurance which always made Ninian feel relaxed. 'From trees beside the Water of Leith,' she went on. 'Remember?'

He nodded. 'Of course...' Walks together last summer, talking—about themselves, about music, his music; but then, come autumn, as leaves first turned gold and then fell into the swirling water, Jane began her alternative lifestyle, her sense of a new self emerging.

She selected powdery flowers, leaves and long stalks with the precision he loved. 'I dried them in the microwave...a bit incongruous, when you think of it.'

He laughed. 'You're never incongruous, Jane... Our green-and-white teapot. I see you still use it.'

'Of course. The very thing for herbal teas. It's essential to use the right sort of pot. Do you know,' she added, carefully putting the lid in place, 'I really identify with this teapot. It's a vessel. Like me singing your music...'

'So-o,' he said slowly, his eyes on her face. 'Jane,' he interrupted, 'would it be inappropriate to tell you you're the loveliest woman I know? There, don't be put out. I didn't mean to upset you.'

Her blue eyes looked troubled. 'Oh, Ninian, that's sweet. But please . . . I need space, inner space, you know.' She set the pot on the table. 'But do sit down.' And she smiled up at him as he helped her ease her chair into the table, seating himself opposite. 'You must be hungry. You walked. And you've been working. Here . . .' She offered him bread in a basket, cheese on a board, salad, soya spread. 'Tell me about it.'

'Only ideas so far,' he said as she poured pale liquid into hand-thrown pottery. 'A counterpoint to last year's Jacobite music. George III . . . I've been gripped by some old newspaper cuttings about his health.'

'Insane for years, poor king. There's a paradox there . . .'

'Oh? I don't quite see . . .' *But you do, Jane, that's what drew me to you: your insight and intelligence.*

'The monarch had powers of healing. Wasn't there a disease Charles I was supposed to be able to cure? Scrofula. Sounds ghastly, doesn't it?' she smiled.

'It does indeed!' But his face was animated. 'Paradox, you said, and you're so right, because the Stuarts were the very ones afflicted with illness. Mary, Queen of Scots, James . . . Jane, you've given me an idea.'

'I see I can be your guru as well as giving you lunch!' she smiled. 'Synchronicity, you see. Have some more cheese. I was awfully pleased when I discovered it in our local shop. I'd only ever seen it in Jenners . . .'

He took the cheese. 'It's delicious. Thanks . . . You used to be so serious, but it seems you're a tease, after all,' he added with a smile.

But there was sadness in his voice as he pleaded, 'Synchronicity, you said. I used to think that was our special gift. *Song for Jane*. Us. But now . . .'

'This isn't a parting,' she said. 'Just an interval. You see,' she filled two bowls with some early Spanish strawberries. 'It's spring. Life is blossoming.' Her voice was warm, but she met his eyes with a challenge he hadn't seen before. *What the hell,* he thought, impatiently. But he loved this woman, just being with her . . . 'But,' she was saying, her eyes on his face, 'I have to withdraw, let everything lie fallow.'

'There's nothing the matter with lying fallow. But I must admit,' he confessed, pausing before savouring the strawberries, 'I don't go a bundle on all this inner stuff.'

'Oh, but you should!' She fingered the jade necklace he'd given her. 'Green,' she said. 'It was our colour. But purple's important too. Purple for passion,' she smiled. 'Though actually, it's a dream colour I personally associate with sickness.'

He looked at her, astonished. 'Jane, you amaze me! Purple is connected with the disease those poor old kings and queens suffered. Porphyria, you know—a metabolic disturbance.'

'Relatedness,' Jane said calmly. 'Would you like some sugar for these strawberries? My journey's only just beginning. But I sense your tension. You're uptight, hostile. Let that go, release it. I'm sure you'll find music coming from sources you've never dreamt of.'

Now he was angry. 'Come on, Jane. You know as well as I do—art is a discipline, not some kind of mumbo jumbo witchcraft.'

'And I've been crushed by it,' she said evenly. 'Ninian, you're an intuitive person. But you think like a metronome,' she said, adding, in spite of his sharp intake of breath, his growing anger, 'but then, you're male . . .'

'Of course I'm bloody male—and you . . .'

She interrupted him, speaking urgently, with emphasis, 'That's what I mean. It's the wrong sort of power. You're drawing on the phallic stuff which builds missiles, makes wars.'

He pushed his chair back. It scraped on the wooden floor. 'I can't accept that,' he protested. 'That's going too far . . .'

'That's why we need this interval,' she repeated.

He got to his feet. 'I'm going home. I need to walk, to think. I'm sorry.'

47

'I'm sorry too.' She escorted him to the door. 'Even though there's been discord, it's been good to talk. May I make a suggestion? Go to that new place of yours—seek wisdom in the west.'

He remembered Kate, then, and her pilgrimage, how he'd assured her that the waters of healing lay not in Greece but in Coroskirr. Why not follow his own advice? Surely in Coroskirr, far from any distraction, he would find the music which had begun to flow that morning.

He held out his hand and within that formal gesture managed to capture Jane's. His natural good humour reasserted itself. 'Okay Jane, I'll seek wisdom—and if I find it . . .'

'You won't need me when you are wise,' she said, lightly kissing his cheek. 'You'll be yourself, complete. I might just complement that wholeness, though . . .' And with that teasing half promise Ninian had to be content.

He headed for home. It was uphill all the way. He found himself churning over their recent argument.

'Don't you see,' he pleaded to an imaginary Jane. 'The only thing which matters to me is music. Everything else has to be a means to an end.'

Her response would be too painful, too challenging. *I don't matter either—you just want me for your music.*

Was he selfish? Yes, he couldn't deny it, couldn't help it, either. Art, like grief, gnaws at the heart of being, consuming energy, relationships, life itself. And the artist has to consent. The freedom to create costs everything . . .

That's what Jane was objecting to. He heard her voice in his head, cool, almost superior: *You won't need me . . . You'll be yourself, complete.* What was the woman wanting? A celibate monk? *I might complement that wholeness.* Aye, well, very gracious . . .

I'm thirty-four, he reminded himself. *Are all relationships to end like this?*

He was nearly home. He passed Indian restaurants, lingered outside a kebab carry-out. A vegetarian carry-out would be fine for his evening meal.

Clanging unheeded above the six o'clock traffic, a single bell alerted him to thoughts beyond hunger: to a hunger beyond thought.

Today was Thursday, not Sunday. A feast then... Of course, Ascension: a festival ignored by the workaday world.

Ninian, a believer not in dogma but in beauty, found the drama and symbols which express God as subversive in complacent Edinburgh as any alternative lifestyle. He heeded the summons of the bell, opened heavy doors, to discover the smell of incense, shimmer of candlelight. He crossed himself and bent his knee; for the body is also an instrument, and gesture and touch may signify assent.

There were less than a dozen people scattered through the Victorian Gothic gloom. Mainly women, he noticed; and, of the men, he was the only one in trousers. Two Franciscans in brown habits; the others were clergy in alb or lace.

Jane had brought him here, for once schooldays were over Ninian had attended church only perfunctorily. But Benediction in this Episcopal church, Jane's voice chanting plainsong beside him in the pew, had taken him back to the religious feelings of early adolescence. He found, not certainty, but a signpost—a map charting a country where music, if one heard it aright, also had its source.

Jane had challenged this source. *You're drawing on the phallic stuff which builds missiles, makes wars.*

Well, Jane, I'll do what you suggested, go to Coroskirr. Between his half-closed eyes and the glimmer of candles came a picture of that tawny girl with hazel eyes ... There had been a lithe and easy grace about her, in spite of a certain hesitancy; enthusiasm and eagerness, too, and a pleasant, singing quality in her English voice.

He pulled his thoughts back to the service: 'So may we also in heart and mind thither ascend and with him continually dwell ...' The melody of those old words fell pleasingly on Ninian's ear, and he gave himself up to the movement and colour, sound and smell of Ascension-tide.

The carry-out afterwards was very satisfying. He sat on the

grass of the Meadows to eat, watched long-haired girls in bright tunics and *shalwar* play on swings, senior citizens walk staid dogs, students on bikes, on foot, on the grass . . . and went home to brew Indian tea (not a hint of herbs in his enamel pot), pack a couple of bags, and check his car oil and tyres for the journey west.

*

'Porridge for breakfast! You must have been up for hours!'

It was nine o'clock, another warm day. Morag, busy baking scones, laughed. 'I'm usually up early, and it's no trouble at all . . . What a good talk we had last night!'

'I enjoyed it too,' Kate assured her. 'Part of the Coroskirr magic.'

Kate had gone down to the shore again last night and Morag had joined her, watching the sun dip behind the high hills of Rhum. Their talk had been slow and comfortable, talk of the old days, when the air had been filled with the smell of peat fires.

They had talked about their work too—Morag's nursing, Kate's underfunded language research—and then, at home by the fire, Morag had told Kate about a man long ago, 'Who might . . . Well, but the war, so many things changed . . .'

And Kate, talking about Alastair, found herself telling her aunt about her own lost babies, about Kumar . . .

'He was lovely. Refined and controlled. There was something almost crystal clear about him. He had a beautiful voice. "Bengali is a sweet language," he used to say. His English sang . . . Yours does, too,' she'd added with a smile, 'and Donald's. I told Alastair I'd probably go and see him—if your kind offer of the car's still on.'

'Of course, Kate. But go on. Did your parents ever meet your friend?'

'No, unfortunately. It might have helped—but term time's too busy. Then things sort of speeded up, and then, well, he got a letter to say his father hadn't long to live.'

'That was before you'd become pregnant?' Morag had queried.

'I thought I might be, but I wasn't totally sure. It was only three weeks after our holiday. I think I knew, though.'

'You felt the changes within you?' There was a world of understanding in Morag's voice, thought Kate, pushing her tangled curls back from her face, flushed by the fire. Yes, I knew, she thought, I felt life within me, closer than a heart-beat, deeper than breath.

But still she couldn't quite tell even someone as sympathetic as her great aunt exactly how she had felt: excited, lonely, a bit afraid. 'You're very understanding,' she said aloud. 'It would have been a scandal here in Coroskirr when you were young.'

'A very great scandal,' Morag agreed. 'Which isn't to say such things didn't happen. But it would only have been whispered. The lassie would have been forced to give up her baby. Maybe her mother would have brought it up, pretending it was her own. Or she'd have hidden herself away in Glasgow and never come back.'

'The good old days,' Kate commented wryly.

'Human nature doesn't change; just the way we handle things, the kind of lies we tell . . . So the father was dying, away in Pakistan . . .?'

'Bangladesh,' Kate corrected. 'Yes. Kumar knew he had cancer. He was very worried, of course. But the letter sealed it, said they'd tried surgery and it hadn't been a success.'

'So it wasn't a good moment to tell him?'

'No. He'd have been overwhelmed. He was incredibly soft. But well, you know how strong the family thing is for Asians. He showed me the letter.' She broke off, then turned her hazel eyes to meet her aunt's listening face. 'It's odd the things you notice when your world's falling apart . . . The address was in foreign writing, thin purplish ink. Purple of sorrow, I thought.

' "They have arranged marriage for me. I have to go that side . . ." He was so upset his English went to pieces, I remember noticing that. And how his hands shook.'

51

'Ah,' said Morag sympathetically. 'Torn in two, the soul.'

'Yes,' agreed Kate, her eyes on the fire. *Those supple fingers trembled like tears . . . Purple ink—the touch of his love in that white bed was purple, deep purple . . . He turned my whole being to purple. I'd kissed his fingers, weeping and laughing till I brought him his climax . . .*

'Of course I told him he had to go . . . There were tears in his eyes, Aunt Morag. He didn't want to leave me. I felt so bad for him.'

'And so you didn't tell him. You let him go. Kate, you were strong.'

'I didn't think so.' But then Kate looked up at her aunt, her fine soft hair wind-blown from clear plastic combs, her determined face full of feeling. 'It was the only thing I could do . . . But if I was being strong, perhaps my Coroskirr blood helped. Highland women had to be strong, didn't they? I can see that from you. Besides, I know from things Grandad said.'

'Aye, well, he was thrawn, right enough. But that's what they always said of us Coroskirr MacDonalds. There's a wee streak of that has passed on to you, I can see,' she added with a smile.

'Thrawn?'

'A right pig-headed lot,' her aunt interpreted.

So this morning in Morag's sunny kitchen, Kate, cotton jersey tucked into a summer skirt, reminded her aunt, 'Last night you said I was strong. Thrawn,' she added, pronouncing the vowel in the English way. 'I think *you* are. I love it here, but I couldn't live on my own like you. It would drive me bonkers.'

Morag laughed and poured herself out a cup of tea, pulling a chair beside Kate. 'Och, well, it's not so bad. I have neighbours. Some of the holiday folk spend a good part of the year here.'

'But the darkest, loneliest part of the year you're on your own,' Kate argued.

'That's so. The car's a great blessing, as I've mentioned. I try to get out most days, unless the weather's too bad, to see folks in Achnacrois—Donald, of course, and others who are elderly, shut in. Alastair came last Christmas, the first time he's ever been free to come away here.'

'Of course . . . He must have missed his wee Joey.'

Morag sighed, her green eyes sad. 'He did, Kate, he did. Aye,' her voice echoed her sorrow, 'it was a quiet Christmas right enough.'

'No street lights,' mused Kate. 'No shops. Just the sea . . .'

'And the black dark. I listen to the midnight service on the radio. It was a foreign service, a Mass, from somewhere away in Europe. Of course, Christmas wasn't a holiday in Scotland when I was a child . . .'

'Wasn't a holiday?' Kate echoed in surprise.

'Hogmanay was the thing—bringing in the new year. Och, but here we are, back in the old days and your holiday's just slipping away. And it smells as if the scones are ready. I'll take them out, Kate, and then I'll get you the car keys.'

'Thanks . . . those scones smell good!'

'Let's have one with some butter. There . . . Now, you go off and explore . . .'

*

Kate set off a bit uncertainly, unsure of the controls, unsure of a road whose every bend came as a surprise. You could never quite tell where the next twist might be. It seemed to run at random.

Alastair and she had come down that steep shoulder. She paused to look about her, then edged the car forward. Downhill, then up. The Mull hills shimmered on the horizon. She caught a glimpse of the sea she had crossed in the small ferry.

And thought she saw, cutting across the hillside towards Achnacrois, a solitary hiker. Well, she was here on holiday, so why shouldn't other people be? But it hadn't seemed as though anyone else were staying in Coroskirr. Could it be Alastair?

He doesn't seem to have a car ... a rusty bike, he said yesterday. I'd have given him a lift, if he'd wanted ... I wonder if he minded when I asked about his daughter. He listened to me, he seemed to care ...

What was his wife like? A grudging person, Aunt Morag had said. But perhaps she'd been made to feel that way, ground down by expectations of her as the minister's wife. 'Can't be an easy role,' Kate had agreed, and Morag had added with truth that Alastair had probably been too caught up with his own hurts to have realized what was going wrong.

'Just the same,' Morag had said. 'I doubt she ever loved him.'

'So why did they marry?'

'Och, well,' Morag had tried to explain, 'young people in church groups often get thrown together.'

And Alastair, set on becoming a minister, had seemed a 'good catch', Kate had surmised, reading between the lines. Neither he nor Isabel had known how hollow their marriage, his work, would turn out to be.

Kate turned the car towards the line of houses, many empty, some totally deserted, which was the township of Achnacrois.

Donald's house lay to the far left, beside the church, not far from the road down to the harbour. Kate turned right, giving way to a shepherd with a long hazel stick and two collie dogs, who waved his thanks.

She pulled up outside the shop.

There didn't seem much else at Achnacrois. 'The field by the cross,' she recalled, hearing Alastair's explanation. She could ask in the shop where it was ...

She went inside and looked around. There was very little on the shelves and everything was so overpriced that Kate was taken aback. Apples rotted in a box. The only vegetables were potatoes which had seen better days.

However, she'd better buy something, Kate thought, choosing some postcards.

She waited at the till. A woman appeared from the back

of the shop. She cut across Kate's attempt at a greeting with a curt, 'Aye?'

'Just these postcards,' Kate said hastily, stifling a need to apologize for disturbing this atmosphere of non-doing. 'It's another lovely day,' she heard herself prattle.

The woman didn't answer. She handed Kate her change. Kate noticed the dirt beneath her fingernails and glanced at the sausages turning puce under plastic in an empty storage rack beside the till.

'Thank you,' she began, and drew back as a sandy-haired man with a roll-up stuck between his pursed lips carried a small bottle of calor gas out on his shoulder. He bumped against Kate, who apologized quickly, 'Oh, sorry.'

But it hadn't been her fault!

She slid her purse and postcards into her bag. Pride, perhaps, or the feeling that she wasn't going to let them intimidate her, made her linger beside the rack where the postcards were displayed. Thrawn, a right pig-headed lot ... Her MacDonald cussedness came to her rescue, and she made a show of looking through the goods, noticing some music cassettes. She pulled them out. Pipe bands, something in Gaelic, and, newly released, *Jacobite Airs* by Ninian Bruce.

That man again! *My business is music ... Do I detect a change of key?*

Ninian. That salmon-skin belt. Long supple fingers ... Like Kumar. That was it! The resemblance was in the refinement—in Ninian's case, the refinement of hands which have learnt discipline and control.

Without turning round, Kate felt hostility directed at her from the man with the calor gas. The woman had disappeared. Kate felt angry, wanted to challenge him, 'What's the matter? Is it me? Or does my choice of music annoy you? If you can't be nice to customers you shouldn't run a shop.'

But maybe the man was a customer too, perhaps a local who had it in for her because she was a tourist.

She put the cassette back and forced herself to walk steadily out of the shop, but she couldn't help feeling shaken as she got back into the car. The man followed her, pulled out his fag, spat and changed his gas bottle from one shoulder to the other as he swung off the road, obviously preferring the hills. He looked young enough to be the son of the woman behind the till.

Kate started the engine. *No wonder Aunt Morag said the shop's a disaster*, she thought. But the sense of unease persisted. She decided to drive along the road a bit. No use visiting Donald while she was feeling shaken like this.

The road climbed steeply towards a headland and petered out. A track wound down towards a sheltered bay. Still feeling upset at the hostility she had encountered, Kate pulled the car into a viewing-point and clambered down towards the shore.

Mull came clearly into view, and from her vantage-point Kate could see the ruined castle beside Achnacrois harbour. On her way down to the bay she passed a cluster of roofless drystone cottages, where people had once wrested a livelihood from rock and water, their way of life perfectly adapted to these windswept shores. Who could exist so independently today? That shop wouldn't help the survival rate, Kate told herself, trying to imagine winter nights without electric light. Easy enough: you huddled beneath covers of wool or down and slept. And if you woke, you moved towards your partner and engendered new life to be reared and fed in those stark stone nests.

Birth, and death. There were graves here too, long since gone to grass. A huddle of stunted standing stones showed that this bay had been settled for centuries. When would they have been put there, she wondered. A thousand, even two thousand, years before Christ? Kate tried to telescope time . . .

Close to the shore, beside some sort of walled enclosure, she found a single standing stone, facing the sea: an aged monarch worn down to a silent frown.

She noticed crude carvings someone had once made: a cross and animals—a dog perhaps, and beside it something

56

like a deer. Kate reached out to trace the symbols which time had almost obliterated, but dropped her hand. To touch was to intrude, to stake a claim, possess. She stepped back, climbed the broken wall into the space enclosed and overgrown: a place apart. And perhaps because it was a place in all this wilderness, it drew her in ...

...To find Christ crucified on a fallen stone, exposed to rain and sun, feet overgrown with moss, face weathered into agelessness. The breeze from the sea tugged Kate's curls loose from their clasp. Her hair fell across her face as she bent to have a closer look.

It was beautiful, a work of art as well as of devotion, unvisited, unvenerated. The figure wore no crown of thorns. Lacking this instrument of ignominious punishment, dunce's cap, the head assumed a timeless dignity, a look sometimes seen on the face of those who are wise—as the face of Donald Cameron might be, if it were not for the shutters which guarded his faded eyes.

For Donald had about him (and this was what drew Kate to him) the singleness of one who knows how to keep a lifetime's vigil for the morning that will come, as simple and serene as this Christ.

Kate tried to scrape moss away, dirtying and breaking her nails. *Neglected, cast away,* she thought, *like the babies I did not mourn.* She let her hand caress the sun-warmed face of the Christ before she wandered across the shore to find a sheltered spot where she could sunbathe with the sound of the sea in her ears.

Feeling thirsty, she drank from a nearby burn whose banks were bright with primroses. Guessing Donald would have had his lunch by now, Kate went back to the car, blessing the sycamore above for its shade, and drove off to come upon the only car she had seen that day, heading towards the shop.

Kate stopped, tried to reverse, fumbling with unfamiliar gears. The driver, sunroof rolled back, looked round, eased back and waved her on.

As she drew level they recognized each other. Ninian

wound his window down, and Kate stopped.

'Hi...'

'It's yourself,' Ninian returned. 'How's it going? Everything all right?'

'It's fantastic... But you didn't tell me you planned to come west too.'

He switched off his engine. 'You know how it is. The best laid schemes...'

His smile made her colour rise. *Let's keep things in proportion*, she told herself—but switched off her engine too. 'It's nice to see you,' she told him sincerely, 'but if you're heading for that store you're in for a shock. It's a terrible place.'

'I need matches for the gas. Think they'll have any?'

'They haven't got much. Grotty potatoes. Oh, and music,' she added, with a smile which showed that she'd guessed something about him. '*Jacobite Airs* by Ninian Bruce.'

'Ah.' He returned her smile.

'I met a man the day before yesterday who told me his business was music,' teased Kate.

'So you put two and two together...'

'Not too difficult. Actually I heard something by the same guy on the radio the other night. *A Song for Jane*. I liked it, Ninian. So that *is* you? Your work, I mean?'

'Yes,' he admitted. 'I'm glad you liked it.'

'Oh, but dozens of people must tell you that. It's quite a coincidence, though, isn't it? First the radio, then the shop.'

'Shows a certain amount of good will—the shop, I mean.'

'Why?'

'I'm an enemy. One of the hated landlords. I've just inherited this neck of the woods. Or bogs. It's a bit embarrassing.' He smiled disarmingly, but Kate wasn't going to be won over so easily.

'I suppose it depends who you're talking to.'

'Oh, Kate, I didn't mean it that way! Come on, don't be my enemy. I need people on my side. Specially someone as charming and vibrant as you.'

58

'Thank you! You're winning me over by the minute!' Then her face relaxed into a smile. 'No, seriously. In Edinburgh—you gave me such a warm welcome. I appreciated that, you know.'

'Nice of you to say so. Tell me, where can I find you in Coroskirr?'

'I'm sure you'll see me around! There's just one other person beside me and my great-aunt. Actually I noticed some guy in the hills—I wondered where he'd sprung from . . . I'm in the last house along that track at the end of the road.'

'Then we're neighbours. *Seaview*—that's where I'm based. It's over the cliff, in the next bay, Port-na-Tuinne. Maybe you've noticed.'

'I've not been that far along the Coroskirr shore.' Port-na-Tuinne, the Bay of the Wave. Alastair, who had named hilltops and islands, had not pointed out the bay where his brother Kenneth had launched a canoe into stormy seas.

'Pity. Port-na-Tuinne's phenomenal. Probably the love-liest of all the Coroskirr bays. Terribly dramatic. Anyhow, I'll have the pleasure of showing you around,' he added in that warm voice, which had sharpened with annoyance at the noise in Waverley Station, she recalled. 'Where are you heading for now? You've obviously been to the shop.'

'Yes. And the bay.' She pointed. 'There's a carving of Christ . . . Woefully neglected, though.'

'Wonder if I'm responsible for cleaning it up? Perhaps I should have a look at it some time.'

'Yes, you should.'

Those dark blue eyes held hers. 'Will you come with me, Kate?'

'Of course!'

His smile showed his pleasure. 'That's kind of you. I'll be so pleased to have your reactions to the new inheritance. Maybe tomorrow?'

'Sounds okay.'

'I'd better get on, get those matches, unpack. I've got a heap of paperwork to do.'

'Any new music?'

'I hope so . . . Ah, Kate, I hope so very much!'

And you didn't need a musical ear to catch the ambiguity and invitation in his voice.

Kate felt her colour rise once more. She started the engine, ground the gears. 'It's my aunt's car,' she explained through the open window. 'See you soon, Ninian.'

She waved and drove on. Ninian watched her in his driving mirror. *Couldn't see her legs, but the head and shoulders were pretty good . . . Perhaps it's as well we had two doors between us. I knew she'd be here, but I didn't think we'd meet so soon, or that the effect would be so . . . Well, why not? Jane's left me in a bad space, as she'd say . . . Matches,* he told himself firmly. *And poor King George. Music and the duties of the estate . . .* Ninian pulled himself together and cruised towards the shop.

*

Jimmy McCann walked back to Coroskirr with his gas bottle. He took his time, stopping on the way to have a packet of crisps, a bite of cheese. The pie in his pack was still defrosting. He drank a couple of cans of Export, took a swig from a half bottle, pulled on his roll-up. That job he'd done, which had sent him on the run, had netted big bucks. Bad luck for Jimmy and his pals that security guard had got in the way. *Worse luck for the guy,* thought Jimmy, as he stretched out for a doze in the sun. And good about his great-granny. He'd told the incomers, Annie and Tam Wilson in the shop, when he'd bought yon wee calor gas heater, that he was up tracing his ancestors and staying in the old family croft. The laird's house suited him fine, lying empty yonder, totally secluded. He'd been careful not to light fires, used an old paraffin lamp behind closed curtains. So he was living in style. No cashflow problems . . . Lambs bleated about him. A lark sang above him. The sun shone on him. Empty hillsides cradled him, and Jimmy slept soundly in the hills behind Coroskirr.

5

Donald was sitting outside his house, his lunch on a small table beside him.

Seeing Kate he eased himself to his feet, his face shining with welcome. 'Come away, Kate. There's a pot of tea, a plate of pancakes. What's this?' he protested as Kate sat on the grass beside him. 'Will you not have a chair?'

'I prefer the ground,' Kate assured her host.

'Let me fetch a rug. There's one in the room.'

'I'll get it. Oh, and I suppose we'll need another cup.'

Kate went into the front room with its view over the Sound of Mull, its old-fashioned furniture, family photographs, books: *Reader's Digests*; authors Kate didn't know—Neil Munro, Neil Gunn; a much worn leather bound book, *The Loveliness of Christ* . . . A low fire smouldered in the hearth. On her way to the kitchen Kate glanced quickly at a photograph of Alastair, solemn in a dark jacket and stiff plastic collar. Not a good likeness, she decided, no hint of the man who seemed so at home among the rocks and hills of his beloved Coroskirr. And there was his daughter, Joey, complete with gap-toothed grin and crooked school tie.

The room was well cleaned, the kitchen too. Did Donald manage to do housework, Kate wondered as she hurried out with a mug from the kitchen, a plate and the rug.

Donald poured her tea. 'Do you take sugar? I have a

terrible memory nowadays. I'm more in the past than the present, it seems. You'll have a pancake? Ailidh, the home help, made them. She's a grand soul.'

'I'm glad you have someone to help. Does she come every day?'

'Two mornings a week. And what's new with you, Kate?'

'I love Coroskirr,' Kate began and saw Donald smile, well pleased. 'Alastair and I had a walk yesterday,' she went on.

'Alastair—ah.' And she noticed a breath of a sigh—was there always this sadness between father and son?

'We had a good time,' she countered. 'I've been exploring a bit today. I met Ninian Bruce.'

'The laird himself? That's more than many of the locals have done.'

The laird himself . . . Dark hair and his easy style. 'Any new music?' 'Ah, Kate, I hope so, very much!'

'It seems he's a musician,' Donald was saying.

'Yes, they had a cassette of his in the shop.'

'Aye, Ailidh tells me they sell his music there. So you were in the shop?'

'They weren't very friendly.'

'So I've heard. There have been one or two unfortunate happenings. The police were seen, even.'

'I shouldn't think they're overworked up here. The police, I mean.'

'They might not agree. The distance, you know,' he smiled. 'But you'd be surprised. Debt, depression, drink . . . these kind of dark dramas.'

'You're well informed,' Kate observed.

'Put it down to nosiness, an ex-teacher who can't stop meddling. Will you have another pancake?'

'They're delicious.'

'Aye, Ailidh's a good baker—almost as good as your Aunt Morag.'

'You can say that again!' Kate told him between bites. 'I'll be putting on pounds!'

'There's no sign of it yet,' Donald assured her.

'You were a teacher in Glasgow, weren't you? It must have been hard to live there after Coroskirr.'

'It was at first,' Donald agreed.

'Couldn't you have taught here?' Their talk moved as lightly as the May sunshine, dappling through rowan blossom above Kate's head. A blackbird sang near by, and a wagtail hopped down but, too shy to investigate, whirred away.

'I planned to—but I met Margaret. And the war came ... But I think the pull south began way before that. The First War ...'

'It's the far croonin' that's pullin' me away.' The song marched through Kate's mind. Dedicated 'to the lads in France', as if war were a Boy Scout camp. *'Gone to grave-yards ev'ry one. When will they ever learn? When will they e-ver learn?'*

Yet waves still wash rock and headland; and hillsides are rich with wild flowers: purple-spotted orchid, marsh mallow, foxglove, bell heather, thyme, harebell, speedwell, bog cotton, yellow iris, water-mint, wild hyacinth—a criss-cross embroidery into which is threaded the sound of burn water running towards silver sand, foaming surf, the endless sea.

Coroskirr. Another age, another way of life. Kate had heard hints of this far-off world in her Sussex childhood; those bare bones had been fleshed out by Morag last night, and now by Donald, whose talk—and this was one reason why Kate welcomed it—gave immediacy to the heritage she longed to share.

Boys who could bring home from the burn a clutch of brown trout, girls who could knit hose on four needles and carry on their backs babies, driftwood, seaware, peat—learnt English fairy tales, arithmetic, history in the southern tongue to which their native speech gave the music which sang in Donald's voice—captivating Kate.

A music caricatured in comedy: *'Ach, Tonal, will you pe hafing a wee dram?'*

'For me the first notion of Glasgow began when I was a boy

63

of, och, maybe ten or twelve,' said Donald. 'My mother sent me to find carrageen.'

'That's seaweed, isn't it?' Kate took the last of her tea and settled back to hear Donald's tale.

'Short, with small leaves. It's made into jelly.'

'How is it done?'

'My mother used to spread it out to dry, then she'd pinch it into a panful of milk and boil it.'

'Was it nice?'

'A distinctive flavour, cool to taste. As I'm tasting the old days now, thanks to you,' he smiled.

'I am too—and that's what I wanted to do . . . Tell me about your mother.'

'A worker, like all the women. Her hands were never idle, until arthritis knotted them. She lost two babies. My elder brother was killed in the war . . . But I'm forgetting to ask if you would like more pancakes or tea.'

'I couldn't, thanks; but tell Ailidh her pancakes went down a treat. Could your mother speak English?'

'A little. She hadn't much schooling. Her brothers got the boots and heavy coat when it was wet. It was her faith and not the schoolhouse that taught my mother,' Donald reminisced. 'She loved the old family Bible. What was the sense of stories of Dick Whittington and streets of gold when the only road Mother knew stopped way short of Coroskirr?'

'She was a woman at home in her own world,' Kate said warmly, and Donald smiled, well pleased.

'That's so, but it was a world that was changing, as you've been hearing. Young ones grew up, left home. I suppose I knew my turn would come,' he paused, and added with a smile, 'It took a mad artist in a cave to show me the way.'

'A mad artist?' Kate repeated.

'He was not a Highlander, though he spoke to me in a kind of wild Gaelic. I'd met very few strangers, and certainly none that ever spoke our language.'

'Where was the cave?'

'Along the shore, where those sheer cliffs are . . .'

'The *sgurr* that gives Coroskirr its name?'

'You're well taught,' he approved.

'Alastair . . . So, you went to the cave? Was that when you were looking for carrageen?'

'Ah yes, right enough, I was forgetting. Aye, I went for the carrageen, and on the way home I thought I'd take a wee turn into the cave. I found it lit,' Donald went on.

'Candles?' queried Kate.

'Cruisies, as we call those lamps of rushes and oil. Old-fashioned, even then. I'd only seen them put to use in the byre. I mind it yet: the oats spread about and the young men (your grandfather would have been with them, I suppose) threshing, their raised arms caught in the light of the cruisies, sweat running down them.'

Blackness of the shed, yellow light, yellow oats, honeyed arms rising and falling with the flail, the *buailtean* as Donald called it, 'the little striker': an ancient pastoral pattern of toil and grain.

'You mustn't think of fields like you have in the south. Just strips of earth we'd turned ourselves with wooden tools.'

'No ploughs?'

'No horses. No road.'

'Subsistence farming,' said Kate.

'You could say so indeed,' Donald agreed. 'A strong sense of community, hunger a reality, thrift a necessity. Nothing was ever wasted. "The earth was gnawn to the quick", the old books say. But we're off on another tack. Where were we?'

'Still in the cave,' Kate reminded him, shifting on the rug, lifting her throat to the sun.

'Ah, yes. And not even at the artist yet. Well, Kate, those damp walls were covered with paintings the like of which I'd never seen, and the artist was as weird as his work. Sick. I could see that even in the poor light. Half-starved.'

'Weren't you scared?'

'A wee bit, but curious too. The smell of drink, hardly a smell I knew, was on his breath. But I don't think he was drunk. His eyes . . . that's what I remember most. His face was ghastly. His teeth were yellow and mostly missing, but his eyes were alive and they suffered.'

'You could tell that, even then?' Kate put in, and thought: *the suffering still matters to him—all pain, except the knotted-up heart of his son.*

Aloud she said, 'My mother would say you're one for lame dogs. That's what she always says about me.' *Kate has to have her lame dogs.* She could hear her mother's voice, edgy, exasperated.

'I brought a tramp home once,' she told Donald, and watched his slow, appreciative smile.

'A tramp? Well, now.'

There was a wealth of understanding in those words, and Kate laughed. 'I collected a few strays when I was a student too—but Mum doesn't know about them.'

No wonder. It had been bad enough when they found out she was planning to go on holiday with an Indian friend. 'You're bringing no bloody Hindu into this house,' her father had told her. And her mother had pleaded, 'Suppose you have children, what will they turn out to be?' And then the shattering news of her pregnancy. Her mother, trying to be diplomatic, piled on the emotional blackmail: 'Won't you consider, well, you know, I only want what's best for you— but what about a termination?' And her father's rumbled refrain: 'Think of your career.' She'd backed off, *thrawn*, as her great-aunt would say. 'I'll manage.' And in the end they'd supported her at a distance, bought a cot and a pram. Which had to be sent back . . . 'And it's just as well.' Kate could still hear her mother's relief.

Donald broke into her thoughts.

'You need no mad artist to teach you compassion, Kate. I saw it in you at once. Yes, I see the compassion and I know there's been sorrow in your life. I long to tell you that Christ can bring healing, but I'm a poor example of that, am I not?'

'No, you're not,' Kate countered. 'You talked so beautifully the other day about that "great and splendid brightness". I'm sure you're right, and,' she added impulsively,

'I'm sure Christ *can* bring healing—especially to you. But I suppose it isn't always easy to let it happen . . .'

There was a long silence between them. The May sunlight touched them. The wind tossed the rowan blossom. Burn water sang from somewhere near by. Kate hesitated and then said in a rush, 'Come back to Coroskirr. For your own sake—and for Alastair . . .' Her voice trailed away. 'I'm sorry. I shouldn't have said that. Tell me about the artist and the pictures he'd done.'

'The artist. Aye . . .' Donald seemed in another world. Kate waited. Kumar had taught her a dimension of patience, in the main lost to the Western world. *But not to this man, still as the stone carving of Christ down at the shore. I'll see that cross again tomorrow with Ninian. I wonder what he'll think of it. I guess he's its owner now.*

'Kate, Catriona, as we would call you. You are my artist. Go back to Coroskirr, you're saying . . . To the days that were, the good folk I knew, the loved ones I've lost—that can never be.'

Kate laid her hand on his knee. 'It can't be; of course, it can't be. The old days have gone.' Her eyes searched his. How she longed to say, 'Think of what's happening around you, think of the son who didn't drown . . .' Instead she said, thinking how feeble she sounded, 'Donald, it was your home, and it's so beautiful . . .'

Donald was moved. He patted her hand. 'Beautiful indeed. Kate, *m'eudail*. I'll think over what you've said, but beyond that I'll make no promises.'

'That's nice of you—even to think. So what had the artist painted?'

'Hell,' said Donald, simply. 'He said so himself. "Look, laddie, I have painted hell."'

'Did he say that in Gaelic?'

'Yes, and his voice was harsh and strange. He showed me horrible, nightmarish shapes: the poor of the big cities. That was the nightmare which had led him away to Coroskirr. His grandfather had been Highland—like your own,' Donald added. 'He told me about *Glaschu*, lapsing into his native

Glaswegian. "Never leave here, sonny. Never gae intae thae toons. The land wull waste, if youse ying yins leave." '

'I'm not sure if I understand. He was asking you not to go. But you went.'

'I couldn't ignore his paintings, you see. He searched among sacking and he gave me a picture. I have it yet, Kate, though I fear it is not good art. Yet the man's soul is in it. A crofter holding a lamb, his stick a cross . . .

' "Who is this, *ille?*" he asked and I said, "The Lord", although the minister never preached him so. "*Cait a bheil e?*" he asked. "Where is he?" '

'What did you say?'

Donald smiled. 'In the Bible, and in our own hearts, and in the kirk on the Lord's Day . . . But I could see this didn't pleased him. He gripped my arm so hard I had the marks of it the next day. "Is he there when waves dash small boats against rocks? When sickness visits the schoolroom? When a mother dies bearing her wean?" ' Donald paused. 'He was agitated, wild, but he became calmer when I told him, "Yes, he is there." He gave me his painting of Christ the crofter, and in return I pulled from my pocket a treasured possession, a Gospel in Gaelic some missionary had given out. And that was all. My mother sent me back next day with meal and crowdie, but he had gone. But when the time came for me to leave Coroskirr, I minded yon artist. I knew that he had been sent for a sign.'

'What did he show you?'

'That there's love to be found, even in the heart of hell,' Donald said simply.

But Ninian might have added: that art has purpose and meaning.

'Margaret showed me that too,' Donald went on.

'Tell me about Margaret,' Kate invited.

*

1938. Every year silence had reigned at 11 a.m. on the

eleventh day of the eleventh month in classrooms and factories, offices and banks, out on the streets. In 1938 a nation on the brink of war stopped work to remember; a generation of women had already learnt to stay single.

But the young ones had cut their hair, raised hemlines, abandoned stays. And danced. The Plaza, Barrowland, the Palais. 'Are you dancin?' 'Are you askin?' They moved to melodies they would forever recall with nostalgia, and even in old age would take to the dance floor, white-headed, well-padded, stiffer—to dance in ways their grandchildren might laugh at, but envy.

Women whose mothers had been worn down with the bearing of children learnt to limit their families. Newly-built bungalows mushroomed on farm and moor. Housewives here installed modern cookers, bought Ewbank sweepers; while in overcrowded tenement buildings in the heart of grey Glasgow young wives awoke each morning to dislodge black bugs and cockroaches by banging with their brooms against the walls, while their men tramped the streets for work, or stood in hopeless dole queues—for unemployment spread like sickness across the whole Central Belt, producing decay and despair . . .

'Tell me about Margaret, you said. Margaret came into my life like the brown-haired girl of some of our songs. I met her in city streets, where I was far from my ease.'

'Homesick?' Kate suggested.

Donald nodded. 'The sickness of the heart for the dear place, ill at ease too with students from moneyed homes.'

So the nineteen-year-old student shrank into himself, and, used all his life to doing without, managed on less than enough, in order to bring small, ill-afforded luxuries home each long summer vacation.

Each Sunday he walked to the Highland church where he heard his own language.

One Sunday evening, Margaret was invited there to sing a solo. The tune she chose was based on a Gaelic melody, and the Glasgow girl's singing brought to Donald's mind treeless shores which provided poor grazing for rough-coated cattle; brought to mind also the long tradition in which melodies sung at cradle and sickle, milking and butter-making, waulking and rowing were woven into art forms both passionate and tender, bawdy and mocking, echoes of a culture whose bards had in the end been branded as vagabonds . . .

But although Donald's thoughts were filled with faraway places, his eyes contemplated the singer. She was about his age, sombrely dressed. Her cheeks beneath her hat brim were flushed. Her brown eyes were solemn.

'Two things impressed me,' Donald told Kate. 'She'd chosen that old Gaelic melody. And I could tell she wasn't feared to stand there and sing.'

'That's nice and positive,' agreed Kate. 'So, what happened next?'

'We met by chance, not long after—and indeed she was never out of my thoughts as I walked to my studies or sat at my books—I'll not call it swotting, for my mind wasn't on history. I was walking to the Gaelic service as usual, and there she was, going to her own church with a whole crowd of urchins. They were barefoot, as we had been also, all through our schooldays. But in the city, where gas lights gleamed on wet cobbles, it seemed a bad thing to me that children had no shoes.'

And a good thing that the slender girl was a friend of such children. He lifted his Highland bonnet, bade her 'Good Evening' and might have walked on, but one of the urchins begged, 'Gaunae show us yon big buik, mister.'

'Yon's no a buik,' piped up a child with a snotty nose and torn shorts several sizes too large. 'It's a Bible, but. They a' have big black Bibles in Auntie Margaret's wee hall, an' we get a cup of tea efter . . .'

'You get a scone an' a',' a little girl added, and Donald found himself swept along to a Mission Hall adorned with texts and guttering gas lamps.

'I couldn't resist those children,' Donald said, simply.

No more defences, thought Kate.

'Lame dogs?' she suggested, but Donald smiled and shook his head. 'Ah no, I was the lame dog. They had something to teach me . . .'

'Oh, Donald . . .' said Kate, moved.

After the service, along with the children and some odds and ends of humanity, Donald was drawn into Margaret's family.

Ushered into a warm front room in a tenement, Donald, who 'managed on his own' at weekends (which mostly meant managing without), felt the wallpaper with its plentiful framed texts spin round him, excused himself and stood outside on the stairway, where Margaret's mother followed him.

'When did you last have a guid dinner?' she demanded. Highland pride struggled with inborn honesty, but the lady plainly expected an answer.

'I missed the shops yesterday,' Donald hedged.

Almost at once cold meat loaf, hard-boiled eggs, potato scones and oatcakes appeared on the hospitable table and Donald was sat down to be fed while the urchins had greedy mouths and fingers wiped.

Everyone who could be seated squeezed round the table. Three unshaven men, out of work and sleeping rough. A toothless Irish woman with a puny child under her shawl. A couple of lads with coal under their nails lifted china cups with fingers more used to clutching tankards—while Margaret, her two sisters, a maiden aunt or two, and her mother hovered with pots of tea . . .

For Donald this was the first of many such meals. The living-room with its black-leaded range at which the women-folk dried their unfashionably long hair on Saturday nights became a second home. And soon Donald was bringing others to the never-failing welcome, the frequent singing of Sankey and Moody songs, the freely spoken prayers. Glasgow's rain and fog, kindliness and squalor, fostered his faith and fed his life for almost half a century.

'Would I have chosen differently today, you're asking? Perhaps. I was taught, you see, to think my own language had nothing to offer the modern world. It seemed selfish to teach Gaelic in a Highland school when, as yon artist saw so clearly, city children were imprisoned in the heart of hell. Maybe I was wrong. It's hard to say. Anyway, it's too late now.'

'*Too late* has a sad sound,' commented Kate.

Donald gave her a searching look. Was he thinking again of her suggestion that he visit his birthplace; return, as she had not dared say, to let the healing happen at the very place of pain, Port-na-Tuinne, the bay of breaking waves? Kate could almost feel the old schoolmaster saying, 'Wait now; let's think again.'

'You know,' he reflected. 'It used to be that the weight of years brought wisdom.'

'It still does, in some cultures. And, Donald, you've got wisdom and dignity.'

'That's kind of you, Kate,' he said, and he was smiling now. 'And yet, I'm thinking it's you that has the goodness to give up a day of your holiday for an old fellow like me.'

'I'm enjoying every minute,' Kate assured him. 'It's in my blood, too. I only heard little snippets when I was a child. It all seemed far away, strange; and yet, as I told Aunt Morag, I couldn't help thinking; "this is my story too—I belong." But go on, you were talking about old age and wisdom.'

'Well, there's old age and foolishness too, is there not?' he said with a sad smile, and Kate noticed small criss-cross veins on his high cheekbones, his teeth—all his own, slightly uneven, gaps at both sides.

'Dementia,' she agreed. 'But no one can help getting like that.'

'No, and you know, I sometimes think this present day is both kind and cruel. It provides a scientific label for every problem—but then tidies it away.'

'We need our armour, I suppose,' Kate interjected, enjoying this exchange of ideas, getting to know a mind whose intelligence had been tutored by a dual culture. Yet

Donald's personal sorrow had turned his gaze turn inward, except when he talked of the need of others—and then his compassion showed in his face.

'Kate,' said Donald, obviously enjoying their talk too, 'what I'm trying to say is that one of the dangers of old age is we get encased in armour, like a shell.'

'Cut off from new ideas, you mean?'

'Wrapped up in ourselves, more like. A shell like a crab,' Donald went on. 'And of course, don't they say that crabs go backwards?'

'That sounds hard. You were talking about being marginalized. That's how old people are made to feel. Tidied away, like you said . . .'

'Afraid of the young,' said Donald. 'That's the worst of it. Seeing young folk as potential muggers.'

'But you didn't retire here because of that, did you?'

Donald shook his head. His blue eyes clouded: 'Kenneth's name is on a stone in the kirkyard here.'

'I see.' Kate pulled at the grass stalks around her, head bent, thick curls tumbling over her face.

My babies have no burial place, nor was there a funeral. No wonder! I couldn't have sat through that meaningless formality. But now I see, being here, that remembrance might have made sense of their non-being, or even, flung away like foam, the wind and the sea might have sung for them . . .

Grief, like age, needs armour.

Donald's voice, saying her name in his own language, broke her thoughts. 'Catriona, your visit's made me look forward, not back.'

She looked up at him, surprised. The sun fell full on her face. And this was how Alastair saw her as he opened the garden gate.

'I'll have to go,' Alastair heard Kate say as he pushed his bike up the path. 'It's been so nice talking to you. I don't want Aunt Morag to worry. Her car, you know.'

'You're very thoughtful,' Donald praised her. 'But, look, here's Alastair, and doesn't he looked pleased with himself!'

Alastair's face had creased into a smile. 'So this is where it's all happening! How are you, Dad? You've a visitor, I see.' And turning to Kate he confessed, with that self-mocking smile she'd noted yesterday, 'I half-hoped I'd see you.' The ride over the rough road had heightened his colour. He looked fit and relaxed as he clasped her hand. 'You *are* good,' he said, his firm grasp lasting a moment or two longer than a mere good-day, 'visiting my father. I bet you've had a rare time to yourself, Dad.'

'We've talked the afternoon away,' said Donald with a smile, and Kate added quickly, 'I've enjoyed every moment.'

'Surely this isn't you away already, Kate?' asked Alastair, propping his bike against the wall of the house, and his father added, 'You'll be needing a wee cup of tea, I'm sure.'

Kate shook her head. Sunlight picked out the amber glints in her hair, and she saw Alastair's look, warm with appreciation. Saw—and connected it not with herself, but with his concern for his father. *What a great relationship here,* she thought. *And yet Donald always looks so sad when he mentions Alastair . . .* Aloud, she said, 'I'd better get off. Aunt Morag will be wondering why I'm taking so long.'

'Ah well, it would be wrong of us to keep you back,' said Donald, shaking hands. 'Thank you for the visit, Kate—and I'll not forget what you said. I'll think it over.'

'I'm so glad,' she said. Alastair escorted her to her car.

'I can see you've done Dad a power of good.' Then, changing the subject, he added, 'I looked out those old papers, if you still want to see them.'

'Yes, I'd love to.'

'Fine. Are we still on for this evening?'

'Oh yes, around eightish?' Kate settled into the driver's seat. 'Though it seems a shame to be indoors.'

He bent towards her, talking through the open door, his face animated. 'No reason why we should . . .' Then, half-jokingly, 'You know the way home? I'm looking forward to this evening!' He stood watching as she headed back towards Coroskirr.

74

6

Coroskirr... Ninian's heart lifted as he eased his car over the last brae with its glimpse of sea and islands, expanse of sand. Fantastic. The world's end... How true, he thought, his mind flashing to his first meeting with Kate. Surely the Well at the World's End is here—and maybe we'll find it together...

He changed gears, bumping between ruts and potholes along the track which wound past Morag MacDonald's cottage, to rise steeply up over the cliff which plunged dramatically down to the sea. Here was a last wide sweep of islands. The craggy outlines of Eigg were etched out by the sun, but clouds hid the peaks of Rhum and blotted out the Cuillins of Skye. Ninian's attention was focused on the track as he navigated the car down towards Port-na-Tuinne.

Buoyed up at the prospect of rediscovering his new inheritance, with Kate to share the experience, Ninian pulled up outside. Glad to stretch his legs, he strolled to the back door.

...Which gave before he'd even turned the key. *I definitely locked that door—I remember going back, checking ... What a stink! Reeks of fags. Bloody hell: someone's been dossing here!*

He took in the dismal scene. Cast-off welly boots. Old milk cartons, crumbs, greasy butter paper on the kitchen table. Dishes piled in the sink. Fishing rods tumbled into a corner, their hooks rusty. Sheets of newspaper tossed down beside the soft chair in the kitchen. Sand and soil from someone's feet scrunched all over the place. Grey scum all over the wash hand basin, a splayed out toothbrush, aerosols which Ninian would never use . . . His sense of outrage rose. He went into the master bedroom to find his bed slept in: rumpled blankets, a stained pillow, a tin of fag ends.

Should he phone the police? The phone box was a good fifteen minutes' walk away, past Morag's cottage, right back where the track joined Coroskirr's only road. He didn't fancy edging the car back over that cliff track . . . He'd need change. He fumbled in his pockets. *Of course, I used it in the shop. Rather than hand the woman a fiver, trying to be helpful. Damn fool. And why the heck didn't I get a phone put in?*

What a mess!

He wished he hadn't come. Wished he had Jane with him—or Kate. Someone to commiserate, help put things to rights.

. . .Not least because the melody he'd jotted down in Edinburgh had been singing in his head the whole way west. He felt ready to add to it, wanted to get down to those papers and glean music from old stories.

And if he went to the phone box, left the house abandoned, the guy could come back and nick Ninian's stuff.

Or might he turn nasty? If so, for his own protection Ninian should turn back at once and phone the police.

He opened a window. *At least get rid of the guy's stink!* Sea sounds came to him: the surf, the wind, the crying of seabirds. He watched waves lift and break on the shore. Phenomenal, he'd told Kate. Endless repetition, infinite variation. Paradise on earth—if it weren't for this intruder. And now he felt uneasy. Suppose the guy had a knife?

Ninian shut the door behind him and, choosing to go on foot, locked his car doors, having found some coins in the glove-box, and swung away over the cliffs, passing the cottage where Kate stayed with her aunt.

His head was full of last year's research: his Jacobite music had been written after hours working through the details of those stormy times. Coming away here into the Highlands had brought it all back to him. But the practicalities of life claimed Ninian's attention: the phone box was out of order.

*

'Mr Bruce, do come in. Of course you can use the phone. Come away in. You'll have a cup of tea after your trouble? You say you've met my great-niece, Kate? She's away seeing another of the old originals. Few of us left, right enough . . .'

Morag MacDonald wasn't a woman to stop what she was doing when she talked. This flow of conversation saw Ninian ushered in to use the phone. A cup of tea on a tray with a white cloth, and scones spread with butter and homemade plum jam, were set on a table beside him. A notepad with phone numbers appeared in front of him—and his hostess withdrew to let him make his call.

He dialled the number. Odd snippets of detail about Prince Charles Edward's attempt to gain the Crown ran in his head. A letter from the Prince . . . *I am charged with the care of my friends and enemies. Those who should bury the dead are run away. My Highlanders think it beneath them to do it. I promised to violate no man's property, but come what will I am resolved to suffer no wounded men to lie untended* . . .

Gallantry, chivalry—the wounded who fell on Culloden Field that April day in 1746 were run through with butcher bayonets and left to die. His Jacobite music was incomplete. A lament was called for, thought Ninian, listening to the engaged signal, dialling again. He'd have to avoid cliché, maybe use native instruments: a clarsach, the borun drums so popular in folk music.

'Yes, I want to report a break-in. That's right, break-in. Someone's been using my place as a squat.'

Morag, appearing to pour more tea into Ninian's cup, murmured something to him. 'Aye,' Ninian added into the phone, 'A lady who lives here all the year round tells me she's noticed a slightly-built youngish guy around once or twice. She thought he was on holiday elsewhere, come over the hills for the day . . . An hour's time? At least? Aye, well, I suppose so; it's a good long way, as you say. Yes, I'll be in. Thanks. Cheers.'

He put the phone down. 'An officer will be over to take a report,' he said.

'Would you like to wait here until he arrives?'

Ninian rose to his feet from the low chair. Drums, a clarsach. *It was a grim time*, he could imagine himself saying to Jane. Or was it Kate, the great-niece of this matronly lady who stood in front of him offering hospitality. He could see the family resemblance, something about the colouring, that lift of the chin. 'That's very kind of you, Miss MacDonald, but I'd better get back. Unpack . . .'

'You think so? Well, if you're worried in any way come right across and get back on the phone. There's another old friend, Alastair Cameron, here just now. He's away this afternoon or he'd be able to help, I'm sure.'

'No, no, I'm fine . . .' *A grim time. But you see, poor old King George had a grim time too*. And Kate, or was it Jane, replied, *Sickness, madness, do you mean? But how does it tie in?* And he'd explain, *Good point, because the future George III was only eight when his uncle Butcher Cumberland inflicted all those cruelties . . . But the whole thing is, George rose above the awful humiliation of his illness, whereas Charles Edward simply ran away. I want my music to link the stories, make a bridge. Reconciliation.*

'Thank you, Miss MacDonald, you've been more than kind. I only hope I won't have to impose on you again,' he said, shaking hands, feeling that Morag's deference to the laird required this formal response.

'It's no trouble at all,' she assured him, watching from the door, waving him away.

Burn water purled from the hill. Larks sang for Ninian. Coll and Tiree basked on the horizon. Further north those waters had carried the fugitive Prince away to safety, abandoning his followers who had given everything for his Cause.

Grim days. A nation takes to the hills, 'skulking', lacking hose and linen. Caves conceal chieftains who lie in these dank places and roast seabirds ...

... are herded like sheep to the scaffold, to the immigrant ships. Women who shelter the sick, who tend prisoners, are punished. Wasn't the Skye woman, Anna McKay, forced to stand among redcoat soldiers for three days and nights? And, noted a contemporary, Bishop Robert Forbes, 'contracted such a swelling of her legs that she'll never get the better of.'

But—Ninian's thoughts ran in counterpoint—*so too the Hanoverian king is tormented by keepers, who bind him even though his bloated flesh is so tender he cannot bear the pressure of bed linen or clothing, gag him when he protests, and force him to eat when he is racked with colic so severe that the Queen of Scots herself, suffering from the same undiagnosed disorder two hundred years earlier, called for a midwife, although she had no reason to suppose herself pregnant.*

The monarch's straitjacket ultimately won mercy for the 'mad poor' shackled naked in Bedlam. No mercy, however, relieved Highland families driven into the hills, their homes set on fire. Yet George, recovered from a winter of torment, received the Sacrament that he might pray for forgiveness for his keepers.

Harpsichord music, thought Ninian, striding back over the cliff top towards his Highland eyrie among the rocks, fouled now by this carrion crow. Jacobite themes composed last year, interwoven with the sorrows of the captive King, would bring together a monarch tarred with the stigma of lunacy, and a prince falsified by romance.

Not caring to enter a house to which an intruder (possibly armed) might be returning, Ninian rummaged in the car for his notebook and pen, found a sunny spot to sit within sight of the sea and got down to work, jotting down, scoring out.

There would have to be humour: the laughter of those whose backs are against the wall. *Woodwind*, he scribbled. And, in keeping with the folk style he favoured, he'd add sopranino recorders with their high range, tin whistles and a marked drum beat. That would pick out the Prince's progress in skirts, 'an odd muckle trallup of a carlin', hoisting his petticoats as he forded a burn, and enjoying the joke with his followers. 'For God's sake, Sir, take care, for you will certainly discover yourself!'

Sitting in the sun, among rocks above the bay where breakers foamed with the incoming tide, Ninian enjoyed the joke too and tried to transpose it to melody.

And then, in the end, sorrow. For the Cause soured; the Prince even in hiding was greedy for his dram; and the Hanoverian king drifted into senility, a prisoner in his own castle at Windsor, his white beard sweeping the royal insignia pinned always to his sunken breast.

Even so, mindful of true dignity, this monarch had erased from his prayer book every reference to his royal majesty, and had written instead: 'George, a most miserable sinner.' And so the piece would end, as Ninian had decided in Edinburgh, with a minor chord, haunting and rounded.

He sat back elated, sure of success once rough corners had been smoothed, harmonies shaped. He flexed his right wrist, stretched out his fingers, stiff with so much writing. But the first draft was finished. And still no sign of the police. He looked at his watch. Four o'clock. The tide was full in. Ninian rummaged in the car boot for a beach robe, flung notebook and clothing into the top of the case, pocketed the car key and ran down to the sea.

The cold took his breath away. His flesh shrank. Gasping, he dived into the waves and let himself be carried with the rhythm of the sea, swimming out into the path of sunlight which sparkled across the water.

And now the composer was his own music, at one with the waves. He surfaced some yards out, looked back shorewards. Black rocks rose behind *Seaview*, circled by buzzards. Birds were at home here; and, out at sea, seals. These had their means of survival. Ninian knew that without imported foodstuffs he had no means of living. He could only ever be a visitor to these shores.

He was warmer now, the water seemed more bearable, but it would be unwise to remain too long in this sea. Ninian struck back for the shore.

The sea had invigorated him. Full of wellbeing and a certain expectancy, Ninian pulled his beach robe around him and jogged over grass which was warm in the sunlight. A man's figure came down from the hill towards the laird's house. Ninian stopped short, out of sight on the sea side of the house. What could he do, vulnerable, naked? Who was the guy, anyway? Changed days, he reflected. When crofters unloaded granite to build the blue-grey walls of *Seaview*, everyone would have noticed and welcomed a stranger.

And the lark said in her song, often goes the Christ in the stranger's guise . . . Rubbra's setting of *The Rune of Hospitality* sang itself in Ninian's mind. There could be a perfectly good reason for a man to be walking over the hills . . . Ninian waited, heard the distant sound of a car engine purring. His heart lifted. The police! He waited, straining his ears, heard nothing more, braced himself and walked round the side of the house. His bare feet made no sound.

He found Jimmy McCann peering into his car.

'Nice wee machine, eh?' said Ninian coolly.

Jimmy swung round. Their eyes met. *Keep calm,* Ninian told himself. He tried to speak steadily. 'I've called the police. They're on their way.'

'Ah huvnae done nothin'.'

'Except take over my house.'

Jimmy eyed Ninian. Slowly, deliberately, he fumbled for a tin of tobacco, tapped shreds into a paper, tucked the tin under his arm . . . Ninian waited, willing that car he'd heard to appear. Jimmy struck a match, pulled on his roll-up.

'Ah'll huv tae get ma gear oot.'

Again their eyes met. *Play for time . . . but why the heck hasn't that car appeared?* 'Get your stuff and go,' said Ninian. He opened the door and stood back. 'After you,' he told Jimmy, and propped himself against the sink, watching Jimmy pick up

81

stuff in the kitchen. 'How long have you been here?'

'No' long.'

'Meaning weeks—or months?'

'Ah tellt ye, no' long. You're no' the bloody polis.'

Ninian didn't attempt an answer. He stood waiting, swivelling his ring, wishing a police officer would appear. Jimmy plainly wished otherwise. He bundled his stuff into a rucksack, picked up the wellington boots and one of the fishing rods.

'Hey, do you mind?'

'That's mines,' said Jimmy. He made for the door, half turning towards Ninian. 'A' right for some.' The door shut behind him.

And still the police hadn't come. Ninian surveyed his house gloomily. He was cold from the sea, and shaken. He put on the kettle and went out to the car for the bottle of good malt he'd been keeping since Christmas.

He scanned the hills. No sign of Jimmy. *Let's hope that's the end of him* ... And now, swinging down the track towards him, floral print outlining her shapely legs, hurried Kate. She caught sight of Ninian and came running to him.

'Aunt Morag told me what's happened. I came over at once.'

He smiled, 'That was nice of you. I thought I heard a car a while back. Hey, but forgive this state of undress.'

'You look fine,' she assured him, liking his courtesy. 'Don't say you've been for a swim already? You're brave. Wasn't it cold?'

'Freezing! Actually, I'm just having a wee snifter.'

'A what?' Then she saw the whisky bottle and smiled. 'Is that to calm the shattered nerves or warm you up after the swim?'

'Both. There's a poem I like by a bard from these parts.' He quoted: ' "Though we thatch our bodies against the wind which makes merciless holes, we need a dram too to kindle a fire inside ..." ' I can't give you the Gaelic, alas. Won't you join me?'

'Love to—but I don't really drink whisky,' Kate said, as

Ninian led her into the lounge with its view over the sea. She went over to the window. 'So this is Port-na-Tuinne! It's as beautiful as you said.'

'And how kind of you to focus on it and not on the mess in the house!'

'What a wretched experience!'

'I felt bad about it when I arrived,' he confessed. 'Bad for the wee guy, too, in a way. A real con man, of course. But I mean, och, Kate—it's the same old story. Them and us. Our class-ridden society. How about a cup of tea?'

'Okay, thanks. So you felt bad for him—that's generous,' she said, but her gaze kept going over to the window.

'Want to sit outside?'

'Yes, let's. There's still no sign of the police.'

'I've been waiting for ages. But I've done a power of work.' He raised his glass. '*Slàinte*.'

'Pardon?'

'Your health.'

'Thanks.' But Kate's eyes were still on the waves which boomed and crashed on the shore. 'Donald Cameron... Morag took me to see him... his son was drowned here.'

'In this bay?'

'Yes...' she jerked her thoughts back to the present. 'You seem very calm. You've managed to get work done, you say? And no salmon-skin belt?' she teased, drinking her tea.

'In the car,' he smiled. 'I haven't had time to unpack.'

'Of course not. So, you felt sorry for your unwelcome guest, Ninian?' Kate repeated. 'What was he like?'

'One of life's losers. Kind of hostile. Sandy-haired.'

'Sounds like the man I met in the shop. He gave me the shivers.'

'Don't worry. We're well rid of him. Listen, I'd love to talk to you about my music. Would you like to hear what I've been doing?'

'Of course. But tell me about your house too. Tucked away in this gorgeous bay. How old is it, do you know?'

'It was built in the '20s for a retired tea planter. He got

local men to quarry stone from the hill and bring it down in barrowloads.'

'Sounds like hard labour,' commented Kate, remembering Ninian's words about 'them and us'.

Ninian sipped his whisky. 'It was. And I tell you, it must have been some sight—those wee steamboats, puffers they were called, chugging in on the spring tide with timber and piping. Everything had to be carried by sea,' he added. 'He even imported Shetland ponies to cart his materials across the sand. Can you imagine the sturdy beasts plodding over the cliff top, down to the bay here? It must have been the talk of Coroskirr for years: the sight of these granite walls rising above the surging surf of Port-na-Tuinne,' he added poetically.

'I can imagine,' Kate said with a smile. 'You tell it so vividly.'

Ninian raised his glass. 'I'm inspired by my audience!' he told her.

'Thank you!' Her thoughts flashed to their first meeting. That easy charm. Well, she liked him too. 'How long did the first laird stay?' she asked

'I don't think anyone ever stayed here long. And you know,' Ninian added seriously, cradling his glass in those supple hands, 'the Murray family who owned Achnacrois and Coroskirr last century—there's a story of a curse.'

'Bad news!' Kate said, startled. 'What kind of curse?'

'It wasn't against them specifically, but both Murray sons died—one in a duel. I've got a lot of bumph if you'd like a look. Anyhow, as I said, no one stayed long.'

'Because of the curse? Doesn't that worry you?'

'Och, Scottish history's riddled with curses. And blessings, I may add. Is the tea all right? Anyway, Kate,' he smiled, 'we've got the Well at the World's End here, remember?'

'Of course I remember,' Kate said. *But*, she thought, *I've found Christ carved on a cross, an old man who shared his lifestory with me, his son who heard of my loss and accepted my story*. 'Bless you, Kate. Bless you'—she could hear Alastair's

84

firm voice tinged with a kind of authority, perhaps all the more real because it came from his own sense of failure... Heard herself urge his father that he should come back to Coroskirr—let go of the past... And had a sense that these were signposts on that pilgrimage of hers—failure and blessing—even as Ninian added, 'I've a hunch it might not be too far from here. I'll show you. Anyhow, the house. The last owner was an elderly lady with an interest in Gaelic songs—very distantly related to my family. She left it to me. I talked my brother and my dad into giving me a hand with some painting. I got someone in to attend to the damp. My next task is to get rid of mice and give the place a good airing—after I've removed all traces of my dosser's dirty ways.'

'That's the last thing you want,' Kate agreed, 'especially when you've got all this music going round in your head. You were going to tell me about it.'

Ninian smiled. 'Well, you see, I'm trying to bring two very different stories together. Last year I did some Jacobite pieces; this year it's King George.'

'Which George?'

'The Third.'

'He had porphyria,' said Kate.

'You've heard about it? You must be a fund of general knowledge!'

'I've read a bit about genetic disorders,' Kate said, and it occurred to her that Ninian had never asked her about herself or her own work. 'Blue blood, indeed!' she went on, adding with a smile. 'Purple, more like.'

'You're so right,' Ninian agreed, smiling at this tall English girl whose brown hair fascinated him with its swirl of amber lights. 'The point is, it's thought this disorder was passed into the British royal family by the Stuarts—intermarriage passed it to the Hanoverians, too.'

Ninian paused to take another drink of whisky.

What a man of moods he is! He apologizes for his appearance, says he is sorry for the guy who's been vandalizing his property, talks so vividly—but he's all wrapped up in his music, Kate thought, watching the sunlight sparkle in Ninian's crystal glass, watching the long fingers of his left hand resting against the dark fuzz of hair curled across his chest.

'By the Stuarts?' she echoed. 'A hectic raging in the royal blood, indeed.' Her mouth puckered into that smile of hers, recalling to Ninian's mind the way she'd looked when she told him about putting her hands into cold well water and making that promise to come to Coroskirr.

'Dead right. How apt! As southern rule has been to Scotland! That's the point. The economy which caused the Union in the first place has become a major irritant, as disastrous as the blood disease . . .'

'I'm not with you. Why turn all this into music?'

Jane would have understood, he thought. Kate watched his face darken. *Can he be so moody?* She tried again. 'You mean you want your music to explore this irritant?'

'That's it!' His face cleared. 'Music brings meaning . . . Listen, what's that?'

'A car.' Kate stood up, listening. 'Coming over the cliff. I saw something shine—a metal glint.'

'That'll be the police.' Ninian drained his glass. 'Oh, Kate, it's so nice of you to have come. I can't tell you how it helps. More warming than whisky,' he smiled, pressing his left hand on her shoulder. Standing so close that she felt his breath on her cheek, he said, 'Has anyone told you you're all honey and amber?'

Shades of Kumar. That gentleness . . . those tender fingers . . . But am I ready for this? And yet, there's something . . .

Kate put her hand over his. 'I'm sorry you've had all this hassle. Do come over if you're worried about anything. Oh yes, and Aunt Morag says, now she's had the honour of having had the *laird*,' Kate gave the last word an impish stress, dropping a quick curtsey, 'inside her cottage, maybe you'd like to come round for a meal some time?'

'That would be nice. And I'll see you tomorrow?'

'Yes. Can I get home by the shore? Or isn't it possible at high tide?'

'Should be okay. You may have to scramble a bit.'

'That's all right. See you then, Ninian.'

She was gone, her hair wind-tossed about her—and Ninian turned to meet the police.

*

'So you liked the laird, Aunt Morag?'

'Aye. Handsome too, and polite. Maybe a touch full of himself. I don't mean conceited. Preoccupied.'

Morag and Kate were busy pooling their observations of Ninian over a meal of mince and potatoes.

'I know what you mean. But he's a musician. And of course he'd had that shock. Just think, that guy's been living right next to you! All winter, when you were on your own.'

Morag smiled at Kate's concern. 'Maybe it's as well I didn't know, in the black dark . . . We'll hope the police will sort things out. So you were at Port-na-Tuinne?'

'Yes . . . The one place Alastair didn't show me. You don't think he'll be offended, do you?—you know, I'm seeing him tonight.'

'It might do him good if he went there himself,' said Morag briskly, serving lemon meringue pie hot from the oven. 'I fancy he gives Port-na-Tuinne a wide berth. But at least he comes back to Coroskirr, which is more than his father does.'

'I told Donald to come back,' said Kate, and saw her aunt freeze with astonishment. 'You did what? Told Donald to come back here?'

'Yes, I know it was a bit outrageous. You're a wonderful cook, Aunt Morag. Donald said so too.'

'Old-fashioned,' said Morag. 'None of these quiches and salads you see in the magazines . . . And what did Donald say?'

'Not much.' Kate toyed with her last piece of pie, spooning meringue apart from the lemon filling, preferring to leave the fresh citrus taste till last. 'He said he'd think about it. And I have a feeling he will . . .'

'Well, Kate, if you can get Donald here it'll be a real

miracle. How about just a wee piece more?'

'Oh, Aunt Morag, I'm sorry. I can't. But it'll keep, won't it? Why don't I make coffee while you relax with a second helping?'

'That's how you keep so slim. Well, all right. You're to meet Alastair, you say?'

'Yes, but I'll write some postcards first. I'll sit outside, I think.'

The evening sun, ebbing tide, dreaming Hebrides, took Kate's thoughts back to the past, to the days before those Morag and Donald talked of: the days when few folk lived here, people whose faith had carved Christ on stone, whose language was lost, and so many of their songs.

Yet there's a shadow brooding in this beautiful place. A curse, Ninian said. People were degraded, shipped away, and the ones who were left were educated in a foreign language...

Kate remembered Donald's words. What was the use of London streets paved with gold for Highland children who trekked across peat bog and silver sand to school? *No wonder there's no one left now, apart from Aunt Morag—and that hostile man dossing at Seaview...* And Port-na-Tuinne, the most beautiful bay of all, brought sorrow and loss... It almost seems there's some sinister influence.

Could there be healing too? she wondered. Ninian's music was trying to bring his sense of harmony to an old enmity. How he'd glowered, though, when she hadn't immediately understood. But then the charm, the easy style she liked, drawing her in, inviting her to join him for a drink, smiling at her enthusiasm for the beautiful bay. His compliments. Honey and amber. His hand on her shoulder, and hers on his. (Alastair's hand had lingered in hers that afternoon—but that was surely because he was so pleased about her visit to his father.) She'd seen a kind of compassion in Ninian too. All that talk about 'them and us'. He'd been sorry for his uninvited guest. *One of life's losers.* Donald would have approved. *We are all losers,* Kate could imagine him saying in that musical voice of his. And, she was sure, Donald wouldn't have sent a dosser away until he'd found him somewhere to stay.

Where is the man now? she wondered, slightly uneasy. But it was chilly. Time to put on something warmer and head across the dunes to meet Alastair. Only two postcards written! Never mind. She hadn't any stamps. She would buy some tomorrow, when she was out with Ninian.

Now it was back to Alastair, in whom she'd confided so much, so soon. Too soon, perhaps? No, no ... Her confidence was safe with Alastair—and she'd felt his immediate concern, his sense of one-ness in her loss.

How amazed he'd been yesterday morning over there on the rocks, when she'd showed him she'd understood his loneliness. He'd shredded that small pink flowerhead in his confusion.

I wonder what he'll think if Donald agrees to come here? Kate, Kate, what have you started now? This could be heavy stuff ...

Yet hadn't she read that facing one's hurt was the first step towards healing? If Donald came back, it would be his decision entirely, Kate argued to herself. All she'd done was plant a suggestion like a seed.

She went upstairs to change. Her aunt was sitting by the fire, reading a magazine. She looked up. 'Is that you away now, Kate? Tell Alastair I'm expecting him tomorrow for that job he promised to do on the roof. I wonder, would you mind taking him a piece of that pie? There we are—safe in your pack. Have a good time,' she added, waving as Kate went jogging across the dunes.

7

'She's a good person—a grand lass . . .' Alastair rode home with his father's praises of Kate singing in his mind. Isabel, his wife for a dozen years, had only ever criticized his parents. *Your father's not practical. Your mother . . .* The absolute pits . . .

Accept the death of your marriage, counsellors advised.

But then you have a daughter, a wee Joey, with her gaptoothed grin and shy, awkward ways. Not a big baby: she'd weighed in at under seven pounds. The most devastating loss of all.

Alastair forced the bike up that last steep hill. One in five, he always reckoned. The effort stopped him thinking, but the whole bleak business surged back in his throat, bitter as bile, as he coasted down to Coroskirr, brakes hard on, wary of ruts and the pebbles under his wheels. He pushed his bike into the old byre.

But Kate was coming tonight . . . A girl who had chosen Coroskirr . . . who seemed to enjoy his company . . . The image of her sitting on the ground, looking up at his father, lifted his heart.

Watch out, he warned himself. *You were wrong last time . . .*

She'd been lit up with the sun and her own radiant self . . .

Do you really want to get back into all that again? A certain freedom threaded the bleakness of singleness. And what had he to offer a vibrant girl like Kate? Failure and shame. But she'd shared her story with him, the loss of her babies, not being married. And she'd done it to help him—that was what was so incredible. For a man who was keeping his head down, on the run from too many failures, it was . . .

No, no, he didn't dare dwell on what it was. But she was coming, and Alastair hurried inside to tidy the place up a bit.

She arrived at eight, casual and relaxed, her face with its light scatter of freckles flushed in the evening sun.

'You've been running—barefoot again.'

'I've got boots in my backpack. Oh yes, and something from Aunt Morag. I'm the St Bernard this time,' Kate laughed, easing her shoulders out of the pack. 'Hope it hasn't got squashed,' she said, bringing out a plate wrapped in foil. 'Here we are.'

'Lemon meringue pie! One of my favourites! Morag's spoiling me rotten. And so's her niece,' he added, his lean face lit up with a smile. 'Come on in . . . We'll put the pie in the kitchen and head right out. The shore—or a wee daunder over the clifftops? Or something to drink first?'

Was he being over-anxious? Trying to sound casual and coming across like a right auld sweetie-wife?

But Kate smiled. 'I'm not sure what a *daunder* is, but the clifftops sound all right. I'd better put boots on. Sorry about this,' she added, perching on a kitchen chair to pull on socks and boots. To her surprise he dropped to his knees beside her and fastened her laces. 'Okay? Not too tight? You don't mind?'

'Of course not, but there's no need . . . ' Colouring, she jumped to her feet. 'Shall we go? Do you need to lock the door?'

'Not usually.' *Damn fool*, he chided himself. *Hold back. You're not sixteen* . . . But Kate was saying, 'Ninian—that's the laird—' (the Scots word sounded strange on her English tongue: Alastair savoured its melody with a bitter-sweet delight) 'he's been broken into. A dosser . . .'

They talked about the laird's misfortune as they

trekked across to the northerly headland which had given Coroskirr its name.

'So I've been to Port-na-Tuinne . . . I'm sorry, Alastair. I mean, I know that was the bay where . . .'

'That terrible place . . .'

They lapsed into silence as they zig-zagged across smooth slabs of rock. The wind sang around them. From somewhere further away came the bubbling call of a curlew.

'It all happened so long ago,' Kate ventured. 'Almost a lifetime.'

'Aye, almost a lifetime.'

Kate hesitated, watching the wind tug his fine straight hair back from his temples. He looked fit, lean . . . She turned to him, touched the thick sleeve of his sweater. 'Alastair . . .'

'No, Kate. Whatever you're going to say, it's too late.'

She dropped her hand. Were those tears in his eyes, or had the wind reddened them?

'I'm sorry.' She hesitated. 'Too late . . . That's what your father said. And I told him it's not. I asked him to come back to Coroskirr—what a fool I was . . .' Her voice died away. They stopped. Kate focused her gaze on clifftops and islands. Evening light veined the cliffs of Eigg, picked out a farmhouse, softened sheer hillsides, but Alastair sounded agitated as he said, 'So that's what he meant about thinking it over. Jings! That *would* take the lid off things, him coming back here.'

'Fools rush in . . .'

'No, Kate. You're no fool. But it's too close . . . Too sore.'

'Too close, too sore, too late . . . No, it's not fair to probe.'

He shot a look in her direction. 'Oh, yes it's fair. From you of all people, it's fair. Because you *know*. You've been there . . .' His gaze went back to the sea. 'It's just, I'm finding it hard . . .'

The silence between them was filled again with sea sounds, comfortable and windswept; filled too with wide skies and distant islands.

'The edge of the world,' said Kate. 'No wonder you come

again and again.'

He narrowed his eyes as though he wanted to look right into the heart of it. 'I can never have too much of it,' he said simply. And as they walked towards a rise where a scattering of rocks proclaimed earlier settlement, Alastair said, 'I let Kenneth's death ruin my life. I know I did.'

'You were young,' she said at once. 'You didn't really want to be a ...minister,' she hesitated over the unfamiliar term. 'You thought it was right—but you couldn't live Kenneth's life for him.'

He looked at her curiously. 'Do you go to church?'

'Not often—though lately I've thought about it. Ever since my sister got married last Christmas.'

'A sister. Just the two of you?'

'Yes. Fiona's two years younger. A speech therapist. She'd been living with Mike for a couple of years.'

'But they're married now?'

'Mm. A church wedding. Not a white one, though. It was Christmas, as I say, and our little village church ... Dark arches dating back to Norman times ... holly ... candles ... Mike sings madrigals. Not for a living, he's a dentist. His group sang at the wedding. Byrd. Something seemed to shiver inside me. It wasn't nostalgia,' she tried to explain, sensing his interest. 'Something more poignant. I find it here too, all this immensity. And at the cross too.'

'So you found the cross?' he asked.

'Overgrown and neglected. But it made me wish I could pray.' Kate was finding it easy to confide in this man who had offered his blessing yesterday. Then: 'I'm going to show the cross to Ninian tomorrow,'—and couldn't know how she knocked him back.

Ninian. The laird. That's you told, mister.

'Ah yes,' he said, carefully.

Kate heard the change in his voice, and glanced at him, but said nothing more until they had dipped into a lonely bay among rugged cliffs.

She felt his closeness as they walked on in silence, their feet scrunching over shingle. *We were getting deep back there,* she thought. *And he seems glad to talk—like when I mentioned his little girl. He's locked in his hurts, like his father. But we were on the right tack* . . . She struggled to find the right words. 'You said you let that terrible accident ruin your life—and you were only fourteen. Aunt Morag's told me,' she explained. 'So young to take on such an enormous burden . . .'

And no, she hadn't made her meaning clear. 'Burden?' he queried.

'Well, wasn't it? A hard life—and not the one you really wanted.'

'A total sham,' he said bitterly.

'A sham? I don't think so. Shall I tell you something?' They were at the water's edge. Slow waves lifted lazily, leaving lace on shining shells. A cormorant coasted above the tide. Seagulls cried. Far out at sea a single sail dipped by.

'So alone . . . so green and clear,' Kate mused.

He shot her a glance, and she turned to face him.

'I don't know how to say this . . . I've never met anyone quite like you, Alastair.'

His face wore that half-rueful smile of his, and Kate smiled back. 'I'm not doing very well, am I?' she told him.

'I don't know . . . I'm wondering what's coming next.'

Kate hesitated again. How could she say, *I think you do yourself down* . . . 'You did . . . well . . . you know, the thing you thought best,' she said. 'And there's strength in that, Alastair.' The words were coming more easily now. 'That's it: strength,' she went on. 'You took all that blame on your shoulders—deciding to follow your brother's calling. Not yours.'

'Aye, what a mistake,' he said bitterly.

'Maybe, but totally unselfish,' Kate told him warmly. 'You felt you were being a sham . . . That's one thing you're not. I don't see anything phoney in you.'

He was walking very slowly now and, after a long pause, he said, 'So, may I ask: what *do* you see?'

Kate touched his arm lightly. 'Someone who's been

scourged,' she said gently. 'Who sees his life as a waste, when perhaps it wasn't . . .' She hesitated again, and added, 'Definitely someone strong.'

'A dour Scot,' he suggested.

Kate smiled, 'Perhaps, a bit,' she confessed, and then she added, teasing him. 'Don't they talk about the hounds of God? That's you. A greyhound.'

'Never!' He was laughing now. 'Gone to the dogs! That says it all.'

She laughed with him, but then her eyes sobered. 'That's what my father said about me. "Gone to the dogs, her and her Paki lover . . ." He was Asian, you see. Bangladeshi, actually. It was an eye-opener—I'd never thought my parents were so racist.' And then, as they crossed the bay and perched on rocks at the foot of the cliffs, she challenged him with an almost embarrassing directness—perhaps she was feeling defensive, in case she'd praised him too warmly, been too personal . . . 'Maybe that's what you think too—about me and Kumar, I mean. Only to be expected—a fallen woman.'

Alastair drew back, shocked. 'A fallen woman! You? No: if I thought anything about your love affair, it would be to think how brave . . . Brave,' he repeated. He was groping for words now, words which would sound right to her. 'You respect people for the way they are . . .'

'You think so? You *really* think so? Oh, Alastair . . .' And it was she who drew back from the passion which lit the face she'd seen so troubled and closed.

'Kate . . .' he began, and checked himself. He bent and sifted the shingle with searching fingers. 'Here we are. And here. See, these wee cowrie shells? They're quite hard to find. Take them, Kate. Souvenirs of Coroskirr. Joey calls this Shelly Bay. Oyster shells, and cowries, groaty buckies, they're called.'

'Don't talk about souvenirs. I don't want to think of leaving!' She crouched behind him and examined the shells he had poured into her open hand. 'You know, I met Ninian, the laird, quite by chance in a salad bar in Edinburgh on my way here. We decided I was going on a pilgrimage. And shells are for pilgrims. "Give me my scallop shell of quiet . . ." Do you know that?' But Alastair shook his head. And again the warning voice: *the laird. Hold back. This is not for you.*

Sensing again the change in his mood, Kate put the shells away, and said, 'You were telling me that prehistoric people settled on this headland. And now those boulders are all that's left. But there's still a feel that people lived here. I suppose they ate shellfish and things. Where would they bury their dead, Alastair?'

'Aye, where? Dig four inches and you hit solid rock.' He straightened and pointed out an easy climb up over the cliffs. Rowan blossom brushed against Kate as she negotiated the rocks. 'Peat preserves you for ever.'

'And sand blows away. Sea burials, then, like the Vikings?' suggested Kate. 'But at least they weren't shipped away like the people last century. No memorial stones for them.'

Alastair looked at her, 'Do you know, Kate, all these years I've been coming here, I've never thought of that. No memorial in the kirkyard. Just a few names in the parish records—as you'll see. Shall we head back?'

'Let's have one last look at the view. What are those islands way in the distance?'

'Uist and Barra . . .'

'Uist and Barra,' Kate repeated. 'Islands of dreams. But didn't you say that if we see them clearly it means the weather's going to break?'

'I think it will hold for a few days yet . . .'

They were heading for the cluster of cottages where Alastair stayed, skirting old peat cuttings and pausing every so often to watch the sun sink lower, flush the horizon with light.

At the cottage Kate stopped. 'Another memorable walk. Thank you . . . And I've got my shells . . .'

'Thank *you*,' he said with emphasis, standing back to let her enter.

'Have a seat,' he offered, ushering her into the front room.

Papers lay neatly stacked on a low table. A chair was pulled up to a picture window facing the most southerly coastline.

Alastair plugged in a heater and pulled it over towards Kate. 'What can I offer you? Sherry? Or would you prefer tea or coffee?'

Kate accepted sherry. Alastair offered peanuts which they both pretended weren't soft.

He's tensed up, formal. He was more at ease outside . . . 'What about the old papers you mentioned?' Kate asked, lightly.

'Here we are.' He lifted a large leatherbound notebook from the table, switched on the overhead light.

Kate took the book in careful hands, opened it and read aloud, ' "1775. This being the first week day that the Session met . . ." Look at that: the first "s" is an "f" . . . "The Minister exhorted the Elders to Love and Unanimity amongst themselves and advised them to be regular and circumspect in their Walk and Conversation . . ." Alastair, this is a gem! *Circumspect in Walk and Conversation . . .* And the writing, too: genuine old copperplate. Where on earth did you get it?'

'From the Session Clerk. It's about 200 years old.'

'Yes . . . 1776. It's amazing! But surely it should be stored in some sort of archive?'

'Probably. But here it is for you.' Alastair sat back with a quiet smile.

'I'll look after it, I promise.'

'I know . . .' She was pulling off her warm top. Her head was hidden in some sort of fluffy velour, her tee-shirt rode up. He glimpsed a taut midriff, and now she was smoothing her hair with quick casual fingers, bending to take up the book again. He saw the outline of her round small breast.

'Listen to this.' She was animated, engrossed. ' "1783. The necessities of the poor now induce the Session to distribute their funds small as they are. Whereupon the following persons were fixed upon as being the most distressed objects in the parish . . ." *Objects,*' Kate repeated, looking across at Alastair, her eyes sparking indignation. 'That's terrible.'

'Objects of charity,' he explained, his mouth lifting in a smile of amusement at Kate's outburst.

'Some charity! But listen... "Passage of paupers to Glasgow. Herding lambs donated to the poor... blind, cripple, ill of sore foot, papist, bedrid, deaf, dumb and idiot, changeling." Oh, Alastair, *changeling*. That's a child stolen by the fairies and this is, let me see, what year, 1789...'

'I remember that bit about the changeling...'

'And you made a copy of all this once, you said?'

'Aye, it was a wet summer. Here.' He showed her a jotter covered with pages of careful handwriting. Kate turned the pages with interest. *I have Ninian's writing in my diary, the laird captured in ink. Alastair has given me shells and the loan of a valuable old book*... She turned back to the original.

'You went to a lot of trouble to get this for me...'

'No sweat. I cycled over after I'd cut Dad's grass. And maybe there was something for me in it—the Session Clerk told me that the charge here's coming vacant. It covers Achnacrois and Coroskirr—and other wee places too.'

'How exciting! So you might come and work here?'

'Yes. It's been my dream for a long time,' Alastair said slowly. 'I took up teaching for Isabel's sake—trying to save the marriage,' he added. 'The denomination I belong to allows a divorced person to minister—though you're still a non-person. Everyone wondering what went wrong. No one wanting to be the one to ask. Only, if I ever have a charge again, it could be here. The Kirk Session have known my family for years.'

'And respect you, I'm sure,' Kate said warmly. 'So it's not too late, Alastair. This time, follow your dream!'

'You think so?'

'Of course!' Their eyes met. *This is high-powered stuff. Careful, Kate.*

She's beautiful. I've touched her hands, her feet. Quick, furtive touches. Glimpsed her breast... little, rounded.... She's seen my hands tremble. She doesn't know it's because of her... Dear God, she must never know. I can't impose on her...

But can I do what she's saying?

'You're telling me to forget the past. Forget! Kate,' he leant forward, his hands held out in front of him, his eyes searching her face. 'You're saying I've to put all my failure behind me. My shame. That I'm entitled to my dreams, a man like me who feels tainted...' His voice died away, but Kate's eyes held his. 'That's exactly what I'm saying. *Of course* you're entitled to your dreams. But you *must* put the past behind you. Not forget it. Face it, then let it go. That's what I'm trying to do.' But then she looked away. 'I know it's hard for you.'

Alastair's hands dropped to his knees. 'Hard. Aye, it's hard all right...' There was a long silence between them. Kate turned back to the papers. Suddenly her voice broke into his thoughts.

'Alastair, look, listen: you must listen to this.' She jumped to her feet and stood beside him, leaning over him, thrusting the book at him, her hands and voice shaking. ' "1837," ' she read aloud, pointing her slim finger at the careful script. ' "Board and lying-in charges for Catriona MacDonald and Bastard Twins whose paternity has not yet been established." *Twins... Catriona...* That's my name... And MacDonald too. Perhaps she was directly related. And she wasn't married...' A giveaway that, but Kate was too absorbed in her namesake's story to care, and Alastair was absorbed too. Kate was so close he could feel the warmth of her. A woman so close, and this woman... 'Now what's this?' she was saying. ' "Two pounds",' she read, ' "Seven"—that's shillings isn't it? "and ten"—what's that?—"and a half pence". That's what they gave her, all noted down, not forgetting the ten and a half pence.'

'Tenpence ha'penny,' he corrected, smiling up at her.

'Is it? That old money! But Catriona MacDonald. My name,' she repeated. 'Twins. My story's here, Alastair. *Whose paternity has not yet been established...* What prudery!'

'Thrift, not prudery,' he ventured, his smile spreading

across his whole face.

'Thrift!' she repeated indignantly.

'Good Scots thrift,' he assured her, laughing now. 'Kate MacDonald, our Catriona . . .'

'*Bastard twins*,' she exploded. Her eyes filled with tears.

He put out his hand. He wasn't begging, now. No longer a plaintiff, beseeching to be allowed to follow his dreams. He touched her arm, stroking very gently. 'They were beautiful wee lassies, I'm sure, Kate, those little baby daughters of yours . . .'

'Oh, Alastair!' Her voice shook. She sat down. 'They were beautiful. They were darlings. And I didn't hold them. Didn't touch them. Didn't even bury them. Didn't give them names . . .' She was crying quietly, her shoulders shaking. He passed her a box of tissues. 'It's all right, Kate, don't cry . . .' he murmured. She blew her nose, and looked at him, unashamed to show her tear-streaked face. 'I've got to cry. I can't help it. I was crying for them on those rocks, you know, when you brought me coffee.'

'That's maybe why you looked so chilled. How about some coffee now? Another wee sherry?'

'No, no. I'd better go.' She smiled through her tears. 'Look at the sky . . . washed with light. Amber and emerald. Except we can't see properly through the glass, with the electric light.'

'It'll be dark across the dunes.' He was pulling on his jacket, opening a drawer, rummaging for a torch.

'I may take this book, mayn't I?'

'Of course. Here, let me find a bag.' He produced a plastic bag, held it open, practical, matter-of-fact, but Kate knew that her tears had touched him, and, she hoped, helped him too. *But let's keep this light,* she thought, and said, trying to sound matter-of-fact too, 'It's the age of the poly bag.' Adding as she eased the book inside, 'They used real leather in those days; ink you can still read after two hundred years. But treated people as *objects*! Anyway, thank you again for going to so much trouble getting this for me.'

100

'Not at all.' He took the bag from her.

'Are you coming, too?'

'Of course.' He pulled the door behind them and switched on the torch.

'Let's have one last look at the shore.'

She stumbled and his arm went under hers, but on the sand they stood apart, watching the ebbing tide fill rock pool and wave ridges with pale light. Seabirds cried. A sudden screeching: gulls drove a heron from the shore.

'Was there any more about Catriona?' Kate asked finally, as they headed over the dunes. The sky was a patchwork of light and dark: streaks of colour in the far east, purple over the hills, paling as a sliver of moon eased its way through. There was a scattering of stars, and, over the dunes, white smudges—the ubiquitous sheep.

'Not much—a couple more entries.'

'What happened to her?'

'Kate, I have to tell you, they shipped her away.' Alastair's voice came jerkily behind her as they walked over narrow tracks made by the sheep. He shone his torch ahead of her.

'It isn't in the records,' he added, drawing abreast over smoother grass. 'But once, when I was in Edinburgh for the General Assembly, I went into West Register House. I found a list of names of people cleared from here, including Catriona MacDonald and a ten year-old-boy.'

'One of the twins must have died.'

'It seems so.'

They were at Morag's cottage now.

'So where did she go, Catriona and her boy?'

'Australia. To work in gold mines. If they ever got that far. And of course, once there, not many survived. The heat. The new way of life. It's a sad story.'

'A terrible story,' Kate agreed. 'One I knew nothing about. Not even from my grandfather. So all that's left is this book. And her name in the papers you read in Edinburgh. I wonder where she buried her child?'

'I don't know.' He switched off the torch and they were

standing together in this northern never-dark.

'Maybe Ninian will have something about it in his papers,' Kate said. 'I'll ask when I see him tomorrow. Thank you so much for this.'

'You're welcome. Well, I'll maybe see you when I'm up doing the roof.'

'You're very kind to Aunt Morag.'

'She's been good to me,' Alastair told Morag's great-niece gravely. *The laird,* he thought. *But she'll not think there's anything wrong in a wee goodnight kiss.* He took her hand. 'Good night, Kate.' And he brushed his cheek against hers, felt the touch of her skin, her curls.

'Good night, Alastair. I'll give you the book back as soon as possible.'

'No hurry,' he assured her, saw her into the house and turned away.

His own seemed all the emptier on his return. He left the room in darkness and knelt by the chair where she had sat, his face resting against the cushion, his eyes on the last sunset rays lingering far in the west. It was a long time before he went to his bed.

8

'So you see,' Kate was saying to her aunt next morning, 'Alastair goes to so much trouble to get the parish book for me, and I find my namesake. It's uncanny.' She propped a plate into the plastic rack on the draining-board. 'I've used too much liquid soap again, I'm sorry. All these suds. I'm not used to this soft water.'

'That's all right,' Morag, sieving flour, reassured her niece. 'I was in London once. I couldn't get used to the water there—so hard.'

'Give me Coroskirr any day. I wonder if Catriona got thrown out by her family? She must have met with so much disapproval.'

'She will have, indeed,' Morag agreed. 'So you're off with the laird today?'

'Yes, any moment.' Kate rubbed her hands on her linen shorts, and raced upstairs.

Morag smiled indulgently as strains of Hebridean folk-song echoed through her usually silent house, followed by a shout of, 'He'll be here any moment—I heard the car coming over the cliff road. Is my camera down there?'

'On the sideboard,' Morag called back. Kate hurried downstairs, crammed her camera into her bag, kissed her aunt and rushed outside as Ninian pulled up.

She deserves some happiness, she's had a bad time, Morag

thought—too discreet to wave them off.

'Hi! How are things after the hassle? How did it go with the police?'

'Not bad. I've about fumigated the place now.'

'You've obviously managed to unpack,' Kate said, noticing his belt.

'And had another swim this morning,' Ninian smiled.

'I must follow your good example,' she teased.

'That would be nice,' he told her with a sideways glance. 'I swam nude.'

'Skinny dipping. Oh.' Kate laughed, then pointed to his ring. 'That ring? *A Song for Jane*?'

'Fair enough,' he smiled, and was telling her about Jane as Alastair cycled along the track towards them. Ninian slowed. Alastair lifted his right hand in thanks, saw Kate in the passenger seat, and waved.

Kate wound down the window. 'Have a good day on the roof!' she called. He nodded with a smile which somehow didn't quite reach his eyes, wobbled over a rut and was gone.

'That's Alastair Cameron,' Kate said as Ninian drove on.

Again he shot her a glance. 'Here on his own?'

'That's a loaded question, isn't it? Alastair's a family friend. I went to see his father yesterday, the person I told you about, whose son was drowned.'

His good humour returned. 'You know more people here than me . . .'

. . . *Jane*, Kate was thinking. *Clearly a gifted person, streets above me. Am I jealous? He's very attractive . . .*

'Where are we off to?' Ninian went on.

'I have to buy stamps . . . Then there's the cross,' Kate suggested. 'And what about our pilgrimage to the healing well?'

'I don't think we need go far to find it. Or at least where I think it might be,' Ninian said. 'Okay, the great metropolis, Achnacrois.'

The road wound ahead of them, dipping up and down.

'So, Jane wants a space. An interval?'

Ninian changed gears. His hand brushed her knee. 'You're a beautiful woman, Kate. When I saw those long legs of yours getting in beside me today I couldn't believe my luck. Why don't we stop for a moment?'

He pulled into a passing-place, rolled back the sun roof and switched off the engine. Birdsong and the skirl of burn water filled the air.

'Remember how we met in Brewster's Bar? There was an immediate rapport. Quite honestly, I've come here just now because of you.'

Kate sat still, looking ahead. Hazels grew beside the burn. Trying to defuse the atmosphere, she pointed, 'Look, Ninian. Hazels of wisdom, wasn't it? And the salmon of knowledge is round your waist.'

He smiled, 'Which comes first, wisdom or knowledge?'

'The tree of Knowledge grew in Paradise... But Eve wasn't wise when she ate it.'

'*Felix culpa*. The happy fault.'

'The happy—wait a minute. "Adam lay y-bounden",' she said, quoting the medieval carol, sure he'd know it; and she was right—he was delighted. His hand was on her right leg, his long fingers touching her bare knee. His fine tenor voice sang teasingly, 'Four thousand winter...' Kate added her voice, 'Thought he not too long...' He laughed, increasing the pressure of his fingers on her knee. 'Well done, Kate. "And all was for an apple..."' Shall we go on?'

'An apple that he took...' They sang with their faces turned to one another, as their voices sent the old English words dancing above the plashing of the Highland burn.

'So our pilgrim Kate's a singer?' Ninian queried.

'Nothing serious... I couldn't compare with Jane,' she told him. *In more ways than one*...

She wondered whether to lift his hand away. Instead she twiddled his ring. 'Not a wedding ring, so what...?'

'Just an old family thing. You don't mind?'

'Mind?'

'My hand on your knee?'

Kate smiled, 'I knew there were good vibes when I accepted your invitation to come with you today.' But then she gave his fingers a warning tap, 'Not too fast, though, Ninian. Go easy.'

'Pity. I like the fast lane.' He removed his hand, let his fingers curl round hers, lifting her hand towards him. 'Don't you?'

Kate shook her head. 'I'm not eighteen any more.'

He looked at her shrewdly, 'Once bitten?'

'Or something,' she fielded. 'Shall we taste this famous Highland spring water then?'

'Why not?'

They stood among the hazels with nodding catkins, the fresh green of larches. Ninian bent to fill a plastic mug he had found in the car. Primroses starred the bank. *Be careful, Kate,* she told herself. *You've been hurt before.*

Ninian turned to her, smiling, offering the mug. '*Slàinte*—your health!'

'Thanks. To us and Coroskirr. Blessings upon us. You see, I haven't forgotten what you wished me over the apple juice. And the water *is* good. Try it.' She passed him the mug. 'Will the Well at the World's End taste like this?'

'Better,' he assured her, turning to refill the mug.

'So where is our healing spring, do you think?'

'Between your house and mine. And that's nothing if not symbolic, don't you agree?' He started the engine and they drove on. '*The Well at the World's End.* I want to set it to music when I've finished my other piece. I'm here to write, after all, it's not just an alibi,' he said, with a glancing smile. 'By the way, on the left there, the old graveyard—a grave there's supposed to have been cursed.'

'The curse you were telling me about . . . Ohhh! Ninian!'

Kate shuddered, braced herself. Neither had noticed an oncoming van approach at speed, forcing them off the single track road.

Ninian braked sharply. The car slithered. A few feet further and they would have plunged into a bog. Here, a narrow strip of gravel had been used to make the road slightly wider, and the car righted itself inches from the edge.

'That was deliberate!' Kate gasped. She looked behind them, but the van had disappeared round one of the many bends in the road. 'Why, Ninian, why? What's it all about?'

He sat very still, his hands clutching the wheel.

'Ninian, are you all right?'

He forced himself to speak. 'Yes, Kate, thanks.'

'No thanks to that driver,' Kate replied fiercely.

'Did you get a sight of him?'

'No, it happened too quickly. A hate attack? Don't you think we should tell the police?'

'Oh, Kate, the police station's thirty miles away. Think what an age it took for them to come out yesterday. And we haven't much to tell. I didn't even notice the make of the van—did you?'

'Only its colour. Quite easy to identify, orangey red. But are you sure you're all right?'

'I'm getting over it. How about you? Would you like to go for a drink or something? The hotel's back that way.'

'Which means turning the car. We're pointing the right way for the cross. Let's go on. Besides, we've had a fright and that place is so peaceful . . .'

'The place of blessing.'

A few minutes later he was smiling again. And he slipped his arm around Kate's waist as they walked down to the bay where the old stone with its crudely carved cross stood facing the sea.

'That's it,' Kate said. 'But the cross I liked is inside this broken down wall.'

They stepped into the walled enclosure. Ninian drew apart, made the sign of the cross, stooping to kiss the nailed feet weathered on the stone. They stood together in a long silence.

'There's peace here,' Kate said, caressing the sun warmed stone. 'Like reading a message you can touch. You obviously feel it too,' she said, adding with a smile, 'You're closer than me.'

'Closer? To him?' He looked surprised. 'Me? No, I'm too selfish, too much a sinner.'

And he bent his knee to the ground as they turned away.

That was the right thing to do, she thought, her mind flashing back to her sister's wedding and that sense of—what had it been?—the mystery yet the familiarity of the Godhead. Now, under the wide arch of the sky, the neglected Christ was a silent offering of love which said 'approach me, I am here'. And Kate found herself wishing that the wounded love of the stone Christ could heal the tragedy which haunted Donald and Alastair.

They lingered for a long moment, then, wanting to have a reminder of this neglected stone, Kate pulled out her camera. 'Wait a minute. I must take a photograph,' she said to Ninian. Then, 'I've been reading your old parish records. Alastair borrowed them for me.'

'Oh?' he said. 'Anything interesting?'

Kate nodded. 'There's a girl mentioned. My namesake. Catriona MacDonald. I'd love to find out more about her. I wondered if you might have information.'

'In my old family papers? I can't promise she'll be mentioned, but you're welcome to borrow them. In fact, the Murray residence is where we're going for lunch.'

They bought Kate's stamps. The shop did not improve on further acquaintance, and they were glad to head away to the fake baronial splendour of the nineteenth-century building which had become a hotel.

'Sir John Murray owned the entire peninsular,' Ninian explained. 'Stags' heads and all,' he added, nodding towards mounted heads in the hall. 'Obviously not into Animal Rights.'

'Nor human ones,' said Kate, crossing the hall. 'Let's sit by the window and look out at the sea.'

They ordered fresh salmon and chilled wine. Ninian raised his glass. '*Slàinte.*'

'*Slàinte,*' Kate repeated.

'You're learning!' He smiled his approval. 'You'll soon

know as much Gaelic as any of us Lowland Scots.'

'*Bahut achcha* . . . And, no, I didn't sneeze.'

Ninian laughed, his teeth white and even. 'So, what did you do?'

'Said, *very good*.'

'In?'

'Punjabi,' she told him assertively, keeping her end up.

'More widely known than Gaelic, that's for sure,' Ninian commented, refilling Kate's glass.

'Thanks.' She sipped the wine, enjoying the flow of talk as much as the silence they'd shared in the walled enclosure. 'How about Asian music?' she asked. 'Will it ever become part of mainstream music, do you think?'

'And not just a side dish to Chicken Madras?' he teased, over his wine.

Kate smiled. *Is he enjoying this too? Or playing along, wishing we could go back to where we were in the car, move into the fast lane?* 'I must say I like the sitar,' she ventured, and thought how lame this sounded.

'Amazing, isn't it?' Ninian agreed. 'Akin to some of the stringed instruments folk groups use. I'm trying to incorporate that sort of sound into the piece I'm working on.'

'Making the marginalized part of the mainstream? I like that. I didn't hear any sitar sounds in *A Song for Jane*,' Kate added, knowing he'd be glad to talk about his work.

'You listened carefully, then?'

'I liked it very much,' Kate told him, sincerely.

He smiled. 'I'm glad.' And squeezed her knee as he got up to pay the bill.

'Please let me pay my share.'

'Not this time. It was my invitation, remember?' Ninian said as they crossed the baronial hall on their way to the car.

Yes, thought Kate, *and I accepted, but I'm not paying my way. Or is my company enough?*

'Thank you for lunch, Ninian,' she told him.

He teased her with a little formal bow and held open the car door. 'Thank you, Kate,' he replied, in a tone which made her wonder if this weren't all a big send-up.

They drove towards the ruined castle Kate had noticed from the ferry, parking the car to walk towards it past warning notices: *Danger. Keep out.* 'It shouldn't be left like this,' objected Kate, clicking her camera once more.

'Send a report to the laird,' suggested Ninian at her side. 'Tell him his property's ruinous.'

She laughed. 'What will his lordship do?'

'His hands are tied,' said Ninian, lacing his fingers through hers. 'But he'll file your findings with pleasure. Oh, Kate.'

And yes, she had known it would come to this: mouth to mouth making music above rocks where waves crashed, claymores once clashed, and galleys brought captives to walls Kate no longer saw clearly. Here too, men and women had made love, harping with body, mouth and finger music both wild and tender.

His arm went round her waist once more. 'You're beautiful, beautiful . . .' She slipped her arm about him and they walked like lovers towards the car. *His touch makes my body sing. Only Kumar ever did that. But am I ready for this music?*

After two winters without a caress, or even much companionship, isolated, experiencing loss, Kate knew herself to be hungry. *You're telling me to forget the past.* Alastair Cameron's voice, pleading, as if he begged for release, echoed in her mind. And her reply: *Face it . . . let it go.* Wasn't this what she had come here to do? And had met Ninian right at the outset, to encourage her on her pilgrimage. Yet it was not Ninian she had told about her babies. *Let it go . . .*

'We fit well together,' she said, and Ninian promptly took this as an encouragement to chart with his supple hand contours he'd been appreciating since their first meeting.

Wanting to stay in neutral, Kate said, lightly, 'We've been to the stately home and the castle. How about a visit to a crofter? Or at least someone brought up on a croft. Donald Cameron. I'm sure he'd love to meet you.'

'I'd be pleased to meet him too,' Ninian said at once. *And, yes,* Kate thought, *he's not so much the artist that he can't feel at*

110

ease with people, which is nice. But the flip side, I suppose, is it's useful *for him to keep in with local people* . . .

With these contradictory thoughts, Kate led Ninian up the path where Alastair had pushed his rusty bike yesterday, his face brightening at the sight of his father's guest.

They found Donald in his kitchen, sorting through yellowing cookery books which took him back to summer 1939, with Margaret singing hymns as she followed one of her mother's recipes for jam, stirring a big copper jelly pan on a newly installed gas cooker.

'6 pounds blackcurrants 3/6. 9 pounds of sugar 2/7. *Since Jesus came into my heart* . . . Total 6/1. *Floods of joy in my soul like sea billows roll* . . . That means if we get 17 pounds of jam it will be $4^1/_4$ d a pound.'

Fourpence farthing a pound that July day, when the world would soon erupt into war and Donald would join the army, postponing wedding plans until VE day.

Kenneth had been born five years later, growing full of the promise of faith and intelligence. Like his father, Kenneth would have chosen to share the lives of people neither father nor son would ever label 'the poor'. The Reverend Geoff Shaw in the Gorbals, Father Borrelli in Naples, the Abbé Pierre and his ragpickers in Paris: these men who pioneered the work of the church in what would become known as 'the inner city' were Kenneth's heroes. His younger brother, driven by a different necessity, preached to congregations who might offer their minister a crystal glass of sherry, but would never give him their hearts.

It was this unfulfilled promise which had hit Donald so hard, robbing even his faith of meaning. Yet did not the old people of the islands say that the drowned have water in plenty: why wash them a second time?

I kept watch for my love, salt for my sorrow; spindrift for his shroud. The deeps are his bed; his linen is not of my making. The beloved of my body is the heart-wound of me . . . Old songs mourning, and perhaps thereby healing grief. Death by drowning, an ever-present reality for those whose commerce is with the sea.

Donald had not returned to the sea which had parted him from his son. But now Kate had come, kinswoman of a man Donald remembered as a dour lad, who'd left the care of ageing parents to his unmarried younger sister. This grand-daughter of Iain MacDonald's was a feeling-hearted girl; and she had asked him directly the thing no one in his own family ever dared: Come back to Coroskirr. And Donald had defended himself, talking about armour.

Armour, he thought now; *when the Lord was stripped naked.* But there was a knocking at the door. No one had ever knocked in the old days; nor even now, though callers were few. And there was Kate herself, with a dark-haired man she was introducing as Ninian Bruce, the laird.

'Come in, come in. You'll be having some tea, I'm sure.'

Now they were sitting round the kitchen table. Kate was switching on the kettle and the laird was quoting that old thing Edinburgh housewives were supposed to have said: *You'll have had your tea?* And Donald was thinking: *They seem well suited. Maybe this man will help the lass get over her sorrow.* The young ones asked about the old days, and Donald thought how times had changed—that the laird should sit in a back kitchen supping his tea. But he would never say such a thing, of course. All the while that challenge was echoing: *Come back to Coroskirr.* And Donald was reasoning: *Strip off the armour. Harness chafes. The body, encased in steel, sweats.* But the word 'armour' had brought to his mind an old Bible verse which kept hammering away inside his head: '*Wherefore take unto you the whole armour of God.*'

'That was very nice,' Ninian said, getting to his feet. 'It was good to meet you, Mr Cameron.'

Kate got up too. She pressed Donald's hand. 'Thank you so much, Donald. I told Ninian we couldn't miss the chance of a talk. Your grass looks very neat now,' she added, as Donald saw them out to the front.

'Aye, Alastair makes a good job of it.' And again there was just the hint of a sigh.

'He cares a lot,' Kate said. 'I know he does.'

'Yes,' said Donald. 'He's always been a good son to his mother and myself.' And he added, almost to himself, 'Maybe too good.'

She was half turning to go, but she checked at this, looking back at the old schoolmaster, his shoulders stooped in his soft tweed jacket, his blue eyes which she'd so often seen looking inwards, back to the past, filled with something: a question, perhaps. Kate couldn't be sure.

'You see,' Donald said. 'I'm still thinking over what you said.'

Kate smiled. 'It isn't too late. I'm sure it isn't.'

Was she telling an invisible Alastair that too? 'Thanks again,' she called, and followed Ninian down to the car.

Donald watched them go. He turned back into his kitchen, and minded too late about the picture. He'd had it looked out, all ready for Kate, since she'd been so interested in the story. Well, perhaps it was meant to be. He would bring the painting himself when he came to Coroskirr. He put the cookery books away and went into his bedroom for his Bible.

*

'Nice old boy. I'm glad you introduced me. Where now, Kate?'

'The Well at the World's End, of course,' she said, and Ninian laughed and turned the car back towards Coroskirr.

They passed Morag's house, and pulled to the side of the road just short of the cliff road.

'I think it could be somewhere here.'

A grassy hillside sloped down between Morag's white cottage and the cliff road to *Seaview*. A cuckoo called from a fold in the hill. Islands shimmered on the horizon. 'We're guarded by hilltops and islands,' commented Ninian, as they made their way across the hillside to a small burn. 'This small rise here is marked on my map as Cnoc-na-cille.'

'Translate,' said Kate, walking beside him, and neither of

them knew that Alastair Cameron, straightening from his day's work on the roof, saw the laird put his arm around the shoulders of the girl he . . . the girl.

'*Cnoc* means a small hill. Knoll, perhaps. And *cille* means cell. A monk's cell: you know, those beehive sort of things the old Celtic monks made.'

'I'm not sure that I do, but never mind.'

'Let's sit here, beside the burn, and you can tell me if you think I'm right about the Well at the World's End being here.'

The hillside, Cnoc-na-cille, was filled with the crying of lambs. Sheep tore the springy grass. The wind was gentle, the sun strong and kind, and the burn threaded a living seam through the hill, pouring out from some hidden source.

'It's never dry,' Ninian began, as Kate was saying, 'So this is it: the Well at the World's End? Just an ordinary burn. A spring, I suppose, not at all like my Greek well.'

'No goats,' said Ninian, with a smile. 'Just as well,' he teased her. 'Smelly animals. Randy too.'

She looked at him with an answering smile. 'There's the smell of wild thyme,' she countered, crushing a leaf between her fingers. 'Perhaps we have to taste the water for its healing properties to be revealed,' she suggested, cupping her hands under the swift flowing water. 'It's cold.' The water trickled through her fingers. She scooped up a mouthful, drank, turned back to Ninian. 'It *is* a special place, Ninian, guarded by hilltops and islands, as you said. And the water is sweet and clear.'

'Let me taste this sweet water!' He caught hold of her hand, wet and cold from the water, bent his mouth to her palm, tilted her head back and she was crushed by his kiss. His hand touched her breasts. 'I want to drink *your* sweetness, Kate.'

'I know. I want it too.' But even as she said it she was holding back, taking control of his hands, putting them into her own.

'What is it then, Kate?'

'Give me time, Ninian. I'm confused. Uncertain. This

114

beautiful place.'

'Let's make it even more beautiful.' His handsome features darkened with disappointment. 'And there isn't much time. You're here—for how long?'

'Ten days. Ninian, I told you, go easy.'

He stood back. 'I'm sorry, I just need more time,' Kate repeated. 'A pilgrimage,' she pleaded. 'Remember? You said so yourself. I'm really sorry.' She added with a flash of laughter, 'Jane's making her inner journey. Kate's on pilgrimage.'

'And poor Ninian stays celibate,' he smiled. 'But I won't push you to anything you don't want.'

'Thanks.' Kate turned back to the water, making small waterfalls pour round her fingers. '*Grace*, you said,' she reminded him. '*To aid a pilgrim is to share the grace*. What is grace, Ninian?'

He sat on a boulder. 'I could say it's what you're denying me,' he chided, and she flushed. 'It's given to the undeserving,' he went on. 'That's certainly me.'

She looked up. A smile played around his lips. 'Sorry, Kate. I didn't want to rush you. It's just you've—well, taken me by storm.' He held his hand out, and she took it, laying her other hand lightly against his chest.

'You have that effect on me too. That's what I'm afraid of. If it weren't so good, I . . .'

'You'd say "yes" and we could let it happen?' he teased.

'No, no, not that at all.'

'I know. I was joking. That was unkind. Okay, so it's good but we mustn't give way to it? Well, I've got music to work on as well.'

'You were saying you've got ideas based round our healing spring,' Kate prompted.

'Yes.' He relaxed on the rock, and she settled back, rubbing her wet hands against her shorts.

'Well, I came across the story in an obscure reference to Columba,' he began and, glad of this return to neutral, Kate commented, 'I thought Columba was associated with Iona.'

115

'Of course, but he didn't stay there, naturally. In fact there are almost as many references to him round these coasts as there are to Bruce and his spider.'

'Bruce? One of your ancestors?'

'I doubt it.' His voice was tinged with impatience and Kate drew back a little. *Does he think I'm such a fool of a Sassenach?* She could almost hear the tetchy way her grandfather used to talk: anyone south of the Highland Line who annoyed him was a *damn fool Sassenach*. Old stories from history surfaced in her memory. 'Of course! King Robert the Bruce. The Battle of Bannockburn. He watched the spider spin its web. And learnt patience,' she said, adding, with a lift of her chin which her great-aunt would have recognized as pure Coroskirr MacDonald. 'A Bruce characteristic, perhaps?'

Ninian laughed. 'Okay, Kate, you win! Where were we? Columba. Well, a monk whose name I can't recall came to Coroskirr and baptized Pictish peasants beside a healing well. Which may have been this spring. See the boulders lying scattered around? And it may be this unknown brother who built his cell here on the hill. Anyhow, the story goes that a Pictish princess came along. The Picts were matrilineal.'

'In what way?' Kate asked, her fingers pulling at a piece of wild thyme, its scent pungent and good in her nostrils.

Ninian flashed her one of his warm smiles, 'Sorry, that's getting a bit technical. It's that just the kingship passed through women. But the point is: this princess had borne only dead children,' he continued in the same matter-of-fact tone.

And why shouldn't it be matter-of-fact? Dead children. Had borne only dead children ... My story again. Catriona last night. A princess now ... Kate wondered if her face had changed. If she'd given any sign. But Ninian went on. 'She was baptized along with the peasants. And my guess is it was here—though the name of the hill and the scattered boulders are the only clues.'

'But why should a princess choose to be baptized here?' queried Kate.

Ninian looked at her in surprise. 'I don't know. I suppose she . . .' But then his face changed. He caught Kate's hand. 'Of course! That's it! She was a pilgrim, like you. I like it! The story ends simply by saying she became a mediator in the quarrels of kings. And that the poor loved her. She'd found grace and received wisdom, obviously. And it all happened here, between your house and mine, at the world's end.'

'Tell me,' said Kate, and Ninian slipped his arm round Kate's shoulder. 'See, Kate, how you fill me with music.'

'Not me. The music's yours. So are the ideas. I'm glad you're building it around the story of a woman.' *A woman who has borne only dead children.*

'Well, listen, here's this woman who belongs to the court. Maybe it was over the headland: a heap of stones, no mod cons, but still a centre of power.'

'Right. So what does she see?'

'A dirty wee man, whose breath when you get close enough stinks of bad diet.'

'Ragged and rancid. But she was probably a bit niffy too.'

'Yes, and so was the crowd gathered round him,' Ninian went on, and they were in unison, as they'd been when they'd sung their carol together.

'But the buzzards would have been circling round the rocks, just like now, and the burn water would be flowing, larks singing. And the sea and the islands. Completely unchanged. And the smell of thyme, maybe. Can you put smells into music?' she teased him and he smiled too.

'Aye, and empty the concert hall in two seconds!'

'So, what does the princess hear on the hill?' Kate returned to the story.

'The wrinkled man, who's barefoot, of course, takes a child into his arms. Utters a threefold blessing. Remember, three is a sacred number. The princess hears three words . . .'

'What were they?'

'Father, Son, Spirit. Power, Love, Wisdom,' said Ninian. 'She knows about power, but she's never heard of it being rooted in a Trinity of love. And she's seeking love, as well as

117

wisdom. So she comes closer to listen. Finds herself the centre of attention. The peasants look at the silver at her throat, the bronze on her arms. The monk places his hands on her head, gives her his blessing. She feels wanted, accepted. Feels strength flow from his fingers. She's a princess but she kisses the hands of the ragged ambassador of the High King of Heaven. Now, she thinks, I shall bear children.'

'No, no,' Kate interrupted. 'It's a wonderful story, Ninian, and it seems to me you compose from stories. But don't define her in terms of her ability to bear children.'

'Fair enough,' he smiled. 'How, then?'

'You said she became a mediator, received grace and wisdom. I'll tell you how the story ends.'

'Please.'

'She offers him an honoured place in her fortress, better clothes, a warm sheepskin for the winter. Am I doing all right?' she added, and Ninian said, 'You're doing splendidly.'

'But he refuses,' Kate went on. ' "Give your wealth to these peasants and their children," he says. So she takes them into her hall and feeds them.'

'And receives blessing,' Ninian ended. 'The blessing of the poor. Great! Now I just have to turn that to music.'

'You'll do it,' said Kate warmly. 'You'll call it *Well-Blessing*, and it'll wow your audiences.'

'I'll dedicate it to Kate . . .'

'What would Jane have to say? She's only asked for an interval,' Kate reminded him.

'True.' But his mood had changed now. He got to his feet with a touch of his old impatience. 'Shall I walk you home?'

'Do you know, I think I'll stay here a bit longer. This is what the pilgrimage was for,' Kate reminded him. 'I can't just hurry away. Thank you for today, Ninian. I've enjoyed it so much.'

He raised his hand in farewell and walked towards the car. She heard him start the engine, drive off. She turned back to the music of the burn and scooped up water, touching her lips with fingers wet from the Well at the World's End. She thought of Ninian's story—power, love, wisdom, rooted in the Trinity—rooted in mercy, thought Kate, remembering Christ carved on the neglected stone cross.

Mercy. That Christ on stone is held prisoner so that the world might be transfused with mercy—as the burn water runs seaward through the veins of the hill. And no one notices. But it is so, it really is so, and that means nothing's wasted, not even two little lives which in the end never were.

'Beautiful wee lassies...' She heard Alastair's voice, tender, understanding. Heard Ninian's: 'Grace is what you're denying me...'

Ninian, Ninian, you touch me like a lover. You showed me the well. We shared the legend. Don't try to bind me. Let me be free.

If Ninian were right, and there had been a holy well here, with only scattered boulders left to mark the place, Catriona would surely have known of it. What would Alastair think? Would he understand if she told him the story? Would he receive the mercy? From somewhere close by a lark soared, singing. Kate made her way home, opening the front door to the sound of Gaelic. Her great-aunt was speaking on the phone. An odd English word intruded, 'Ephesians? *Cuiribh umaibh uìle armachd Dhè.*' Fine, Donald, fine.'

She turned to Kate, her face soft with wonder. 'That was Donald. I can't believe it. He's coming to Coroskirr on Sunday. It's because of yourself, Kate, he says. It's all your doing.'

9

Well-music, thought Ninian, as he edged the car along the cliff road. *Kate's got something there. You'll call it* Well-Blessing ... It would be a short piece: a tone poem. Structure would be important: it would have to be free; just as birdsong, burn water, the sound of the waves, the blowing of westerly winds have their own inner rhythm. Ninian parked the car, still pondering. 'The wind bloweth where it listeth.' Tomorrow, he reflected, his thoughts going off at a tangent, would be the Sunday before Pentecost. He supposed he'd go to church, a Presbyterian service, up here. Back to the music, though: Jane would applaud this fluid structure, one which wasn't goal-orientated, undergirded by the metronome. *You think like a metronome.* Jane's jibe still rankled. *I'll dedicate this piece to you,* he'd promised Kate. But was he really writing it for Jane? No, for the music itself, he reminded himself, opening the back door.

Someone's been here ... Not again. He was sure he caught the stale smell of tobacco. He went into the lounge—and stopped short in a rush of impotent anger.

White paint, irregular letters, defaced the front windows. The lounge was in a mess: furniture overthrown, papers scattered about. Ninian stared around him, stunned and furious. The view, the beautiful view out to Port-na-Tuinne was defaced by these crude letters with their hostile message. *Get out. Go home, snob.*

It's that dosser, that damn wee weasel. How dare he? What right has he? It'll have been him who tried to force us off the road today. I'll have to tell the police. He's had it this time. I'd know him anywhere, and so would Kate.

Ninian took a step towards the door, but checked himself. Stupid, there would be no sign of anyone now. His music, that was the important thing. *Song for a Sad King.* He snatched up his manuscript book. A scorch mark singed the cover. *God help him when I get my hands on him.* But the manuscript was intact. Ninian scanned page after page. 'I am in great difficulty how I should dispose of my wounded prisoners.' Inverted chords splintered into five-tone harmonies. Yes, he'd freed the timing here, he noted. Done it instinctively, he now realised, influenced no doubt by the rhythms of folk music as he'd tried to tell how the servant girl, Anna McKay, stood three days and nights among enemy soldiers. 'I promised to violate no man's property...' Charles Edward had written. Ninian's property had been violated, all right. But, thank God, the music was intact within the singed cover of the book.

Was anything missing? He hardly knew. The house and its contents were still unfamiliar. Drawers were pulled open. He looked round him at random. The whisky bottle was empty. That half-finished malt. He'd only had one glass out of it yesterday. *I'll put poison in it next time,* Ninian vowed. And, the same old problem: no phone. Its lack added to his frustration. *Get out* ... Not likely.

Phone, yes, he'd go and phone. If the damned thing was working. If not, he'd have to trouble Morag MacDonald again. He looked at his watch. After five. Would the police still be on duty in this outpost? Anyhow, he'd have to do something, and then there'd be all this mess to tidy: a miserable waste of time. And who knew if a worse attack might not follow? Ninian pulled on a patchwork body-warmer, stowed his manuscript book safely inside its large inner pocket, locked the door (futility) and headed back over the cliff road, passing the MacDonald cottage, where Kate and her great-aunt were rejoicing at Donald's news.

'A miracle, an answer to prayer,' Morag declared, over a celebratory cup of tea.

'What will Alastair say? Oh, what will he say?'

'He'll not be able to believe it, that's for sure.'

'Sunday—that's tomorrow. So soon.'

'Aye, our service is at noon. Will you come with us, Kate?'

'Of course, I'd like to. Listen, there's someone at the door.'

'Who could that be?' Morag got to her feet. 'Unless the holiday folk are around, no one visits me, except the postman. And he never knocks.' Morag went to the door. Kate heard her say, 'Come away in, Mr Bruce.' Heard Ninian's voice, 'I'm sorry to bother you, Miss MacDonald. The phone's still out of order.'

'Of course, you're welcome to use ours.'

Kate hurried into the hallway. 'Hi, Ninian . . .'

'You'll have some tea?' her aunt was saying. 'We're just after a cup . . .'

'Thank you very much. I'd better phone first. The police again . . .'

'Is something wrong, Ninian? Hey, I like your patchwork jacket.'

'Put on for a purpose.' He opened his jacket to show her its deep pockets. 'To keep my music safe.'

'Safe?' Kate echoed. 'Not another dosser?'

'I've been vandalized.'

'Now sit right down,' Morag smoothed the dralon-padded chair beside the phone. 'Here's the book. And you can be drinking this. By the look of you you're needing a good *couppa* . . . And a pancake won't go amiss, I'm sure,' she added, passing a plate.

'Indeed it won't. Thanks very much.' Ninian sat down. Morag's Highland etiquette forbade her to ask any more questions, but Kate said, 'It's just one thing after another. Vandalized. Who by?'

'Your guess is as good as mine,' he said, heavily.

'Do you think there's some sort of a hate network aimed at you? The dosser, the incident with that van today. And there was that burnt-out cottage. Aunt Morag thinks it's because the owners planned to start a salmon farm.'

'So some folk are saying,' said Morag, returning to the fireside. 'What are those people called?' she said from the living-room door. 'Animal Rights?'

'But why attack me?' And he added wryly, 'I'm a vegetarian.'

'Poor Ninian. You can't win,' Kate told him, turning away. But he caught hold of her hand as he dialled the number. 'No, don't go. Yes, hello ... They've put me through to their 24-hour service. Hello. Yes, Ninian Bruce. *Seaview*, Coroskirr. That's right, I was on to you yesterday. I'm afraid there's been another break-in.'

Kate watched the fingers of his left hand worrying at the flex of the phone as he told his story. *Those long fingers—and that voice of his! Smooth as cream, coming from a throat of music. Like a thrush! He'd laugh at that comparison.*

'Let me give you some more tea.' She carried his cup and plate into the living-room and Ninian followed her. 'They'll be sending someone along to take a report,' he said.

'Sit down and finish your tea, Mr Bruce,' said Morag, offering an armchair. 'It will be a good while before the police get here. Can we offer you your evening meal? I have eggs.'

'You're filling me up with these delicious pancakes...' Ninian was saying, taking another from Kate, his lips shaping the words *You're delicious too.*

Footsteps scrunched outside. The back door opened. Alastair appeared.

'The roof ... a final check. Oh, sorry, I didn't know ...'

'Alastair, this is Ninian Bruce,' said Kate. '*Seaview*'s been broken into again.'

The men shook hands. 'Vandalized,' explained Kate. 'We're waiting for the police. Ninian, don't you think it might be helpful if you let us see the scene? We could be witnesses,' she added.

'Yes, that's true,' said Ninian, thoughtfully.

'Aye,' Morag agreed. 'Independent witnesses are always useful.'

'Don't you agree, Alastair; it would be good to have a look at *Seaview*?' Kate said. 'And, listen, we've got news for you,' she added, drawing him in.

His eyes were on her face. *She's lovely, so spontaneous. Lucky Ninian. I wonder if she likes his snazzy gear—yon coat of many colours. And here's me in working things.*

'You've done a great job on the roof,' Kate went on, touching his arm. 'Aunt Morag told me you've been hard at it all day.'

'No problem,' he assured her, and she warmed to his smile. 'So,' she said, 'will you come?'

'It would certainly be useful,' Ninian echoed Morag's words. 'Though I'm afraid the mess speaks for itself,' he added wryly, as they left the house and crossed the greensward in front of Morag's cottage.

The wind had got up. Kate shivered, tucking her arm through Ninian's and Alastair's, 'The weather's against us too. But look, Cnoc-na-Cille. Ninian tells me it's the Well at the World's End. Do you know about it, Alastair?'

'Tell me,' he invited.

'You must ask Ninian.'

'A story I came across,' said Ninian. 'Kate and I were putting it to music.'

Aye, and some music, the laird's arm around her. But Kate's arm was firmly through his old sleeve, as much as through the crushy cotton of the composer's Indian shirt. And now they were on the cliff road, and Kate released their arms, and Ninian went ahead, as they dipped down towards Port-na-Tuinne.

'Ninian's writing music,' she told Alastair.

Ninian overheard and paused. 'Trying to,' he corrected, looking over his shoulder. 'It's not so easy when your house is wrecked,' he added, striding further ahead.

'It's hard for him,' Kate said. Then, 'Alastair, I'm sure

124

you'll know: what is grace?'

And heard Ninian's voice in her mind: *grace is what you're denying me.*

Alastair looked at Ninian's distant patchwork back. 'Grace?' he said carefully, not looking at Kate. 'I'm not sure that I know. The theory, yes: God's mercy. The practice: no.' *Dare I tell her, dare I say: grace is you—everything you could offer me?*

'Ninian says it's given to the undeserving,' Kate said, and her hand was on his arm again.

'Yes, that's certainly true.' And now he turned his face towards her, hurrying a little to catch Ninian up.

'Kate . . .' *I love you. I want to lift those fingers from my arm and kiss them. I want more than your fingers. Yet you don't need to give me anything at all. Every moment I'm with you is grace, is heaven.*

'Port-na-Tuinne,' she was saying. 'Alastair, we're going to Port-na-Tuinne.'

He answered with a smile, 'I know.'

'You'll see it from the windows,' she said. 'The bay where . . . you never go . . .' Her voice trailed away, and she noticed that reddening about his eyes once again, but the wind was against them and it was certainly strong.

'Listen, I must tell you, quickly while we're still on our own. Your father's coming to Coroskirr. After church tomorrow. He phoned to tell Aunt Morag. She's delighted; but, Alastair, how will it be for you?' And now she challenged him. 'I'm going to ask you something. Be pleased too, Alastair.'

He had slowed his pace, but at this he stood stock still. 'I can't take it all in, Kate.' A roughness edged his voice. 'After so long—it's too hard.'

Hard to be walking beside this woman and not to touch her; to remember how he'd seen her with the laird; to hold back when feelings he'd stifled for years were throbbing through him so unexpectedly. Isabel had made him feel a failure . . . *Well, that's all I am,* he reminded himself. The day that white envelope from the court had plopped through the letter-box in his silent flat, telling him his marriage was over. Like a death, only no funeral. And never, ever to dream another relationship might be possible. Especially not after the failure of the first. But Kate had changed all that. That was her gift. *But she mustn't know. She must not know. She and the laird . . . they're so right for one another. Morag seems pleased about it too. I can't be the one to ruin this for her—after all she's been through.*

He thrust his hands into his pockets—*that defensive gesture,* Kate thought, noticing. His mouth had set in a firm line. 'Don't worry about me, Kate,' he said, brusquely. 'Don't let it worry you.'

She looked hurt. 'But it does, Alastair.'

He quickened his pace. *Your boyfriend will wonder what's keeping us.* But he didn't say it. Couldn't.

They walked down to *Seaview* in silence. Those shorts she was wearing set off her slim legs. *Hold off,* he told himself. *She's not for you. Who are you to think like this after the mess you've made?*

Mess. Well, there was mess in the laird's house, the view of the bay hidden by that hateful graffiti. 'No wonder you're upset,' Alastair told Ninian. 'Attacks on property don't leave visible scars, but they hurt just the same.'

Kate heard the concern in his voice. 'Your parish must really miss you,' she said, and Ninian looked round in surprise.

'Are you a clergyman, Alastair? I'd never have guessed.'

Alastair laughed. 'No wonder, dressed like this.'

But Kate was holding out a dog-eared jotter. 'Look, it was lying here by the door. Is this one of yours, Ninian?'

Ninian flipped through the pages. 'Of course not! D'you think I'm capable of this crap?'

She flushed, but she was getting used to Ninian's mood swings. Alastair defended her quickly. 'How was Kate to know what was in it?'

'Maybe it's evidence to show the police,' Kate said lightly, and, leaning over Ninian's arm, fanned the jotter out so that Alastair could see the untutored writing: *Poems*:

They tore out the willow tree
to make a motorway.
Where's left for me?
I'm here to stay.
They'll never send me away.

'That's proof it was written by your dosser,' said Kate. 'Listen to this next one. It's saying the same thing.' And she read:

Purple mountains in the west
the sea is green and blue
empty sand I leave
footprints like a castaway.
This is the home my people left
but I will always stay.

'Aye, well, there's plenty of us would agree with that,' Alastair commented dryly. 'But there's ways and means of staying.'

'Who is he? He's obviously got family connections here,' Kate pointed out.

'You're right, Kate, and that should give the police a lead,' said Ninian. 'Especially in a small community like this. Well done, finding this book.' And he flashed her one of his warm smiles.

She smiled back. 'It's rather sad. If the dosser did write this, it shows you were right in calling him one of life's losers. Your father would think so too, wouldn't he?' she went on, turning to Alastair. 'Ninian and I went to see him this afternoon.'

'Did you? Thanks very much. I bet the old man was pleased.'

'Were you brought up here?' asked Ninian, laying the jotter on the table, and moving towards the door. Alastair went with him. Kate lingered to have one more look through

127

the lined pages, in a vague hope of finding some clue as to the book's owner.

'Only for holidays,' Alastair was saying. And Kate read, in the same untutored handwriting:

They took my old man away. For life.
Life for life. The doors are closed.
I'll break down bars.
I'll shatter glass.
I'll reach the stars.

'There's determination there. He'll stop at nothing. Ninian, Ninian, you must take care.'

*

'He's a poofter,' Jimmy tossed back his whisky. 'This place wull be full o' yuppies.'

'Aye,' agreed Tam, 'Nae use tae us, ken. They bulk buy in the supermairkets, load up their caravettes, never shop here. No, Jimmy, no' for me,' he added, as Jimmy offered another dram. 'I'm no' wanting to get like *her*.' Tam nodded across at his wife Annie, her sunken cheeks flushed from the heat of the electric fire. 'She's been at it a' day.' A bell rang in the shop, and Tam got to his feet. ' "We'll run a garage and a shop," she said, when I won the pools money. "Get away frae it all; a nice wee life on the West Coast. Plenty fishing and nae worries"— I don't think.'

'Aye, it's hard on you,' Jimmy agreed. 'So I can get a loan o' the van?'

'Nae probs. You did a fine wee re-spray. You're wanting it for the night's fishing?'

'Aye. I'll drop thae messages off at the auld man's for you.'
'Thanks, pal.'

It was a shame for Tam, Jimmy reflected, going out to the van. Terrible when a woman let herself get like that, worse than having no woman at all.

No woman, and no life of your own. On the run. He'd

started off for Glasgow that morning in the orange van—
going to pick up stuff for Tam, wanting to suss out the scene.
But he'd seen a headline in the *Record,* recognized a face in a
photograph. 'Wanted man held for questioning...' One of
his pals had been lifted. And so Jimmy turned back to
Achnacrois.

Tam believed the story about fishing. Jimmy had brought
Tam and Annie trout before. So Tam hadn't minded lending
the van. And agreed to the re-spray. Green merged in with
the landscape. Jimmy reckoned there were plenty places
along this coast where he could hide.

He swung up Donald's path with messages he'd ordered
by phone.

Donald was in the kitchen, organizing his outing to
Coroskirr. The messages were for Morag, to say thank you
for the dinner she'd be giving him. And on the kitchen table,
beside a small envelope marked *Freewill Offering*, was the
painting he'd promised Kate.

'Messages frae Tam's!'

'On the table here. That's fine, thank you very much. It's
very good of you to deliver them. It's a bonny day again.'

'Aye, it is that,' agreed Jimmy, who hadn't noticed.

'Though that's quite a wind now. You'll be new here? And,
yet, there's something familiar about you. I feel I've seen you
before.'

Was he right in thinking a look of alarm crossed Jimmy's
thin face? Always ready to put another at their ease, Donald
added, 'Ah well, maybe not. My mind plays tricks these days.
I must be thinking of someone else. Thank you for the
messages. How much am I owing?'

'Settle wi' Tam.' Jimmy turned away.

'Call by any time!' Donald waved Jimmy down the path—
not before Jimmy's practised eye had taken stock of the room.
Books but no video. Not worth coming back.

Left alone, when it was no longer possible to establish
facts, Donald had it. Rab. That was it. Rab McCann. This
young man was a slighter, sandier version of the fourteen-

year-old redhead Donald remembered: sly, yet there'd been a streak which made Rab stand out. 1947, and Donald, newly qualified, was teaching the class about the cattle drovers bringing their beasts down through Scotland. At going home time, when rain drizzled down high steamy windows and gas lamps glimmered in the puddled streets, Rab had lingered to volunteer, for Donald's ears alone. 'Ma granny's frae the Heilans, sir.'

It would never do to admit it in front of his pals, be derided as a *teuchter*. It was a big enough thing to stay and talk to the teacher, be a *sook*; but there was a softness in the boy's pinched face as he confided, 'She's tellt us aboot thae wee black coos eating seaweed and that.'

Above the sound of rattling trams, the carthorses trundling by with coal and paper boys shouting, 'Ev'ning pep-iir!' Rab McCann added, 'She's frae Coroskirr.'

And when, a little later, Donald wrote a school report on Rab McCann to be presented in the Sheriff court, he noted: 'The boy displays a hard exterior, but his basic nature is sensitive.'

He'd have to ask the home help, Ailidh, if anyone called McCann had come to work in the shop.

*

Jimmy headed back to the shop to pick up paraffin. It was just on closing time. Ailidh was in the shop, leaning across the counter talking to Tam. Local people tended not to have too much to say to Tam and even less to Annie, but Ailidh talked to everyone.

'Such a good man, Donald Cameron,' she was saying. 'One of the old school. Taught in Clydeside all those years . . . And is your wife still no weel, Mr Wilson? A sad business, right enough . . .'

'Whit a gas-bag,' Tam said, locking the door behind Ailidh. 'Listen, pal, would you give me a wee hand? I hate tae ask, but . . . It's Annie, ken. Bevvied.'

Jimmy gave Tam a hand to heave Annie from the floor into her bed. 'Thanks. It's nae joke. I'm tellin ye, I'm gettin oot. Selling up. Fancy yer chances?'

'No' me,' said Jimmy and took the road to Coroskirr. He pulled off near the most northerly headland, bumped the van across a gully and took to the hills, with his calor gas, paraffin and a small rucksack. He'd found a small croft, remote and isolated, long since gone to grass. But the home help's words echoed in Jimmy's head. The old man whose house he'd just been in had taught down by the Clyde where Granny McCann had brought up her large family. Jimmy was half in mind to turn back and speak to him. But . . .

He unloaded and hiked across to the back of the hillside they called Cnoc-na-cille. Telephone cables connected Morag MacDonald's cottage to the rest of the world. An eagle was reported to have its eyrie on the crag there. It would be something to see an eagle.

His Da had said so once. That was when Rab had had a bust-up with Alec and Robert and he and Isa had walked out. 'We're no wanted here.' Rab had said, but Jimmy had called, 'Wait, Da! I'm comin' wi' you.'

And so he'd left Alec, Robert, Jean and Danny and gone off with his father, Isa and the new baby. They'd caught a bus to the docks where Rab had grown up with Granny McCann from Coroskirr. 'Coroskirr's up north. Mind the photie above the fireplace? There are eagles there, Jimmy.'

But things had changed since Granny McCann bore her thirteen children in a single end. Rab rented a room from some foreign landlord. Rab, Isa and the baby shared the recess bed. Jimmy lay on a blanket on the floor with Isa's coat on top of him. No one knew where he was, not the school, nor the Welfare, nor the police, not even his own mother, back home with her kids now that Rab, his fancy woman and yon puir wee bastard wean of hers were away.

One night Jimmy woke up to the sound of shattering glass. Isa was out at the Bingo. The baby was yelling. Jimmy shoved a half-empty bottle into its mouth, pushed the pillow higher under its head, went over to the window and stuck his head out. A crowd had gathered round the pub below. Sirens wailed. An ambulance with a police panda car raced down the street.

Jimmy rushed downstairs. A man had been murdered, people told him. A fight in the pub. The police were looking for the killer. 'A red-heided bloke.'

Much later that night, Rab staggered in. A wound gaped across his cheek. Isa screamed. 'He'll bleed to death! He should be in the casualty.' Jimmy tried to help Isa clean his father up, but the police called and took Rab away.

The day they tried him, Jimmy hung about on the steps outside the Sheriff court. Isa didn't go. She said she wasn't feeling well and, of course, there was the baby, a red-head like his father, crawling around, getting into everything.

Rab McCann was given a lifesentence. Jimmy learnt his father's fate from boys in the gangs round about. They made Jimmy their leader. He chose the nickname Eagle.

*

'This is very kind,' Ninian said to Morag over a meal of poached eggs and hastily defrosted smoked haddock from Morag's fridge-freezer. Alastair had declined to join them.

'Please,' Kate had added her plea to her great-aunt's invitation. 'You've been working on the roof all day.'

' "The labourer's worthy of his hire",' Morag had said, but Alastair wouldn't be persuaded, and Kate sensed his reluctance to intrude. But as he said goodbye, she went up to him and kissed his cheek. A smile had flooded his face. 'Thank you, Kate,' he'd said softly, turning away.

'Is he feeling bad about his father coming tomorrow?' Kate had asked her aunt anxiously in the kitchen. Morag shook her head and sighed. 'I don't know what's going on inside his head at all.'

As the meal was ending, they heard a car engine above the noise of the wind. 'That'll be the police,' said Morag, keeking out of the kitchen window. 'Aye, that's them.'

Ninian put down his cup, and stood up. 'I'd better go. Thanks so much.'

'I'll come across later and help tidy up,' Kate offered.

'That would be great.' And he hurried away.

Morag started to wash the dishes. 'No, no, Kate. You'll be needed by the laird any time,' she said, refusing Kate's offer of help.

'I'll go across to the burn. I'll be able to see the back of *Seaview* from there,' said Kate. She pulled on her tracksuit and made her way across the sloping shoulder of Cnoc-na-Cille. It was sheltered here, out of the wind. The police car was just visible, parked behind Ninian's house. The investigation was obviously taking time.

It looks as if there's some sort of hate-campaign—so close to the burn where the princess was baptized. Cnoc-na-Cille: it's been Coroskirr's holy place for so long.

Kneeling beside the burn Kate listened to its music, to the wind gusting across sheep-cropped grass, smelt wild thyme and heard larksong scribbled like psalms across this wide sky with its shifting patterns of cloud and light.

Words sprang up, unbidden, within her to form a prayer: *Lord, have mercy . . .*

. . . on Ninian and his music. May there be no hate. And Alastair . . . 'They were beautiful wee lassies, I'm sure, Kate, those little baby daughters of yours,' he'd said so tenderly in his Glasgow voice, Kate recalled, and she tried to hold him in the centre of her prayer. *May there be deep mercy for Alastair.*

'Kate!'

She looked up. And there *was* Alastair, striding over the hill, wearing the climbing breeches she'd first seen him in.

He hunkered down beside her. 'I'm sorry, I seem to make a habit of this—disturbing you.'

Kate smiled. ' "This is holy ground", Alastair—isn't that from the Bible?'

'Our wee burn?' Alastair looked puzzled and Kate said, 'You don't understand, do you?'

'Not really,' he admitted. 'Tell me about it,' he added, scooping up a handful of burn water. 'Our wee burn,' he said again. 'We always thought it was the sweetest water in the world.'

Kate smiled at this. *There's this good sense of ease between us,* she thought. *We're relaxed. No pressure. I'm so glad he's come along here just at this moment . . .*

'You belong as much as me,' Alastair was saying. 'For all the English voice,' he added with a smile. 'You hardly heard an English accent up here. Just on the radio, or television. I love your voice, Kate, especially when you use Scots words.'

'I wish I knew more. They're so expressive. Alastair, when I was on holiday in Greece last year I came across an old well. And I made a promise to come to Coroskirr.'

'Amn't I glad! Go on.'

Kate smiled, and continued, 'Remember I told you, it was like being a pilgrim? Well, let me tell you what I've found.'

'What *have* you found?'

'The Well at the World's End,' she smiled. 'All right, it's just an ordinary burn, but—see those stones? Ninian says there may have been a well here. He found an old legend, you see. And the name of the hill, Cnoc-na-Cille. I wondered whether the golden apples of the old Celtic legends—Avalon, Arthur's Isle of Apples, the place of blessing, you know . . .?' She broke off. Alastair didn't know, but he nodded, absorbing her words, not wanting to break the spell of being with her. 'Whether the apples of blessing could be healing after loss.' She warmed to her tale. 'I thought of Ophelia, too. Rue, you know. Being sorry—repentance, wouldn't you say?' She saw he was listening intently, and she put her hand out in a quick gesture, lightly brushing his, as she quoted, ' "O, you must wear your rue with a difference . . ." And I think you must too, Alastair,' she said seriously, and Alastair nodded again, his eyes never leaving her face.

'You told me about the cross—Achnacrois,' Kate went on. 'I'm so glad. I love that carving of Christ, Alastair. I showed him to Ninian. He kissed his feet, went down on his knee. And he was right, you see. God isn't just in churches bound up in a black Bible and one's best performance, shiny shoes, Sunday best.' Kate paused. 'That's what my grandfather thought. The way he was brought up. I think he hated God. Maybe that's why he never wanted to come back. That's sad, isn't it? But your father's not like that. Nor is Aunt Morag. And of course, nor are you. Ninian didn't even guess you're a minister,' Kate added with a smile.

'No wonder!' he said, bitterly, but then he relaxed, glancing down at small pebbles he was turning in his hands. 'But that's what I've been doing—for far too long. Going through the motions. Keeping God bottled up. How wrong.' He dropped the pebbles. His hand went out towards her. 'You've shown me otherwise. And now you're telling me about saying sorry. Oh, you're right, Kate. But it's not so easy—finding forgiveness . . . But who am I to say that to you? You know, Kate, everything about you is a gift! And when you kissed me—Kate, you've no idea how much it meant!—in front of the laird, in front of Morag . . . That's when I knew I had to see you, Kate. There's just one night left. Would you like the boat trip we've mentioned?'

'Of course—but, Alastair, just one night?'

'Morag will run me to the ferry first thing Monday morning. There's tomorrow, I know, but it's the Sabbath.'

'I don't see . . .'

'Och, it wouldnae matter, but it's in my blood: we never took the boat out on the Lord's Day.'

'I see. Of course, I'd love a trip. But—almost your last day. And tomorrow . . .'

'Aye, tomorrow . . . It's going to be *some day*! Is that the police car away? Will we see if we can do anything to help the laird?'

They walked down over the cliff road to see Ninian.

10

'Come in,' Ninian welcomed them, and added, turning to Alastair, 'Sorry your visits to *Seaview* have been chaos and trauma.'

'Not your fault—how did it go?'

'A youngish chap took painstakingly detailed notes.'

'Did you tell him about the orange van?' Kate asked. 'And the notebook?'

'I told you, he noted everything. A real P.C. Plod. Could have been someone else in that van, of course.'

'I'm sure it was your dosser. But what's the matter, Ninian? Are you all right? You seem very off-hand.'

'I've just been grilled by a guy intent on doing his duty,' Ninian said, stiffly.

Alastair looked at them. *Must he be so huffy?* 'Can we give you a hand here, Ninian?' he offered. 'I've white spirit . . . I'll have a shot at those windows, if you like.'

'Thanks. This calls for music.' Ninian slid a cassette into his machine.

'Music while we work,' Kate said, sweeping broken glass into a bin. And felt she was trying too hard to keep things casual. *Why am I glad that Alastair's here? Is it because he's so clearly on my side? Or because of the vibes between Ninian and me—I'm not sure I can handle being on our own.*

She picked up cutlery, tidied things back into drawers.

Alastair scraped away at the window, his back partly turned to her. The music lilted into the room: 'O flower o' Scotland . . . and sent him homewards tae think again . . . '

'A great song,' commented Alastair. 'A wee bit too nationalistic for you, maybe, Kate?'

'No. I'm all for nationalism. Especially when a small country's dominated by a bigger one,' she added, with a smile which Alastair returned as he turned back to work. 'I knew it,' he said, but now Ninian, bending over the desk, exclaimed, 'Here's stuff that would interest you, Kate. Old papers. My goodness, I never knew *these* were here!'

'A diary.' Kate came over to have a look.

'Aye, I knew about that. I was planning on lending it to you, in fact. But, look, letters. Here's one from Sir John Murray's eldest son,' he added, with real interest in his voice. 'It's about a duel. Here, have a read.'

'You must have a look too, Alastair,' said Kate, taking the letter from Ninian. *He should be included in this. It's not right for him to be doing Ninian's dirty work while we're chatting here.* And looking towards Alastair, Kate saw that the bay, so full of tragedy for the Cameron family, was emerging into view as he erased the graffiti from the glass.

'Look at this old letter, Alastair,' Kate repeated, holding out a paper brown with age, covered with scrawling handwriting.

'I can hardly make this out,' she said. 'Here you are, Ninian, see if you can read it to us.'

And so Ninian read:

My dear and only Brother
I am this day to settle the difference with F. This business has given my Father and Lady Peggy much anxiety. I feel more for their distress than for my own demise. Say farewell to Father. I am sure there never existed a father more good nor generous . . .'

Ninian paused. A gust of wind rattled the window. They

heard the rising waves of Port-na-Tuinne crash on the shore, and Kate shivered. 'Poor boy. He clearly didn't make it.'

'No,' said Ninian. 'But crofting folk here—the Clearances, you know—never had any reason to believe that Sir John Murray was good or generous.'

'Reassuring words—coming from you, Ninian,' said Alastair.

Ninian smiled. 'Thanks! I'd offer you a dram—good malt, if yon wee vandal hadn't got there first!'

They laughed. 'We'll buy another bottle,' said Kate. 'But, you know, dram makes me think of that poem you quoted— about clothes to thatch the body and whisky to kindle a fire within.'

'Oh, yes, it's by a very colourful character,' Ninian was saying, when Alastair gave them the verse in the original Gaelic. '*S fheudar dram òlmar linnigeadh cleibh . . .*'

'You know the Gaelic, Alastair? I'm impressed,' said Ninian.

'Not at all. He was a local bard, after all,' Alastair said, turning back to the window and talking as he worked away with white spirit. 'He joined the Prince too, and the redcoats burnt his house. They even killed the cat so that the family would have "neither fur nor flesh to sustain them",' he quoted, feelingly.

'That's heavy,' said Kate. She turned back to the paper and took up the story, written in another, less hasty, more legible hand. ' "They tossed up and Captain Murray won. He fired and shot Mr F under the left breast. F opened his jacket and declared himself mortally wounded. He then raised his pistol and shot Captain Murray . . ." But this must have been against the rules,' she went on, 'because, listen: "This conduct has been universally reprobated, but it is all of a piece with the rascal's character." *Universally reprobated,*' she repeated, ' *. . .all in a piece with the rascal's character . . .* It sounds like those old parish records. What was it? "Circumspect in their Walk and Conversation." '

'Good Presbyterian characteristics,' said Ninian. 'Very

boring.' And his hand slyly crept round Kate's back. She felt one long finger edge under the waistband of her trousers.

And couldn't relax into his touch. *This is what I was afraid of. He stirs me, yes, but not now, not with Alastair here. It isn't fair.*

'*Touche pas . . .*' she said softly, and Ninian smiled, spreading his trespassing hand in mock innocence. A question? Or an invitation?

Kate shook her head, and glanced towards Alastair. His back was still turned. 'Almost done,' he said. 'Do read on, Kate. Is there any more?'

'Let Ninian read it.' She put the paper into Ninian's open hands and crossed over to Alastair. 'You've made a good job of this window. And there's the bay, the beautiful bay.'

'Aye, we can see it again, thanks to you!' said Ninian. 'Take these old papers, Kate. They'll be safer with you,' he added, sliding them into a bag. He came and put his arms round their shoulders. 'Great work, folks!' he said, in a mock Hollywood accent. 'How about a swim? The sun's out. The tide's in. Let's go for it, eh? Thanks so much for all your help.'

'A swim sounds good,' said Kate. 'How about it, Alastair?'

But he declined, with a shake of his head and the smile which reminded her so much of his father. Oh, but couldn't they forget that old hurt, shake off the past and live again?

'I'll get the boat ready,' he told Kate.

'Of course! I'd almost forgotten! Okay, I'll see you soon!'

She raced back to Morag's, the wind tugging at her clothes, her hair. The evening sun was golden in the west. Kate dumped the papers in the living-room. 'Take a look at these papers, Aunt Morag, if you've got a minute,' she called, running upstairs to change into her bikini, snatch up a towel and rush to the bay where Ninian waited, already in swimming trunks.

'Fantastic!' he told her.

'Yes. It's a wonderful evening.'

'Not the evening. You. Didn't you like it when I let that stray finger explore a little? I thought you did, but then you pulled away . . .'

She looked at him, confused. What could she say? *Yes, I liked it, and wanted more, but it wasn't the right moment . . . We weren't alone. Alastair was there . . .* And knew he'd pick her up: *Alastair—so that's it!* She shook her head, and perhaps with a desire to shake off too many contradictory thoughts, ran into the sea, hesitating only for a moment as the cold water made her gasp. Then she dived into the foaming surf, swimming out through the surge of those lifting waves, bright with the westering sun.

And Ninian was beside her, turning his head towards her, shaking water from his eyes, racing back over the deserted shore, tossing her a towel and saying, as she rubbed herself dry, 'Come to bed with me, my mermaid, my woman of the sea.'

'No, Ninian,' she shivered. *Yet what right have I to play the prude? Why should we not make our own music on this magic, silver shore?*

'Kate, this chastity thing's no good. Not with someone like you. At least let me look at you . . .'

'Not here, not yet, please, Ninian.'

'Why, Kate, why?'

'I'm cold,' she shivered, feeling ridiculous now. 'Don't hurry me.'

'But you're going out with Alastair Cameron?'

Kate squeezed the ends of her hair and huddled into her towel. 'It's his last free evening.' *And, anyway, why shouldn't I?* But she didn't say so. 'I've got all your old papers to read too,' she told him through chattering teeth. 'I'm frozen. I'll need to get dry. Bye, Ninian.'

She hurried home to pull on her warmest clothing and shake her hair dry in front of the fire. 'You'll have a hot drink, too, Kate, for it's cold out at sea in that wee boat,' Morag said. 'I've been trying to phone Donald, but there's some fault in the line. I can't get through. But it was nothing that can't wait till tomorrow.'

'Pity. You could have told him how pleased we are.' Kate

tugged a comb through her hair. 'Though I still don't know what Alastair thinks about it . . .'

'Well, there's many years of prayer gone into Donald's decision,' Morag observed, giving Kate a hug.

'Your prayers, Aunt Morag,' Kate said, and her aunt kissed her before she hurried down to the shore.

Alastair had pushed the boat down to the water's edge. 'How was the swim?'

'Cold! I froze. But good. Here, let me help,' she offered, as Alastair put his weight behind the boat to give it a final push into the sea.

'I wouldn't dream of it,' he told her firmly. 'I'm well used to it.'

'I know . . .'

The swell lifted the boat. Alastair helped Kate aboard. 'It's no great shakes, this boat,' he apologized, holding out his hand to steady her as the boat dipped. He helped her fasten her life jacket before he took the oars, navigating half-hidden treacherous rocks.

The waves slapped against the boat. 'This is great!' Kate smiled.

Alastair nodded, pleased, tugging the cord to start the outboard. They chugged out into the open sea. He handled the boat with easy assurance, taking a southerly course. The lighthouse was clearly visible, and on the left the white sweep of sand: Port-na-Tuinne, with the laird's stone house squatting at its edge. *Ninian, desperate to make love.* Was she right to deny him, wondered Kate. *To aid a pilgrim is to share the grace* . . . He'd love it if she applied those words to him! He was so polished, always with the right word. Could she ever match him?

Alastair switched off the engine. The noise died away. The boat rocked on the waves.

'Nice,' approved Kate. 'Sea sounds and islands. Good to savour. Why have we stopped?'

'Thought we might try some fishing.'

He showed her how to cast, play out the line.

'It's gone taut.'

He reached over, controlling the boat lightly with one hand, with the other helping Kate wind the fish in. 'A mackerel,' he said, expertly catching hold of the silver-blue fish. They fished successfully for the next ten minutes.

'Your aunt likes a freshly caught fish.'

'Straight from the sea. Couldn't be fresher,' Kate agreed.

'Is that us, then?' Alastair said a bit later, winding in the line. 'We'll leave some supper for the seals.'

'Seals?'

'There's one over there. See, coming up now.' He pointed. She followed his gaze. 'What wise sad eyes!'

He nodded. 'Aye, you're right. Will we go further out?'

'Yes, please! Oh, Alastair, I never want to go south again.'

'I know the feeling.'

They headed towards the crimsoning west, islands swinging into view whichever way they looked.

And now Alastair turned off the engine again. 'Look, Kate, porpoises,' he said, keeping his voice down. 'Just for you,' he added bending towards her, aware of how sounds carry.

'Magic!' she breathed. 'Creatures of myth. Such grace!'

'Aye—come to greet a woman of grace.'

'That's a nice compliment.'

'It's true,' he assured her. He had shifted across beside her. She felt him rocking in the rhythm of the waves. *The silence, these rare, shining creatures hold us both. And if we were in trouble, if a wave capsized this little boat, I know this man would risk his life to keep me safe.*

'Alastair,' she said, and hesitated. 'About tomorrow. Your father coming here. Are you angry with me?'

'Angry with *you*? How could I ever be angry with *you*? But I'll admit I'm a bit worried . . .'

'It'll be all right.' Kate slipped her arm about his shoulder. 'Look at these beautiful creatures! Moving in unison. A bit like us over this business tomorrow?'

'Could I be so lucky!' Then his voice became businesslike. 'That's some wind! We'd better head in. Okay?'

She nodded and Alastair shifted across to the stern, tugging at the starter again. The engine sputtered into action. Alastair set the prow for home, but once they came on shore, Kate said, 'Only one day left for you.'

Alastair paused, his arms full of fishing-tackle. The wind rushed between them. Low clouds hid the sun. The last rays of evening light were like a shaft of slanting steel cutting through cloud breaks into the sea. A single gull circled above them. More came. Then more.

'One day left,' he repeated, hoisting the tackle into his left arm, dropping his knife, a piece of rope. He let them lie on wet sand. 'Does Ninian tell you you're beautiful?' His voice was hoarse. 'I'm sorry. I shouldn't have . . .' His blue eyes were fixed on her face. 'You've given me more than I deserve.'

'Ninian tells me I don't give him enough.' The words were out before she could help it. She bent to pick up his fallen gear.

'Ninian thinks . . .? I can't believe it! Kate, Kate, come out of the wind, just for a moment.' He laid down his tackle, shoved a cover over the fish. 'All this can wait. Kate, I can't believe what I'm hearing.'

'I shouldn't tell tales. But what do *you* want, Alastair?'

'Want? *I want doesn't get*.' He quoted the old adage with a smile. 'What I want can never be. But I would like to ask a favour. Here.'

He drew her into a sheltered place. 'Will you do something for me?' He touched her hair. 'It's so long since . . . and never a woman like you. Kate, will you give me . . .' He uncoiled a strand of her hair, made a gesture like scissors. His fingers were as gentle as a caress. 'One curl, just,' he begged. 'A wee end piece. Would you mind?'

'No, of course n . . .' she began, but he laid a finger on her lips. She tasted salt, heard his voice thicken as he said, 'I'm still thinking about tomorrow. But you'll be there. Healing. Grace. *You* bring it. You've given me hope.'

'I'm glad, Alastair.' She put her hand in his. 'Aunt Morag thinks that you suffered more than anyone,' she said softly. 'I think so too. It wasn't fair. I don't know what will happen tomorrow either. There's all this nasty hate stuff, but surely our prayers—the power of love is stronger?' she said, and added, 'It's all so new to me.'

'It is to me too. I knew the form—and it was empty. You've shown me the heart.' He lifted the hand he held, squeezed it. 'Cold from the Coroskirr sea,' he said, trying to rub it warm. 'You mean so much to me! There, I shouldn't have said that.' He hesitated. 'You'll not forget that wee minding? Just one wee curl. I know I shouldn't ask . . .'

'It's all *right* . . . Of course,' she repeated.

'Thank you. Kate, you're freezing.'

'It was the sea. In it and on it. How the weather's changed! The sky is sad tonight, Alastair, full of foreboding.'

'You're thinking about tomorrow. It'll be all right, you'll see,' he assured her as they walked across the shore.

'Do you think so? I hope so. What have you to do now?'

'Walk you home, out of this wind.'

'That's all right. I'll soon warm up. Let me help you with the boat. Please, Alastair,' she added, seeing he was about to refuse. She helped up-end the boat and beach it among the dunes. They stood at the water's edge and gutted the fish amidst a riot of gulls. 'I've enjoyed this evening,' she said.

'I have too,' he told her.

'Would you like to come in and look over those old papers of Ninian's?' Kate offered as they headed towards Morag's cottage.

'Love to,' he said, 'but there's something else I have to do. I think you'll be pleased.'

'Oh?'

'I'm going to the bay, Kate.'

'To Port-na-Tuinne?'

'To Port-na-Tuinne,' he repeated. He bent to offer her his kiss. She put a hand on his shoulder. 'That terrible place . . . Would you like me to come with you?'

He shook his head. 'This is something I must do on my own.'

'I can see that.' She brushed her cheek against his. 'Dear

144

Alastair, may there be Christ-apples of grace for you there.'

'That's a *you* saying. And I love it.'

'Even if grace is given to the undeserving,' Kate said, remembering Ninian's words, '*You* deserve it, you've worn your rue too long.' And found it hard to leave him.

At the cottage she found Aunt Morag sitting at the fire surrounded by Ninian's papers. 'Alastair's going to Port-na-Tuinne,' said Kate.

Morag took off her glasses. 'Is he now?' she said. Kate could tell she was pleased. A bit troubled too, Kate was sure.

But then her face relaxed and she smiled at Kate. 'Well, Kate, the Camerons have a lot to thank you for.'

'Do you really think so? Not me. Alastair's got so much to give,' she added, squatting down beside her great-aunt, who gave her a quick quizzical smile. 'A lot to give,' Morag echoed. 'Aye, that's so. And his father has never seen it ... But, Kate, these old papers.. There's mention of your namesake. See.'

The fire warmed Kate. She shifted into a more comfortable position, and leafed through the diary Ninian had mentioned.

'Written by *Herself*,' said Morag. 'Lady Peggy Murray, the lady of the house.'

'Whose stately home is a hotel now, full of hideous stags' heads.'

'I've seen her in old portraits—they had an exhibition once.'

'What was she like?'

'She was wearing black. Taffeta, the guide book said, trimmed with sable. How they laundered those gowns ...'

'The mind boggles. Was she pretty?'

Morag paused to consider. 'A mass of greying hair, and a wee cap perched on top. A wee bittie vain, maybe. I fancy she wore the cap to set her hair off, rather than hide it,' Morag added with a smile. 'I've done the same myself. We all wore hats when I was young. Strange to think of it now, isn't it?'

'You had red hair too. It must have been gorgeous ...'

'Och, not at all. Carrots,' smiled Morag. 'I used to get in trouble for it on the ward. We had to wear starched caps. Pulled right down low on our foreheads. They gave us dandruff, too! But, Lady Peggy, well, she had a gentle face. You'll see from the diary she missed Edinburgh and its comforts. The New Town, salons and receptions,' added Morag, showing Kate the firm, regular handwriting.

The Work Table Magazine of Church and Decorative Needlework (1/6) is newly arrived from the Mail together with a copy of the Scotsman. I read eagerly. I note, in order to pass on to Effie McPhee, wife of Sir John's tacksman, Lachlan, instructions on how to treat servants. Avoid all familiarity. Servants should be treated with kindness and with firm dignity.

'*Firm dignity*!' exclaimed Kate, and Morag laughed. 'She sounds a right old horror. Like some of the Ward Sisters I was trained by.'

'Horrendous. But this is worse: listen.' And Kate read aloud:

Here, far from the City and all Culture, we have a race degraded physically and morally, whose homes are no better than a midden heap. Indeed, Effie tells me her husband has to climb over a heap of filth before he can even come at the inmates of these wretched hovels. But Effie forgot herself so much as to say, 'Doubtless Your Ladyship has the best intentions of aiding these creatures,' adding darkly, 'There are those who receive funds from the Poors Box who have no title to it.' She means Catriona MacDonald . . .

Kate looked up. 'So, here she is again, Aunt Morag. Our Catriona . . .' And she went on:

I instructed Cook to give the lass odds and ends of linen

and darned woollens together with a groat for her winter's work with the family wash. The creature has bairns at her breast (I told Effie) however ill-conceived.

'Ill-conceived indeed,' says Mistress McPhee.

I remind Effie that the poor creature is not unmindful of her faults. Cook tells me she lifted her eyes to heaven and uttered (in Erse) many heartfelt prayers and blessings for this bounty.

Effie will have none of this. 'Bounty!' says she. 'Can such as she pay her rent?'

Indeed, a hopeless millstone of debt lies about the necks of the poorer tenantry who have been moved from their former lands by the improvements effected by my husband and his tacksman, but I am made happy by delightful letters from my dear Charlotte. All are well. I thank God for such mercies.

Kate looked at her aunt. 'I suppose for the Murray family it was like having Third World poverty right on your doorstep. Debt and hand-outs: all too familiar.'

'I never thought of it like that,' said Morag. 'But Lady Peggy seems to have been a woman of faith. Look.' Morag read:

Ah, what cause of thankfulness have I to Almighty God for the many blessings I enjoy in health of body and mind! I feel much the absence of dear Charlotte and the children, so many miles away, but my mind is resigned and I derive much comfort from reading and quiet reflection.

'Yes, but, well she was stuck in her own mould, I suppose. Feeling herself one up on Effie, whoever she was. Would she have spoken Gaelic, Aunt Morag—Effie, I mean?'

'Oh yes. And her husband. That's why the curse was put on him, rather than on the laird. He was one of their own, you see.'

'But the laird's sons were both killed. Ninian mentioned the curse as well. Do you know what it was?'

'It was when folk were being cleared. One old woman was so sick. But Lachlan McPhee burnt her thatched roof like all the rest.'

'Smoked out like rats!' Kate said bitterly.

'Aye, they made sure no one would return. There was only one route left: down to the sea and the emigrant ship.'

'Did no one fight?'

'They were starving, Kate. Dropping on their feet. The thing was, folk looked on the chief as their own.'

'Clan loyalty,' said Kate thoughtfully.

Morag nodded. 'That's it. Men would die for their chief. But these new lairds spoke no Gaelic. Even so, folk remembered the old order. There was resistance too, but it was no use. Strong young men were tied up and carted to the quay. Like cattle,' Morag stressed. 'Shipped away for good.'

'They've left their sorrow,' Kate said thoughtfully. 'A sense of loss. *Improvements*, Lady Peggy calls it. Look at the result.' Her finger followed the careful handwriting:

Melancholy indeed is the distress in these parts. Unfed wretches drop from the effects of cold and hunger, never to rise again. Yet it is necessary to exercise vigilance to the point of sternness to prevent charitably donated monies being an encouragement to idleness. Emigration of the indigent and surplus population is the best escape from their distress. So debased is the Highlander that these inhabitants of bleak wastelands are unwilling to leave their native land for the benefits of the wide spaces of Canada, or Australia, that new young nation . . .

Kate broke off. 'Aunt Morag, I'm Highland by blood, if not upbringing; this makes me so angry! *So debased is the Highlander* . . . You know, I asked Alastair if he spoke Gaelic. And he said . . .' (Kate heard his voice in her mind, wistful,

148

self-mocking, warm with pleasure at her company): ' "That *is* the language of heaven"!'

Morag laughed. 'It is indeed . . .'

'You think so too! So something must have stayed alive, some sort of pride, identity.'

Morag shook her head. 'Those are very modern words, Kate. But I'm interested to read Lady Peggy's view. As you say, she belonged to her time. Yet she wanted to help Catriona.'

'Who rewarded her with prayers and blessings! And all she could think of was a new bonnet. Look at this!'

Morag smiled at Kate's indignation and said, 'You read it, Kate. It sounds better in your voice.'

Kate looked surprised. 'Why do you say that, Aunt Morag? I could listen to you all day.' But she read:

Some new features are noted in the bonnets in Paris. The front is very open. Pinked ribbon forms a novel style of trimming. Other bonnets are ornamented with lace, confined at the sides with roses. A new bonnet is necessary, for the Queen is to visit the Highlands. Persons of the better sort are required to attend Her Majesty at every stage of the Royal Tour.

'From then on tourism took over,' Kate interrupted herself to say. 'And now you get the sort of Highland sham I've seen on sale. It's tragic! Oh, but, listen to that wind! Alastair's out in it, alone.'

Morag MacDonald looked across at her great-niece. 'He's away to that bay for your sake,' she said. 'To please you.'

'No?'

'I'm sure of it—though it's maybe not very fair of me to say so. I know Alastair Cameron well. I see his face light up when he's with you. But he'd never tell you so himself.'

You mean so much to me, he'd said. And asked for a piece of her hair.

'He knows you're fond of Mr—Ninian,' Aunt Morag went

on. 'Besides, there's too much self doubt. He wouldn't think he had anything to offer a girl like you. I'm not so sure myself,' she said softly, and then smiled. 'Never you mind me.'

'He's a very good sort of person,' Kate said slowly. 'Practical, down to earth. The more I see him, the more I realise how strong he is,' she added thoughtfully. 'A lot to give, as we were saying. It's not just his father who doesn't see it. He doesn't see it himself.'

11

The tide was far out when Alastair came to Port-na-Tuinne, the Bay of the Wave. It was almost midnight. The laird's windows were in darkness. The wind blew ragged edges of cloud back from the moon. Here and there in the far north-west bare bones of light poked through the purple-black folding of the dark.

He was more weary than he had expected, but now he settled himself to wait, as his grieving father had kept a vain vigil two decades ago.

Alone with the restless sea, Alastair churned over questions which the death of his marriage had forced him to ask. *What a farce! Dead from the beginning*, Isabel had said.

It was too easy to see himself as a victim. There had been times, living with Isabel's coldness, her constant grumbling; then alone and grieving for his Joey, when Alastair's mindset had become passive. *It's not fair*. Kate had said so herself. *Aunt Morag thinks that you suffered more than anyone*, she had said so softly. *I think so too. It wasn't fair*. Kate's love for lost causes, her passionate sense of justice: these were what Alastair's story had sparked in her, he was sure. No more. Nothing more. And that southern voice he loved, her laid-back manner, which made him feel relaxed in her company, bespoke, nonetheless, the cool superiority of the English. *She's not for you*, he told himself for the umpteenth time. And tried to pull his mind away from Kate.

But her presence would not be denied. Her voice echoed in his head. The Kate who challenged him: *Be pleased too, Alastair*. Who encouraged him: *You did the thing you thought best, there's strength in that ... You took all that blame on your shoulders ... totally unselfish ... I don't see anything phoney in you ... Your parish must miss you*, she'd said as well, and couldn't know how that remark would wound him. Earmarked him as a caring professional, and so patently untrue that he'd cringed.

Then he'd found her at the burn, absorbed, intent. And she'd said quite unself-consciously, *This is holy ground*. She'd talked about grace and being sorry. Rue... She'd talked about the old stone cross, too. *I love that Christ. I showed him to Ninian. He kissed his feet*. That had touched Alastair. Maybe helped make up for the laird's (deliberate?) remark about boring Presbyterian characteristics. *But Kate doesn't think I'm boring. That's what's so astounding. She seems to enjoy my company. Sees something in me I've never been able to believe could be there. She shares her private thoughts. She talks about praying—in that lovely fresh, unreligious way of hers*. And then had devastated him again when she'd said, *God isn't just in churches bound up in a black Bible and one's best performance, shiny shoes, Sunday best*.

If only he'd discovered that years ago! The grace that's so often given to children with their sense of justice and wonder, to the simple, to some poets, to the handicapped, to the poor. And since that talk beside the burn about grace and forgiveness, Alastair ached to understand, not the dogma he'd earned his living from, but the naked flame, the burning bush, the 'Christ-apples of grace' which Kate had found in Coroskirr.

'Out of the depths have I cried...' The long night enveloped him. A smirr of rain, gusting wind, damp, cold sand. The tide turned and flowed to the waiting shore as Alastair looked into his hollowest depths...

And found himself facing his brother. He forced himself to

hold on, to remember. Eyes which were neither blue nor brown. Greenish—like the smooth marble found only on Iona, the family used to say. A certain brightness in his manner; a gentle humour which came from their father. Alastair recalled boyhood holidays: the two of them racing barefoot over the dunes. Now he was beginning to see his brother more clearly: his high cheekbones, long face—their father's features, the features of the Gael. His hair was brown and thick like their mother's. 'Kenneth will never be bald,' she used to say.

Memories came thick and fast. Tram rides to school, racing to be first upstairs. No doors or seat for the driver who navigated in all weathers, even pea-souper fogs. Those old trams rattled through Glasgow years after most places had got rid of them, even after Kenneth—had drowned.

He recalled the quarrel, the last words which had passed between them.

Kenneth, with a sixth-year bursary to aim for, wanted to spend the summer studying, hadn't even wanted to come to Coroskirr. But his mother had said she wouldn't get a holiday otherwise. He'd brought his books, but the shore is never a place for study, and a backlog of unfinished work built up.

In addition, Margaret wanted her elder son to help Alastair with his maths: an uphill task, which usually ended in a fight. Then Alastair came with a request that they should launch the boat, and Kenneth, sitting reading in the shelter of the very rocks where Alastair now sat, gave way to resentment. 'No wonder you fail! You can't sit at your books for two minutes. Mum thinks you're the bees-knees. She'd sooner I fail my bursary than you not get your Lower Maths.'

That was so untrue that Alastair had stared at his brother in a stunned silence. Then he'd found his voice. 'You're scared. Coward! Swot!'

Anger. The wind swooping between them, snatching away Kenneth's words, the last Alastair was to hear him speak: 'You think so? You're wrong! I'll prove it to you.'

He shut his book, ran down to their canoe. Alastair waited,

certain that the rough sea would soon force him back. He saw that Kenneth had no life-jacket, and began to shout, but the wind whipped his words away. The breaking waves thundered. Kenneth's canoe was lost from sight.

Alastair had pushed out the rowing boat, a heavy old-fashioned thing which normally took two to launch. He struggled alone, chucked an extra life-jacket inside, pulled on his own. Kenneth's Latin book blew among the rocks. Margaret found it later.

Alastair stayed out on the sea for four hours, praying till he had no words left: *God, let me find him. Save him. Let him be safe. Help, help, help . . .*

But there was nothing. Only the tossing sea, the wild wind, himself, stiff and frozen. Finally he rowed home. His parents were waiting on the shore. The sea punished his bare feet as he pulled the boat in. 'Where have you been? You should never go out without telling us. Where's Kenneth?'

He searched their faces, his last hope gone. 'He hasn't come in already, then?'

'Come *in? Already?* What do you mean? We thought you were together . . .' Rather than grasp the truth they piled on their questions. 'We must get help. We'll search the sea for him.'

'I have . . .'

But they didn't want to hear.

The wind tore round him. *No*, thought Alastair, *they never wanted to hear*. Well, he could identify with denial, disbelief. He'd gone through all that when Isabel told him she wanted a separation. But she hadn't been able to leave it there. She'd been a minister's wife, after all. He had to be seen to carry the blame. The Kirk was at fault too, she'd complained: out of touch with today's world, especially with a more positive role for women. And so, although the Manse Lady had once been a person of importance, Isabel felt herself increasingly stereotyped, undervalued. *I've sacrificed my own chances of a career for you and your work . . .* Her lawyers sent a letter, blaming Alastair for neglect of his marriage, for heaping undue pressure on his wife, for mental cruelty . . .

But Kate's come to Coroskirr, hazel-eyed, curly-haired Kate, with her sorrow, her compassion. And instead of treating me like the tainted being I am, makes me feel like someone strong . . . someone with something to give . . .

He would love her for that alone, even if nothing else were possible between them.

And she kissed me in front of them all, he thought again. *After all these years . . .* A wellspring of joy was beginning to bubble, unexpected, unbidden. 'The wind blows where it will . . .' And so he had come here, to put himself where he might hear that wind of God more clearly, to open his heart, say sorry, 'wear the rue', as Kate would say, keep vigil . . .

*

The wind rattled Kate's bedroom window. She shivered, hugging the hot-water bottle Morag had insisted on filling for her. She'd been sitting up in bed, reading Ninian's papers. Her hands were cold.

Black ink told of a destitute population, drifting in droves to the shore in search of shellfish, to the hill for whatever grasses might be boiled. Wet summers and long winters had caused oats to rot, had blighted the potato crop.

Kate could imagine only too well the features of hunger: pot-bellied children with huge eyes and limbs like shrivelled sticks. The children of Gaeldom, doomed to virtual extinction. The children of Coroskirr; and among them, Catriona MacDonald's fatherless twins . . .

Could imagine Sir John Murray, the laird, riding on horseback around his estate. He carries a black book, a pen and inkpot. He is carrying out improvements, economies, the factor tells the people. This man, Lachlan McPhee, whose wife Effie has turned Catriona from the laird's house, calls at the hovels of the poor. 'The laird,' says Lachlan, choosing his words with care, 'is well skilled in the English method of agriculture, but a district like this, however well stocked with

155

sheep, is not within reach of a market. Australia,' says Lachlan. 'Gold mines. Wealth for you all.'

The poor of Coroskirr, cleared here because of the laird's improvements, have built their houses with their own hands, setting boulder beside boulder, binding turf and heather for thatch. They have not seen paved streets, hardly even a wheeled vehicle. Glasgow seems the end of the world to them. What would they be doing with Australia?

'Think of your children,' says the laird, calling the folk together. Lachlan translates. 'Heaven has bestowed these treasures on you. Would you have them starve?'

So they are doomed for eviction, for the emigrant ship. Will its wooden boards shelter them and their children from the sun of the tropics, from rain and storm? Will salt water cleanse them, quench their thirst?

Handwriting a century and a half old wearied Kate's eyes, but she kept on reading, huddling her shoulders under the bedclothes, turning to the end of Lady Peggy Murray's diary.

Heaven loads us with griefs, although we are assured that we shall never be tried above that which we are able, but that with every testing we have a sure means of escape. On his way home from Australia (whither our indigent population was lately despatched) our dearest son George was lost at sea. The *Adelaide* went down with all aboard her. Thus did our only heir yield his spirit to his Maker, leaving his desolate father to mourn the loss of his son. Sir John is inconsolable, and indeed George was a young man of the highest promise in every way, although happy now beyond our conception.

A son lost at sea. Kate thought of Donald who would be returning to his unvisited Coroskirr, thought of Alastair, standing alone in the bay whose breakers surged and broke endlessly, the Bay of the Wave, of loss. She closed the diary. Old papers were scattered about her bed. She riffled them together and a page from a lined exercise book fell out.

Written in blue ink, probably from a fountain pen, it noted simply:

The blessing said to have been sung by Catriona MacDonald of Coroskirr as she buried her child beside the ancient well at Cnoc-na-Cille, before the cottars were mustered for the emigrant ship. Translated from the oral tradition.

I leave you love of Mary mild
as she nursed her homeless child.
I leave you strength of her gentle Son
who puts peace on the sea and the storm is done.
The grace of the Triune God be ever in this place.

*

Ever in this place. Catriona had gone for ever, but she had left this blessing. A woman who had suffered poverty and shame lost her child just when she was about to be shipped away from her homeland for ever, and left words of grace and forgiveness.

Kate read those words again. So she'd buried her child beside the burn. Ninian was right. There had been a well once, where the boulders lay scattered now. The place where the Pictish princess had been baptized must never have been forgotten. The people with their strong oral tradition had retained the story. And from that source came this woman's prayer, connecting Kate so closely to the past of the land, to her own family's story. Remembering how she'd kept watch by the sea her very first evening, the compulsion she'd felt to go back to the burn today, how prayer had welled in her with the words *Lord, have mercy*, Kate found a pen, a fresh sheet of paper and wrote: 'Praying is like scattering seed in a very deep furrow. The seed may be very slow in growing. Perhaps not till many generations have passed will harvest be won from the seed which prayer and long watching have sown.'

Morag had said so too, she reminded herself: *There's many years of prayer gone into Donald's decision,* she'd told Kate that evening in that matter-of-fact way of hers. Kate turned back to re-read Catriona's blessing. And was certain Donald and her great-aunt would agree that it wasn't just chance which had led her to this prayer the very moment when Alastair was standing down at the shore, facing his past, his loss, perhaps his deepest self. And so she prayed for Alastair: '*I leave you strength of her gentle Son, who puts peace on the sea and the storm is done . . .' Alastair, made strong by self-renunciation— surely he knows the strength of the gentle Son . . . So may the storm of self-doubt die away.*

Kate switched off her light and snuggled down to sleep.

*

Jimmy finished his last quarter-bottle of whisky and turned in to sleep. Tomorrow, he thought. And that was it. He'd have to take off again, up north maybe. *It's a' right for some.* He turned in his sleeping-bag. It was terrible to think of leaving Coroskirr. The weather was wild tonight. It suited his mood.

*

Ninian heard the wind gusting through his sleep. He'd worked on *Well-Blessing* all evening. It was good, he knew, this flowing, seemingly formless form. But he needed to add something vocal. And it would have to be for Jane's voice. That was certain. He needed Jane's voice to sing *Well-Blessing.*

*

The tide foamed closer. Alastair waited, chilled and stiff. He'd faced his brother, his loss, and now he faced himself: a husband who had not kept his marriage vows; a pastor who on his own admission knew nothing of grace; a son who had brought grief to his parents; a brother like Cain. His life had been a waste, and yet in the end, thanks to Kate, he had come full circle to the bay of loss, that terrible place, where the waves were running free with the tide; and the wind which tore around him was the gale of God to set his bound soul free.

Cain. Cursed by the very earth which had drunk his brother's blood. Driven out, a fugitive for ever. 'My punishment is greater than I can bear,' he'd cried. And the Lord put a mark on the condemned man, 'lest any finding him should kill him.'

Put a mark too on his own Son. The branding of scourge and thorn and nail.

Light threaded the sky. The night was nearly done. The wellspring of hope still bubbled. Grace. Apples of grace by the flowing burn. Christ's forgiveness beside the shore. *I knew the form,* Alastair had confessed. And now the heart: *Calvary where Christ was made a curse, removes the curse at last from Cain. From every Cain. From me. Christ became curse and shame and death for me. And I am forgiven. And this is grace, healing, releasing. So I can go on now, apply to the charge, and, if they'll have me, I'll come with empty hands but a full heart—to tell the people, a fresh start is possible. The son who was lost, the feckless younger brother's come home. Forgiven . . .*

Storm clouds darkened (but could not hide) the spreading light of day. Rain drove in on a north-westerly wind. Alastair would be drenched before he'd crossed the shore. He set off nonetheless, looking at his watch when he got home. Four a.m. He'd lasted out till dawn, more or less. He lay down, his body weary, his mind alert, and longed more than anything else for his Bible, which never came on holiday with him.

His thoughts returned to his brother. Perhaps, as he was drowning, eased at length into lassitude, Kenneth had glimpsed the God he'd promised to serve. Perhaps one day they would both understand and laugh and forgive. *You're wrong. I'll prove it to you.* Kenneth's last words were no longer a taunt, a terrible judgment. Alastair could almost smile at them now. *Yes, I was wrong, Kenneth, wrong to believe myself a poor shadow of you, a person with no calling, serving out of duty, not love, the wellsprings blocked off.*

Kate had told him so. He heard her voice, full of praise for him, the man who never looked for approval. *You're entitled to your dreams,* she'd assured him. And told him in no uncertain terms to put the past behind him. *That's what I'm having to do,* she'd said. *Yes, Kate, and that's what has happened to me now. I've made my atonement, not the mockery of those ordination vows uttered with—God knows—a hollow heart, but gladly, freely, knowing myself forgiven. But, dear God, let me not make demands on her. Let me leave her free for whatever new relationship opens up for her—for you have set me free to be your son . . .*

She'd not been ashamed to weep in front of him, he recalled.

He had wept too out on the sea, those four awful hours searching for Kenneth. Then tears and prayer together had dried up inside him. Only guilt and misery had been left. It had seemed that Kenneth's life had been so wastefully wiped out, none of his early promise realised. He had not been ordained. Alastair was the one with the plastic collar. But now, at last: reconciliation. The lost son was home.

12

'It's not a nice day,' observed Morag at breakfast. 'Let's hope it clears up for Donald's visit. Did you sleep well, Kate?'

'Like a log. I've just about read all these old papers . . . You never got round to telling me what the curse against Lachlan McPhee actually was.'

'He'd have ill fortune, his house would be burned, like the homes he set fire to; and after his death his grave would be not be honoured, for the folk he evicted had no memorial stone . . .' Morag began, as though she were reciting an old tale . . . 'Now, who will this be?' she interrupted herself, as a knock came at the back door.

'I'll get it . . .' Kate opened the door.

Ninian was there, his dark hair windswept, his handsome face anxious.

'Sorry to barge in *again*. It's just . . . Is your water supply all right?'

'It's fine,' Morag turned on a tap to demonstrate. 'A wee bit peaty.'

'Don't say something else has gone wrong . . .' said Kate.

'No water. A trickle last night. Nothing this morning.'

'Oh, Ninian, you don't think . . .?'

'I just don't know any more,' he said heavily. 'I need someone who knows about plumbing.'

'Sandy McPherson,' said Morag at once. 'We all send for

Sandy whenever anything goes wrong. He stays across the headland. He knows *Seaview* well,' she added, reassuringly. 'The old lady had him across more than once. Last time it was eels in the tank.'

'Eels?' echoed Kate.

'Baby eels,' said Morag, and the tension eased on Ninian's face.

'Let's hope that's all it is!' he said.

'But you'll still need water,' said Kate.

'You're welcome to use ours. I'll look out some containers. Now, will you have tea or coffee?' asked Morag; and since nothing is settled in the Highlands without a gesture of hospitality Ninian was soon sitting the other side of the table drinking tea with Kate while Morag rummaged around for plastic containers for carrying water.

'Did you get much work done yesterday, after all the hassle?'

'I did indeed. *Well-Blessing*. It's coming together. You're quite right, Kate, there's lots of room for music—and we must add our own,' he added, speaking low.

'Fish for breakfast, everyone?' Alastair opened the back door.

Kate greeted him warmly, then turned to Ninian. 'You won't have had breakfast yet?' And she explained to Alastair. 'Ninian's got no water. Aunt Morag thinks it's eels.'

'Eels? So you'll not be wanting any more fish?' Alastair said with a smile.

'Not at all! I wouldn't say "no" to mackerel. Did you catch all these yourselves?'

'Kate's a great fisherwoman,' Alastair said warmly.

'Beginner's luck,' smiled Kate.

'They're fine big fish,' Morag put in. 'Will I grill you one, Mr—ehm, Ninian?'

'Are you sure it's no trouble?'

'Of course not! You can't cook if there's no water.'

'You've no water at all? Maybe I can take a walk over to the reservoir and see what's wrong,' offered Alastair. His eyes were on Kate. *She's in a dress today. Some sort of soft stuff. Looks lovely* . . .

'Really?' said Ninian. 'But it's terrible weather—ghastly.'

'Och, I'm used to it. It shouldn't take long—and there's plenty time before church. In fact,' Alastair added, turning to Morag, 'I've come to cadge a lift.'

'Of course,' said Morag, pushing the grill pan to and fro. 'At least, I hope so. The starter motor's playing up again. It's often slow when it's wet. I was out this morning trying it . . .'

'What a marvellous smell!' Ninian exclaimed. 'I thought the clergy were supposed to be fishers of *men* . . . Speaking of which: what's the minister like?'

'John MacFarlane's a good sound man,' said Morag. 'It's a pity he's retiring. There's not many left like him.'

Alastair laughed. 'We should have you in the General Assembly. You'd soon set the Kirk to rights.'

Morag shook her head, 'Not me! I'm a Martha, not a Phebe or a Priscilla.'

'Who are they?' asked Kate.

'New Testament women,' Alastair explained, and Ninian added, 'Helpers of St Paul.' Kate saw her aunt look at the laird in surprise which turned to pleasure at his next remark. 'The minister's invited me for lunch. I found a letter posted through the door. He'd called by yesterday afternoon. But I must have missed it in all the *stramash*.'

'Right enough, you saw the minister's car when you were up on the roof, Alastair,' said Morag, and Alastair laughed, 'I kept well out of his road.'

'Now, now,' Morag reproved him. 'That's the fish done,' she added.

'Thanks very much! Mmm! Delicious!'

'How about some more tea?' offered Kate, refilling Ninian's cup. 'Don't you like the minister then, Alastair? Tea for you?'

'Coffee, please, Kate. I'm needing some of the black stuff,' he added as she spooned coffee powder into a mug. 'Late night last night ... The minister? Och, he's okay. It's just, well, I'm on holiday.'

Kate laughed. 'So you don't want to talk shop. Here's your coffee.' *He was out in the bay,* she recalled. *There's a lightness about him. My hair ... He asked for a piece of my hair. I completely forgot ...*

'Thanks.' He took the mug from her. Their fingertips brushed.

'This is the big day,' Kate said, and explained to Ninian. 'Donald's coming. So, you're having lunch with the minister, Ninian?'

'Aye, I'll have to watch my language ...' Morag was sorting out water containers and, with the lady of the house out of earshot, Ninian said, conspiratorially behind his hand, 'Sounds like he's a real sober-sides. Lunch'll be hard work.'

'Not for you, I'm sure,' smiled Kate. 'You must wear your patchwork jacket and your belt of salmon-skin ...'

Ninian laughed. Alastair, sipping his coffee, said softly, 'Aye, that would certainly be unusual gear ...' And the composer went on, 'But, seriously, it's not me as laird I'm worried about. It's the other part.'

The other part. Ninian, all charm and petulance ... Impulsive; used to getting your own way. 'You're closer to him than me,' I said, that time by the cross. 'Closer?' you said, genuinely surprised. 'I'm too selfish, too much a sinner.' And bent your knee to the ground.

'Which part's that?' she teased, and Ninian smiled. 'The musician,' he said. 'The Kirk's not known for its kindness towards the arts—especially if the minister's a good sound man,' he added, bitterly.

But Morag was returning, arms full of assorted plastic bottles. 'Will these do? I'll just give them a wee wash out.'

And Kate was saying, 'I'd better get changed if we've to investigate drains.'

'*You* don't have to ...' Alastair and Ninian were both protesting. She laughed and said, 'I'll lend a hand, but wait till I tell you this: I found a prayer, taken down from the oral tradition, it said, definitely associated with our Catriona. Wait a minute, I'll show you.' She ran upstairs.

'She sounds excited,' said Ninian, and Morag said, 'We read those old papers till late last night. She's fairly caught up in it all.'

But she was watching Alastair, seeing how he followed Kate with his eyes, a little smile playing about his lips. Like Kate she noticed lightness in his manner.

He went over to the sink and washed up his mug. *I wonder if she remembered . . . Her hair . . . Och, it wasn't fair of me to ask . . . I won't remind her . . .*

Upstairs, Kate changed hurriedly into her tracksuit. And hunted for nail scissors. But she didn't want to do this in a rush. She stood in front of the mirror. *What a pity it's such a horrible day . . . Not the weather for grace, more for sorrow.* She took a few slow steady breaths, teasing out the ends of her hair, wanting the action itself to be a gift, a sign that she cared . . . She snipped at her hair, put two curled locks into a tissue, and laid it on the bed. *This is taking too long.* She searched for an envelope, a piece of notepaper, a pen. And wrote: '*I leave you strength of her gentle Son, who puts peace on the sea and the storm is done . . .*' *Dear Alastair, may you find peace in every storm. All my love, Kate.* She licked the flap of the envelope and tried to stick it down. The dampness which seemed to be affecting Morag's car had seeped through everything. Her tracksuit had felt clammy when she pulled it on, and the gum on the envelope had lost its stickiness. She slipped the envelope into her pocket and ran downstairs to show them all Catriona's blessing. The folded envelope rustled against the top of her thigh as she moved. She would have to wait for a chance to catch Alastair on his own.

'Here it is . . . Catriona's blessing.'

'Let me see,' said Ninian. She held the paper out to him. He glanced at it intently. 'Kate, it's beautiful! Imagine, this was among the papers and I never knew! How did I manage to miss it?' He reached up and caught hold of Kate's hand. 'Wonderful! Do you know, I think it's the very thing I'm looking for!' She felt the pressure of his encircling fingers. 'I knew you'd be pleased,' she smiled. 'You must set these words to music.'

'I must indeed! "I give you grace of Mary mild . . ." '

'But that's surely *Gradh Mhic Mhoire* . . .' said Morag.

'What, you don't mean you know the original?' Ninian exclaimed.

'Yes, yes, and I tell you who sang it to me. My grand-mother. Your great-granny, Kate. She had very little Eng-lish, and in her old age she forgot it entirely. I nursed her, you know. Wait a minute . . . Yes, that's it.' And Morag delighted and astonished Ninian by singing the original:

Gradh Mhic Mhoire a bhith leibh,
Feart Chriosda, Mic na daonndachd,
sith nà mara, ciùin an dèidh gaillinn
Gràs Dhé mar Thrì agus mar Aon
bhith mu'n tula, mu'n tàn
bhith mu'n ardraich uile.

'That's how it goes . . .'

Ninian repeated a snatch of the melody. 'I must get this. Do sing it again.'

'Yes, I'd love to hear it again too,' said Kate. 'It's a gorgeous tune, plaintive and haunting. Like Coroskirr. The loss is there, but the melody rises above it.'

'That's exactly it!' exclaimed Ninian, while Alastair, wiping grease from the grill pan with newspaper, cleared the sink—trying not to mind that Ninian and Kate were laughing into each other's eyes as their voices followed the melody.

'That's it! Wonderful, I've got it. Listen.' Ninian sang it through. 'That's the theme. And then . . .' He improvised. 'Yes, something like that.'

Kate joined in, picking up the new cadences. 'Lovely!'

'It certainly is! I can't wait to get it down.'

'You'll have your work cut out if you're going across to the

Point to get Sandy,' Morag pointed out, practical as ever.

'You keep us down to earth as always, Aunt Morag,' laughed Kate, slipping her arm round her aunt's ample waist. 'Quite right, too.'

Alastair heard Kate's laughter, saw her caress, saw Morag's face soften—and tried to give all his attention to the running tap. He helped Kate into her waterproof. They squelched over wet grass, leaning into the wind, weighed down by the water they carried. Alastair walked on his own, keeping carefully apart from Kate and Ninian. *I messed it up before. She's been hurt too. Anyway, they're obviously meant for each other. And she's not remembered*... Well, he'd prayed that he might let her be free. How churlish, then, to feel sad and sour! Alastair let the wind buffet him and tried to relive the joy he'd felt at dawn. But he was tired, unslept. His body and his spirits were low.

'The elements are not in our favour,' said Ninian, setting down his load to open the door.

'No,' Kate agreed, and turned to Alastair who was just catching up with them. 'We need a blessing, Alastair.'

'A blessing?' he queried, dashing rain out of his eyes.

'Aye,' said Ninian, standing back with Alastair to let Kate enter the house.

'A blessing from Alastair,' he repeated.

'I thought it was a plumber we were needing, not the Benediction...' Alastair began. And realized how flat and cynical he sounded. A boring Presbyterian. Especially as Kate was saying, 'Your music will be our blessing, Ninian.'

'I'm away to look at the reservoir,' Alastair said abruptly.

'I'll come too,' said Kate. 'There's another hour before we have to get ready for church. How about you, Ninian?'

He hesitated, 'I'll stay here, if you don't mind. I want to get on with this music while the melody's still fresh in my mind.'

Kate turned to Alastair, 'Well, I like Coroskirr rain. Come on!' She opened the back door.

He put his hand over hers. 'After you,' he said, holding the door for her.

So Kate's coming with me—it's too good to be true... He longed to keep holding her hand, but instead he gestured ahead of them up the hill. 'This way. It's just up the brae. Not far.'

And felt her hand on his arm as they trudged through the wet. 'Stop a moment, Alastair. Look. The sea... Port-na-Tuinne... Lashed by the wind. You were there last night? You know, Catriona's blessing—when I found it I prayed it for you. And, Alastair, the piece of hair you asked for—it's in my pocket. In an envelope. But it'll blow away in this wind.'

'We'll be more sheltered at the reservoir.'

And now he couldn't wait to get there.

'Will you know what's wrong with the water supply?' she asked as they slithered towards some stunted hawthorns and rowans, their blossom bedraggled and limp. The burn had been artificially widened here. Pipes led from this lochan, its inky black water lightly plucked by the odd gust of wind.

'It'll likely be something blocking the outlet pipe. Not very romantic,' he chuckled, straddling a square concrete structure set into the hillside.

'But very important,' she nodded. 'It's just as well we're not all dreamy composers.'

Alastair looked at her quizzically, then almost deliberately turned away to plunge his hand into the water, to grope below water for the grating which protected the opening of the pipe, pulling out weeds.

'The grating's rusted. Stuff must have got into the pipe.'

'Is this stick any use?' Kate asked.

'Thanks.' He wiped his hands on the wet grass and poked around with the stick, fishing out weeds, bits of a bird's nest, a winter's debris from the hill.

'We're getting there,' he said after a bit, straightening. He fished in a pocket for a crumpled paper tissue and rubbed his hands. The rain was almost off. They were out of the wind. Kate had pushed her hood back from her hair. Raindrops clung to her eyebrows. Her cheeks were glowing. He couldn't help himself. After all, she'd mentioned it first. 'Didn't you have something for me, Kate?' he asked.

'Of course.' She groped in her pockets. 'It's got a bit squashed. Here, Alastair.'

'So this is for me?' He held out his hand. His fingers were crinkled from the wet. Shreds of weed still clung to them. He opened the envelope carefully, held the sides apart and looked at the tissue inside. 'A wee note too,' he said, easing it out, reading it silently. Kate watched his face, remembered Aunt Morag's words last night: *He's away to that bay for your sake, to please you. But he'd never tell you so himself. He wouldn't think he had anything to offer a girl like you.*

' "May you find peace in every storm",' he murmured. ' "All my love..." And two wee curls. Thank you, Kate. More than I can say.' He pressed the envelope to his lips.

Kate watched, moved. *He's so gentle ... Why does he think he's got nothing to offer? Does he sense the contrast with Ninian, up-front, in the fast lane?*

'Today's your last day ...' she began, sadly.

He was re-sealing the envelope, taking out his wallet, tucking it away. 'To look at and treasure when prison walls crowd in.'

'Is that Joey's photograph?' He showed it to her, smiling.

'When was it taken?' That at least was neutral.

'Last Christmas,' he said, shutting the wallet, and turning back to the reservoir. He picked up the stick and poked around again, dislodging shreds of wool, small bird bones, a rabbit's jaw, thrusting his stick and his arm further up the pipe.

'This is what's done it!' he said, tugging out a large handful of sodden wool. 'And a wee dead shrew.' He held it in the palm of his hand.

Kate edged closer to look. 'Let me see.' She held out her hand. He dropped it on to her open palm. 'So small and stiff,' she said.

' "Not a sparrow falls",' he quoted. 'Or even a shrew.' He got to his feet. Kate laid the shrew on the ground. And saw Alastair looking at her with great tenderness. Gently he laid his hand on Kate's shoulder. 'Not even two wee babies?' Tears welled into her eyes. 'Nor a drowned brother,' he went on. 'Oh, Kate!'

She didn't trust herself to speak. Just looked at him looking at her.

'The nightmare's over,' he said slowly, and then smiled. 'Look, we've unblocked the reservoir. The water can flow again. And . . . for you?'

She shook her head, struggling to find her voice. 'I—don't know.' She hesitated. 'I thought so at the burn yesterday. Ninian said, "We're guarded by hilltops and islands." That made sense. Like being guarded by God. Endless mercy, flowing like burn water. I hoped you'd come so that I could tell you about it,' she added, meeting his gaze with a smile. 'I thought, *nothing's wasted, not even two little lives* . . . And everything was good. Even this morning, when Ninian and I were singing Catriona's blessing. But I'm not so sure now.'

'Are you not, Kate?' And there was so much concern in his voice, she shook her head, smiling through unshed tears.

'Perhaps . . . But you're . . . at ease . . .'

He nodded, smiling, 'Thanks to you. I'd never have gone to Port-na-Tuinne . . .'

'Let's go there now,' she interrupted. 'Oh, Alastair, let's go! The water's clear now. It's stopped raining. Ninian's busy with his music . . . There's lots of time left. Just after half-past ten,' she added, checking her watch. 'Let's go. Let's run . . .'

She started to run, the wind catching her hair, her feet slithering, righting herself, choking back her tears, laughing, and Alastair ran beside her, clutching at her when she slipped, sliding too.

'Kate, Kate,' he said breathlessly, as they slid down to the bay where the waves churned cream and muddy brown, in the upheaval of rain and wind. ' "Ninian's busy with his music." You've already told me he thinks you don't give him enough . . . Yet I see the way he looks . . . Especially when you sing together.'

'I know ... Oh, the waves, Alastair, the wild, wild waves!'

They turned towards the sea, walking over wet blown sand to the water's edge, to the foam and crash. The wind tore at them. Seagulls swooped, crying, eddying, wing feathers singing.

'Kate. I shouldn't say this. I can't keep quiet any more. Wellsprings, was it? Floodgates, more like. I love you, Kate. Oh, don't worry. I'm not going to extract any promises from you. You've given me those wee curls ...' He tapped his chest, the inner pocket which held his wallet. ' "Deep calls to deep" ... Sorry, I can't seem to stop quoting the Scriptures. Cannae talk sense,' he added, lapsing into his native Glaswegian. 'Oh, Kate, Kate.' His hand slipped under her arm. She turned to him her eyes uncertain, saw his, full of love, started to speak. Once again, as he had done last night, he laid a finger on her lips. 'It'll be love from afar, I promise you. You deserve happiness and I'm not going to be the man to keep your heart's desire from you.'

'I can believe that,' she assured him. 'It's just ...' it was she who was fumbling for words now as they walked slowly across the bay. ' "That terrible place," ' Kate quoted with a smile.

'Terrible—and beautiful,' he told her.

'You think so? You really think so? Yes, I can see you do. And your father's coming ...'

'All because of you,' he reminded her, tucking his hand under her arm. 'How is it with you and Ninian, Kate? Are you not so sure?'

And yes, she thought, *I can confide in Alastair,* but she paused, thinking his question over.

'Ninian and me? Well, yes—and,' she added, giving his arm a squeeze, 'you've a right to ask, after what you've told me. Good vibes, of course. I liked Ninian from the very first. And yet ... I'm not ready. I'm confused. I feel I need more time. But you're going so soon. Will you give me your address?'

'Sure thing!'

171

'And it was good to come here last night?' she queried, knowing the answer already.

'The lost son came home...' he said simply.

She looked puzzled, so he tried to explain: 'I was always in the shadow of my elder brother—trying to be what he might have been. You said it yourself. But now... I'm myself. I've put the past behind me, just like you said. I can face anything now—even Dad's visit,' he added with a smile as they made their way back to *Seaview* to find the water running freely.

'So it was nothing more sinister than a bit of fleece! Thanks so much, Alastair,' said Ninian, taking a break from his *Well-Blessing*. 'Can I offer coffee? Tea?'

Alastair looked at his watch. 'Thanks, Ninian, but I'd better get changed.'

'Sunday best?' asked Ninian.

'Not these days. Something a wee bit more presentable than this, though. Will you be making your own way to church?'

'Yes, I'll be going on to my luncheon date!' he said with a mock grimace. 'Coffee for you, Kate?'

'I'll need to change too. See you!'

'Cheers,' said Ninian, already turning back to his desk.

Alastair parted from Kate at her aunt's cottage. 'Thank you again,' he said, tapping his wallet. 'More than I can say.' His lips brushed her cheek; he lingered, watching her go into the house where Morag was busy with last-minute touches to the meal.

'We got the pipe unblocked,' Kate told her. 'And Alastair did tell me, Aunt Morag. He let me know what he feels.'

Morag laid down the knife she'd been using and put her hands on her niece's shoulders. 'Oh, Kate,' she said. 'And you? How do you feel about it all?'

'Confused,' she said again. 'But he's lit up. He feels that he's free at last...'

'Then I'm sure things will go well for Donald too,' said Morag, releasing Kate, who went upstairs full of unresolved feelings, to change back into the dress which had caught Alastair's attention earlier that morning.

*

Five miles along the coast, Jimmy set off in Tam's resprayed van towards Coroskirr as a single bell sounded from Achnacrois parish church tower.

13

The parish church of Achnacrois was squat and functional. Built in the 1830s, it stood on the site of a much older building. One wall had survived, its thick-set stone spanning a thousand years of Latin plainsong, Gaelic psalms, English sermons.

A rustle of waterproofs, freewill offering envelopes, sweetie papers, accompanied the arrival of the dozen or so elderly folk who braved wind and weather each week to squeeze into varnished pews, and rest cold feet on heating pipes which ran along the floor.

Kate rustled too: with polythene bags. The parish records (to be returned) and Ninian's papers, brought for safe keeping. The last page of Lady Peggy's diary recalled the scene almost a century and a half before:

It is delightful to see the whole building crowded. I humbly trust all may be granted the peace of mind that looks beyond this present vale of tears to the blessed place where sorrow shall be no more.

We are sensible we should give heartfelt thanks to Almighty God for the blessings of good health and a sound mind, and endeavour to use both as a preparation for the fullness of joy which awaits 'beyond the veil'. Dr Colquhoun comforts us with an address composed after much study at the Fount of all Wisdom, giving thanks for news of the safe arrival of an emigrant ship. Thus hath it pleased the Almighty to conduct our poorer tenantry across the swelling bosom of the ocean, while our only heir was swept untimely to a watery grave . . .

*

Rain drove against plain glass windows behind the high pulpit. Bedraggled sheep stood out on the hill.

It's such a shame, thought Kate, *that the weather had to change like this. For Alastair's last day. And Donald's return to Coroskirr.*

He was sitting in the second front pew. Kate saw him as soon as she came into the church, behind Morag and followed by Alastair.

Other people were sitting beside Donald, so they slipped into the row behind. Kate automatically eased forward to kneel, and checked. 'No room,' she whispered, wriggling back on to the pew. 'No kneelers.'

Alastair smiled and shook his head. 'Shampoo and set position only,' he whispered back. She looked mystified, until he bent against the sloping pew, sinking his head into his hands until an elder who bore a large Bible mounted the high pulpit in front of the minister in a black gown, academic hood and white preaching-bands.

Like an Old Dutch Master, Kate thought. *Piety is coloured mute, expressed by the stilling of hands, bowed heads, closed eyes.*

The minister gave out the psalm, the Old Hundred, and the congregation stood to sing. They were at, 'For why? the Lord our God is good . . .' when Ninian appeared. He came in through a side door in full view of them all: his hair was drenched, his colour heightened, rain shone on his face.

Surely he hasn't walked here? Kate wondered. He'd obviously pulled off his waterproof in the church foyer, and moved forward now, bright in his patchwork bodywarmer.

175

She saw old ladies turn their heads, saw red-faced men pause in the psalm. Ninian turned to face the pulpit and the congregation couldn't fail to catch a glimpse of his salmon-skin belt. The laird paused and bowed his wet head—was it to the minister, an apology for his lateness, or to the cross embroidered on a cloth which hung from the pulpit? Knowing Ninian, Kate suspected it was the cross... And felt annoyed. *He shouldn't have done that, it's too theatrical, out of place here,* she thought, remembering how he'd bowed to her outside the hotel, holding the car door open.

Voices buzzed above the psalm as Ninian slipped into his seat. Were folk approving the laird's deference to the minister—and, of course, that he'd come to church at all? Or were they disapproving of his outlandish clothing? Either way, Ninian had made a memorable entry into Achnacrois kirk.

Kate noticed he had no hymn book, and whispered to Alastair, 'Ninian's too late to have been given a book.' He nodded and stretched out of his pew to offer his book to Ninian. Kate held hers so that Alastair could see it too, moving closer to share. He had a good voice, she heard now, but it was Ninian's tenor which filled out the singing: 'And shall from age to a-age e-en-du-ure.'

The psalm done, they sat. The minister prayed. Kate's mind went to the meagre funds paid by this kirk for the birth of Catriona's twins. Her namesake had given thanks here for a pittance which could not sustain her. Ensconced in his high pulpit the silver-haired minister read the Scripture: 'And when the day of Pentecost was fully come... I will pour out my Spirit upon all flesh: and your sons and daughters shall prophesy, and your young men shall see visions, and your old men shall dream dreams...'

Kate glanced at Donald. His head was bent. *He probably knows all this by heart,* she thought. *And his son, too.* Alastair sat beside her, profile raised, intent.

The minister announced a hymn. The congregation rustled back to its feet. The harmonium ground into gear.

'Come down, O, Love Divine . . .'

And now Kate thought, *Christ-apples of grace, these are here too. An unseen dove hovers above Donald's bowed shoulders* . . . 'Oh, Comforter draw near . . .' *Alastair's voice is filled with feeling. Mine blends with his. The dove caresses my great-aunt's workworn hands, for a moment stilled. Its wings brush Alastair* . . . 'Let holy charity, Mine outward vesture be . . .' *I love these words, notice them in a new way today. The invisible dove passes to Ninian, offering the silence in which music dies.* ' . . . wherein the Holy Spirit makes his dwelling . . .'

*

Jimmy drove his van along the track which led past Cnoc-na-Cille. The rocks were black with the rain. Clouds hid the hilltops. The rain lashed the gully and the wind moaned through telegraph wires whose connection, Jimmy knew well, was cut.

On the shore, waves lifted, broke.

Jimmy drove round the back of *Seaview* and parked out of sight at the side of the house, half hidden beneath elders and rowans. He got out of the van and entered the house which had been his illicit home. That jotter of his, the poems, he'd missed them since he'd been forced to gather up his things watched by the laird with that right torn-faced look of his. *After you* . . . Big arse!

Muddy footprints . . . Containers of water around the sink. The laird must have been having trouble with his plumbing. *Sumdy's clogged the cludge* . . . Well, Jimmy wasn't sorry. *A' right for some, he'd told yon sair heid* . . .

Aye, for some . . . Short breeks, dreepin aff his skinny wee backside, sandshoes fastened with bits of wool: Larchgrove Remand Home with its punitive regime, a wee spell in Dr Guthrie's away in Edinburgh, Polmont Borstal—'brisk, disciplined regime'—Barlinnie, Saughton . . . He'd gone through the system, been in the care of the Scottish Home and Health Department, become a statistic to add to the five

177

thousand five hundred others in the prison population, knew the *pigs*, the *screws* . . .

Jimmy took stock of his surroundings, opening and shutting presses, drawers. Listened to the waves in the bay. Wild weather, right enough. No whisky—*bad news*. He rolled a fag and lit it, pocketing the match.

Apart from that one bad time, staying out all night, Robert had never been in any trouble. Nor had their big brother Alec, or Jean. Wee Danny was up before thae Children's Panels, the wee chancer, but he'd never been put away . . .

Jimmy sat down in an armchair, drawing on his fag, his feet up on the coffee table.

He'd been in big houses before, sliding in through windows, a deft hand at snibs, chubb locks, at spotting valuables, feeling his feet sink in soft carpets, running gloved hands over wallpaper thick as the curtains which barely concealed the windows at home. Luxury. The laird lived sparsely in comparison. But that wisnae the point . . . Jimmy tossed his fag end into the empty fireplace.

And surveyed the scene.

Pretending he was the owner, not an intruder. Like that time he'd done the library. It was after they'd taken Rab away and the Young-Young Kings had made *Eagle* their leader . . .

He'd led them through silent streets away from the docks back to the library where he used to find warmth and refuge when he'd been dogging school. They'd broken in swiftly, skilfully. Light filtered in from neon street lights and the stacked shelves loomed like coffins.

'Are you sure, Jimmy?'

And naw, he wisnae sure.

'Aye!' he said, his voice sounding like a shout in that silence.

Yelling, laughing, they set to. Books cascaded to the floor, were ripped up, trampled on. Neatly filed cards joined them. They made paper darts and flung them around like confetti, like a poor-oot at a wedding.

Jimmy went into the office, sat behind the high counter.

He played with a date stamp, kneading it on a purple ink pad, changing all the numbers. '*Youngsie, youngsie, ya b-a-a-ss!*' Jimmy yodelled the gang war cry and the six of them went wild, turning glass-topped tables over, kicking at the chairs. Someone tried to set off the fire extinguisher, but they couldn't get it to work. The next move was a fire, a real fire. They had matches. There was no shortage of paper. Then, as flames licked across the jumble of curling black pages, they fled.

Isa wasn't at home, and nor was his wee red-headed step-brother. Jimmy crawled into the bed. *They'll pit me away like ma Da.*

He was wakened by a man shaking him, yelling in foreign Glaswegian, 'Get oot! There's been nae rent paid. Get on street. Go!'

Jimmy went back to the dried-up canal beside the library. Two police cars were parked outside. He headed for the sooty, bent willow tree, but bulldozers had been busy in Jimmy's old den. A gaping hole was left, and Jimmy looked at it in sad fascination, seeing for the first time how deep the tree's roots had been.

He'd gone back home to his mother. 'Jimmy, oh, son efter a' this time! Tell me aboot it, Jimmy. I know it's no' true. Rab's bad wi' the drink, but he's no' a killer. They've put him away up north. We cannae see him, but. I cannae afford the fares. Come on ben, son, tell me how it's been.'

All Mrs McCann wanted to hear were things which would keep her unshaken in her conviction that Rab McCann had not killed a man. But Jimmy knew.

*

The minister came down from his pulpit and stood level with the congregation to preach his sermon.

'That's good,' Kate whispered to Alastair. He smiled, 'Easier on the neck.'

'More together,' she returned, and he nodded.

The minister read out his text. ' "It shall come to pass in the last days, saith God, I will pour out my Spirit upon all flesh." And where is the evidence of it in Scotland today?'

Out of the corner of her eye, Kate saw Ninian's long fingers drum against the raised edge of the pew. Was he fearing a hell-fire sermon?

'Statistics show falling rolls. Churches are closed, charges joined . . . Indeed, we might say today, as was said by Samuel Rutherford in the early years of our Presbyterian Church's life: "The wind is now in Christ's face in this land; and seeing ye are with him ye cannot expect the lee-side or the sunny side of the brae" . . .'

Kate saw Ninian drop his hands, straighten, listen with interest.

'Rutherford was not meaning the wind of the Spirit, but the wind of adversity. And yet, we are reminded here, the Spirit is poured out on all flesh. It is time for our Kirk to rediscover the vision and the dream, the companionship of Christ, who, says Rutherford, "delighteth to take up fallen bairns and mend broken brows."

'The promise is that the Father, Son and Spirit are with us in our need. Let us delight in their fellowship, which is both friendly and fearful, intimate and infinite. For as this old writer reminds us, "How little of the sea can a child carry in his hand; as little do I take away of my great sea, my boundless and running-over Christ Jesus" . . .'

*

The first blink of sun slanted through wind-driven clouds, and the waves of Coroskirr were lifted towards the light.

Jimmy lit another fag.

The day had finally come when Jimmy and his mother, a restless Danny jumping over them, sat in the crowded waiting-room of the Sheriff court. 'Wanton, violent destruction,' the Sheriff said. 'Thousands of pounds of damage.' The gang were fined, put on probation, given twenty-eight

180

days. Jimmy, with his bad record of non-attendance at school, was sent to Approved School.

He was locked in a cell below the court, sitting on a bench carved with gang slogans. There was nothing else in the cell except a cracked lavatory which could only be flushed from outside.

It had happened at last. They'd locked him up, like his father.

Now he was going to get even. Alone in the laird's front room with the sound of the sea, Jimmy uttered the old, half-forgotten cry, '*Youngsie, youngsie, ya ba-ass!*' He kicked over the coffee table, aimed a paperweight at a photograph. But here was a painting of Coroskirr. He took it down and put it out in the van. Brought in the paraffin. *Youngsie, ya bass!*

The waves of Port-na-Tuinne crashed and foamed.

*

The congregation stood for the final hymn. Morag sang alto, her voice strong and true. Ninian added an improvized harmony. 'I give thee back the life I owe, That in Thy ocean depths its flow, May richer, fuller be ...' Alastair's voice was vibrant with self-giving. *He means every word of this,* Kate thought, and felt tears come to her eyes.

The minister raised his right hand in blessing: 'May you have for your seeking three always in your company, the Father, Son and Holy Spirit ...'

Now they were crowding around the door, greeting one another, shaking hands with the minister.

Ninian greeted Kate with a kiss, Alastair with a handshake. 'Damn car—excuse me—kept cutting out. I had to abandon it on that last hill yonder.'

'Really—and walk the rest?'

He shrugged. 'I'll have to get the minister to tow me home.'

'Aye, it's too bad.' Alastair commiserated. 'Excuse me.' He hurried forward to help Donald down the church steps.

'Did you enjoy the service?' Kate asked Ninian, and

couldn't help adding, 'That was some entrance!'

He laughed. 'A bit O.T.T.. I couldn't help it. I find the Kirk terribly static. Non-participatory.'

'I know—but it means something to the people here,' she returned, a bit defensively.

'At least it wasn't hellfire and damnation,' he conceded. 'Quaint old stuff. Wonder what we'll talk about at lunch? Anyhow, I hope your day goes well. You're having the old boy over, aren't you?'

He's nice enough to remember, Kate thought, *yet he seems much more an outsider than me*.

Morag was saying to the minister. 'That's my great-niece. Iain's grand-daughter,' she added to two very elderly ladies. Kate felt glad of this local contact, making her seem part of the place, as she shook hands with John MacFarlane.

'Are you having a good holiday?'

'Oh, yes . . .'

Two banal words: nothing of sorrow and loss, nothing of her discovery of Coroskirr, past and present, nothing of blessing and grace.

'Kate . . .' Morag ushered her great-niece into conversation with the two old ladies, both sisters, of an age with her grandfather. From where she stood with them among dripping trees she could see Alastair helping Donald into the car, bending through the open door on the passenger side.

Only this morning by the bay, wet and muddy, shadows of tiredness about his eyes, he'd voiced his feelings for her. But he'd forced nothing on her, held himself in check, just as he had done in the boat, with those shining porpoises, come like a gift . . . Good memories, not given to many . . . And standing beside her in church just now, he'd sung, with total conviction, 'I dare not ask to fly from Thee . . .'

Not barren duty, any more, haunted by his brother's ghost. *The nightmare's over for me . . . I've put the past behind me, I'm myself*. A self he'd surrendered to the call of love. But now he was walking towards her as she came through the gates ahead of Morag, who'd lingered to talk to friends.

'Did you enjoy the service, Kate?'

'Very much,' she assured him. He nodded, opening the car door for her. 'I sensed you were—well, maybe *enjoying*'s not the right word. That you felt part of it. And that felt good. I've read your wee note to me again,' he added. 'Catriona's blessing, from Kate . . .'

Kate smiled up at him, easing herself in behind his father. 'How are you, today, Donald?' she asked, touching his shoulder.

He looked back. 'It's yourself, Kate! I'm fine, thank you. Looking forward to Coroskirr. And I have yon wee minding for you. The picture,' he explained. 'It's right here in this bag beside me.'

'May I see it?'

'Of course!' Donald picked it up and Alastair, leaning back in the driving-seat passed the bag back to Kate.

She pulled out a small canvas. 'Christ the crofter . . . Do you know this painting, Alastair?' She held it up for him to see. 'It may not be great art, but there's real feeling in it, as you said, Donald. Do you know, it reminds me of—what was that the minister said—"fallen bairns"?'

' "Christ delighteth to take up fallen bairns",' Donald supplied, and Alastair added, looking back at Kate, ' " . . . and mend broken brows." So you like it, Kate?'

'It's very special,' she assured him. 'It will have pride of place in my flat—except I hate to think of going back.'

Morag appeared and Kate moved up for her in the car. Alastair turned the key. The engine struggled into action, and they took the road to Coroskirr, with Donald straining forward, taking in every tussock, bend and hill, as Morag relayed all the local news, deliberately, Kate knew, keeping conversation neutral and low key.

Alastair said nothing. His hands were steady on the wheel. 'That must be Ninian's car,' Kate pointed to a car abandoned in a passing-place.

'It was nice to see him in the kirk,' said Morag. 'No one said so, but there's plenty would have mentioned it if he hadn't been. He's a good singer, they're all saying, even if his clothes are a bit fanciful...'

'*Creag na Airgit*,' said Donald. 'Goodness, they've built a deer fence right round it.

*

Jimmy recalled the fishing-rods he'd seen lying in a corner of the kitchen. *Yon poofter couldnae catch a cauld never mind a fush*. There was a cellar below the kitchen. Jimmy found his way down and looked around for the rods.

There was no sign of them, but in a far corner on a dusty shelf his torch caught a dull gleam. A bottle. He drew it out by the neck. Thick with dust. He could barely read the label. Old-fashioned print, a brand name Jimmy had never heard of. A pure malt whisky. Brilliant! He took it back up to the front room, rubbed it against his arm, uncorked it, taking a long slug straight from the bottle.

*

Alastair drove up the last steep brae, and now Coroskirr's white shore swung into view, awash in a gleam of sunlight.

'After all these years,' said Donald.

Alastair pulled into the side. 'Will we get out and look?' suggested Donald.

Alastair switched off the engine, and they stood at the edge of the road, looking over to Coroskirr, the view Morag had shown Kate on her first evening.

The wind gusted around them. Waves lifted high white crests and foamed over rocks, a wild sea.

'After all these years,' Donald repeated. 'What an old daftie! The Sgurr of Eigg, Askeval, Alleval yonder on Rhum... Coroskirr.'

Kate tucked her arm into his. 'You've made it, you see...'

He nodded. 'I've made it. Oh, but it's sad and deserted. The houses locked, no reek of peat, no smoke curling upward . . . No children.'

'But a road,' Morag put in.

'Aye, the folk are away, but there's a road. Will we get back into the car?'

'Was there really no road?' asked Kate as they clambered into the car, trying like Morag, to keep talk low-key. And saw Alastair shoot her a grateful look in the driving-mirror.

'No road at all,' said Donald. 'Everything had to be carried. Everything,' he repeated, as Alastair drove slowly down towards Morag's cottage. 'Messages from the carter's van, parcels from Canada and Australia, driftwood, peats, sick beasts—and sick folk too. Even coffins. Right across the bog, over stepping-stones, trying not to jolt the dead . . . Is that the MacDonald cottage that got burnt? Your family, Kate. It's a sorry sight.'

'Never mind. The sun's come out. Coroskirr's put on its brightest face to welcome you,' Kate said, and saw Donald's hand go up to his eyes. He turned towards Alastair. 'Will we take a turn over by, Alastair?'

'Do you feel able for Port-na-Tuinne? The wind's rough.'

'Ready and able . . . Thanks,' Donald said with a flash of humour.

'Drop me off at the house, Alastair.' Morag said, gathering up bags and waterproofs. 'There's tatties to put on, things to see to. You can take the car right over the cliff road and park behind *Seaview*. The laird's not here.'

'He wouldn't mind, anyway,' said Kate, picking up her polythene bags. 'Oh, Alastair—the parish records! I've still got them.'

'It's all right. I'll return them,' Morag said.

'You're not getting out just now, are you Kate?' asked Alastair.

'We-ell,' she hesitated.

'What's that?' asked Donald. 'Are you not coming to Port-na-Tuinne with us?'

So he'd named the place himself, and Kate heard Morag catch her breath, but all she said was, 'Of course Kate's coming with you! Give me those bags, Kate,' she added briskly. 'That's it. Now take your time over the rough ground, Donald. The dinner will be waiting for you.'

Morag got out and hurried up her front path, and as Alastair edged the car carefully along the cliff road Donald half turned round and said something which warmed Kate's heart, 'Kate, my dear, your grandfather Iain left with bitterness, but you've come back with kindness, bringing us all a blessing.'

'You can say that again!' Alastair agreed.

He parked behind *Seaview*, helped his father out. Kate took Donald's arm. 'That was a lovely thing you just said . . .' He nodded, but she heard his breath rasp. 'I hope it's not going to be too much for you . . .'

'I'm fine,' he said staunchly. But Kate motioned with her eyes to Alastair, who took his father's other arm, helping him down to the wild surge of breakers in the bay.

14

The tide was coming in. The wind hurled spray into their faces. Waves crashed into a whirlpool of foam.

They stood in silence, watching the sea. Donald struggled to find his voice. 'Kenneth loved this bay best,' he said sadly, but then he turned towards his younger son. 'Alastair, can you forgive me for what I've done?'

Kate saw Alastair's face fill with distress. 'Let's stand out of the wind,' she suggested. 'It's more sheltered among the rocks. I can see what it's like in winter,' she added, as they walked across the shore. 'Wild but wonderful.'

'Wild and wonderful,' Donald echoed Kate's words, settling himself down on one of the rocks, his eyes on the sea.

Kate perched beside him. Alastair eased himself down to a flat rock and sat hugging his knees.

'All those wasted years,' Donald said with a sigh.

'No, no...' Kate began, and Alastair, like his father looking out to sea, turned to face them. 'The other day Kate said nothing's wasted. She's right. Nothing *is* wasted,' he repeated with emphasis, and the old school teacher gave his son a searching look.

'You mean that, don't you? I was trapped in my loss... The loss of our firstborn. He had so much to give to the Lord, we thought...'

'It's all in the past,' Alastair said, but now his father voiced the thing which had been unspoken between them for so many years. 'You tried so hard to replace Kenneth. And we kept you in his shadow ...'

In spite of his vigil last night, in spite of the grace and forgiveness, the old wound reopened. And Alastair replied, dully, 'Is that so surprising? I killed my brother.'

'No, Alastair,' Kate began, putting a hand out towards him. But she bit back her words and let her hand drop to her knee. *This is for them*, she thought. *I mustn't interfere.*

Donald said, more strongly than she'd heard him speak, 'No! Don't say that. Don't ever say that. A wild sea drowned your brother, not you. The Lord took him: "The Lord giveth and the Lord taketh away." I've said it myself, for others. "He is not lost to you, who is found to Christ." But I wouldn't buy it—as they say nowadays. Then you came to visit me, Kate. What a grand talk we had! And you showed me I'd been using grief like a suit of armour.'

'Surely you're not saying it's wrong to grieve?' asked Alastair, but Kate put in, quickly, 'No, Donald's not saying that. We *must* grieve ...'

'You've shown me that so clearly,' Alastair told her with feeling.

And Donald added, speaking against the tumult of wind and sea, 'Sorrow is fruitful if we let it bring hope to others. But I was too selfish. I'm sorry ...' he glanced up at Alastair, looked away to the sea. 'All these years ...' he said, and went on, half turning towards his son. 'You didn't choose a church in the slums, so I let you think you didn't measure up to your brother. I let you think you were no good. I was so wrong.' And now he was looking Alastair full in the face. 'Let's be clear about this. Wrong,' he repeated firmly, adding with regret, 'Yours was a lonely yoke ... one you should never have shouldered.'

'Please don't, Dad. It's all in the past.'

'I didn't even teach you my native language,' Donald lamented, relapsing into self-pity.

'You taught him your love for Coroskirr,' Kate said, and

saw Alastair's face light up with gratitude. She laid her hand on Donald's arm.

'Last year... I became pregnant... And, no, I'm not married. Alastair knows...' Her hazel eyes held Donald's. 'I lost my babies,' she said simply. 'They were stillborn.' The wind ruffled her hair, billowed her floating skirt around her legs. *How lovely she is,* Alastair thought for the hundredth time. *And how she must care—to tell Dad that.*

But she was still talking. He listened, watched, saw his father fix his eyes on Kate, and there were no shutters now. Donald's face was filled with compassion as Kate went on, 'I've been wanting to tell you about my babies ever since you told me about your son.' She paused, let her hand lie on Donald's arm. 'You see, I understand how it feels too,' she said gently, 'and you know, your faith has been helping me.' She paused again and went on, speaking very slowly, her eyes on Donald's face. 'My first evening in Coroskirr, after you'd told me about your loss, I went down to the sea. I sat along the shore over there. I saw you, Alastair,' she added with a smile. He reached up and touched her hand. 'So Kate was keeping watch, and I didn't know...'

'Yes, keeping watch,' she agreed. 'So much loss. So much beauty too... But I truly felt that God was somewhere in it all.'

Donald laid his hand over hers. 'Go on, Kate.'

'You know I've been reading all the old records—parish notes, family papers and so on? Well, I think...' she broke off. 'Perhaps you won't agree. You told me you're too much a son of the Kirk to believe in Second Sight...'

'Were we not hearing from the Scriptures "your sons and your daughters shall prophesy"?' Donald said with a smile. 'Say what's on your mind, Kate.'

'It's just... well, there was so much loss, as I was saying. A whole culture... It's tragic. But if nothing's wasted perhaps those lost people, Catriona and the others who were shipped away for ever, shed their tears and left their prayers for us. So that we can find peace here in the land they loved. Do you know what I mean?' she asked, and Alastair nodded slowly. She turned to them impulsively. 'Your own loss is part of that, too, both of you. Making us strong, bringing hope . . . Did you know Catriona left a special blessing?' she asked Donald.

'*Gradh Mhic Mhoire* . . .' Alastair supplied for his father's benefit, laying his hand against his jacket pocket, a look of tenderness relaxing the tension around his mouth.

'Ah, *Gradh Mhic Mhoire*,' repeated Donald. 'It's long enough since I heard that.' And he recited:

Gradh Mhic Mhoire a bhith leibh,
Feart Chriosda, Mic na daonndachd,
sìth nà mara, ciùin an dèidh gaillinn
Gràs Dhé mar Thrì agus mar Aon
bhith mu'n tula, mu'n tàn
bhith mu'n ardraich uile.

Donald's voice died away. The waves foamed and boomed: an endless litany of loss and renewal.

And Kate said, very slowly, 'Gaelic at last . . . after all these years. A Gaelic blessing in the bay of loss.' And saw Donald's eyes fill with emotion.

'Port-na-Tuinne,' she went on. 'Do you know—Alastair kept watch here last night?'

Again that searching look. 'Did you, son? Kept watch, here?'

'It was the best thing I could have done!' Alastair said warmly. He smiled, and Kate noticed him lift his head a little, straighten his shoulders as he added firmly. ' "He mends broken brows"—as we were hearing. Thanks for coming here, today, Dad,' he said, rising to put an arm gently around his father's shoulders.

Donald seized his hand. 'Alastair, Alastair . . .' There was a wealth of meaning in those two words, thought Kate. She saw Donald struggle with his feelings, heard him say, very softly, so that she had to bend forward to hear, 'So the place of loss

190

becomes the place of hope . . .'

'I've found it so,' Alastair agreed, helping his father up. 'Now, I don't know about you—but I'm starving. Morag'll have our dinner ready . . .'

'We can come back again,' said Kate, slipping her hand under Donald's arm.

'We can indeed,' Donald agreed, allowing himself to be helped back across the bay.

*

Jimmy tilted the bottle, squinting down its length. Emptied well below the label. Whisky glow was turning to grief. *The auld man died in a pool of blood. Prison riots in Peterheid . . . never got reported on the telly like thae wans in Manchester . . . I'll show the sods. Get even fur ma auld man.* He wiped his mouth, swaying as he got to his feet. The waves of Port-na-Tuinne boomed like the surge of blood and rage inside his head.

*

'Is the laird back?—I see a green van parked on the far side of the house.' Donald's words jerked in fits and starts as the wind tore at him. Alastair paused. 'Are you all right, Dad? Would you like a wee rest? This wind is strong!'

'Blowing a gale,' Kate agreed, as they paused again for breath. 'There's Aunt Morag—out looking for us in front of her house . . . It's not far now. Just round the back of *Seaview* and we're at the car . . . When we get back you must tell me all about Kenneth,' she told Donald.

He paused, listening. 'What's that?'

They heard an engine being revved. Then the sound of tires screeching as brakes were rammed on. The driver, who'd obviously left the engine on, had jumped out in the act of driving away, and came running round the side of *Seaview* towards them, yelling above the wind, the running

191

engine, 'Fire! Get back, it's no' safe. Get back...'

Alastair tried to help his father move away from the house. 'Run for it, Kate. *Seaview*'s on fire.'

But Donald seemed rooted to the ground. 'It's the young McCann.' And he started walking towards Jimmy who still stood there, waving and calling.

'Dad—come back,' Alastair tried to stop him; Kate ran to his side.

Jimmy took a half-step towards Donald. Hesitated. Seemed to want to say something, then spun round, yelling, 'Fire! Get back! Fire.' And raced towards the van as a blast echoed around the hills.

Seabirds screamed. Shards of glass sprayed about them like a storm of arrows. Alastair caught his father in a flying tackle, bringing him to the ground. Kate had thrown herself beside him. He reached out, shielding her head. Flames roared out of shattered windows. The roof blasted right off. Flying masonry rattled like machine-gun fire. Alastair held Kate closer. Jimmy, hands clasped around his whirling head, took a running dive into the van, veered away, tugging at the wheel, scraping his van on overhanging rock as he tried to get past Morag's car, parked in the narrow driveway behind the blaze that was *Seaview*.

He'd poured paraffin over the laird's coffee table—and as the fire spread the calor gas bottle must have caught. Whisky ran like fire in his head. He'd felt cold sober for that one moment of recognition, though, as he'd spotted yon auld guy—delayed his own getaway, trying to warn him. He hardly knew what he was doing now. Muzziness thudded a dull mist across his vision. He fought himself free, revved towards the cliff road, skidded, wrenched the wheel round, birling from side to side of the narrow road with its sheer drop. Christ! He lost control, spun over the cliff edge.

The steering-wheel rammed through his gut. He was flung through the windscreen.

Glass sprayed in fountains halfway up the hillside, glinting like frost among withering primroses, unfurling ferns.

Jimmy's rucksack was hurled right down to the shore. Its contents were scattered around: a painting of Coroskirr, a tin of tobacco, roll-ups, a wallet with a wad of notes.

Seaview was an inferno. Flat on their faces on grass wet from the morning's rain, Alastair and Kate tried to edge Donald away from the heat, the roar of flames, the choking acrid smoke, the flying granite. The wind gusted the fire out towards them, singeing their hair. They crawled further down the slope.

Survival, safety . . . Kate noticed speedwells in the grass.

'We're still alive!' Her voice was shaky. 'Donald . . .?'

'Dad . . .'

Alastair bent over him.

'Is he all right?'

'Angina . . .' Alastair slid his arm under Donald and started to massage his father's chest. There was another explosion. More flames billowed out towards them. Kate dropped down, throwing her arm around Donald, and Alastair flung himself to the ground, a human shield beside his father's inert body.

'Is it safe?' He lifted his head, started kneading, one hand on top of the other, counting automatically one—and . . . Kate watched, distressed, hearing the thumping of Alastair's hands against his father's chest wall. Saw him try to tilt his head back again, pinch his nose, breathe into his blue lips, looked up to see Morag frantically stumbling over the rocks at the shore.

And now she was hurrying up over the grass towards them. 'Arrested again, likely,' she said breathlessly, dropping to her knees beside Donald. 'He's not away, is he? Pray God he's not away. What happened? That bang! I was watching for you . . . The whole house went up. I've been trying to phone. But it's no use. The line's completely dead . . . And there's been a crash, there's a van over the cliff yonder, I saw it in the bracken . . .' Morag's usually calm voice was edgy with distress, as she worked with her hands while Alastair kept on breathing steadily, strongly into Donald's mouth.

'The dosser ... it must have been him—his warped sense of revenge. But he tried to warn us, and now he's ...' Kate slewed round towards the cliffs.

Alastair paused in his breathing, passed his hand wearily over his mouth. Kate dropped to her knees beside Donald. *All our prayers, those moments together on the shore. And now this.*

'He's coming round,' she breathed.

Donald's eyelids flickered. 'Oxygen,' said Morag, working away, the heel of one hand pressured by the other on top. 'He needs oxygen.'

'A doctor ... And that dosser guy ...'

'I doubt he'll have survived,' said Morag.

'What we can do? We'll have to get to a phone. We must tell Ninian too ... What about taking the car?'

'Of course,' said Morag. 'Take it by all means.'

Kate jumped to her feet, edged around the burning house, gathering the folds of her dress about her with one hand, shielding her face with the other from the heat—to find the car a burning wreck.

Her heart sank. She had to edge back round the building, the heat, the stink, the smoke ... And bring this piece of news. 'What are we to do?'

'Take the boat,' Alastair said. He was kneeling beside his father, his arms round his shoulders. Donald had obviously responded. But he was in distress. His face was contorted, his breath rasped painfully.

'We'll carry him home, that's the first thing,' Morag said. 'I've been telling Alastair I have an old canvas bed right at the back of the hall press,' she gave instructions quickly. 'You'll need blankets. And, Kate, in my wardrobe, on the right hand side of the shelf, a polythene bag full of tights. We'll need to bind him on.'

They eased Donald on to the makeshift stretcher, binding him in place. Alastair took one end, Morag and Kate the other, and Kate marvelled at her great-aunt's strength as they began their slow progress across the grass, past the blazing house, fearful of the flames, of jolting their invalid. Then over the rough cliff road, not looking down over the edge and slowly, agonizingly slowly, back to Morag's cottage.

Clouds clung to the hills of Rhum, hilltops Donald had named. Kate remembered how he'd said, 'Everything had to be carried. Messages from the carter's van, driftwood, peats, sick beasts—sick folk too. Even coffins...' And now he would only be barely aware that they were carrying him over the rough tracks of his home.

They carried him into Morag's house, good smells of Sunday lunch wafting from the kitchen, and laid him on a settee in the front room, beside the fire; decided to try the phone again, not because they'd be more successful than Morag, but because the ebb tide of life makes for a surge of activity among the living, and they had to do something.

Kate stood by Alastair as he dialled 999. She recalled her first meeting with Donald—his room with its books and its pictures of Coroskirr. 'The sun shone into my room this afternoon,' he'd said. 'There is a hereafter, a great and splendid brightness...' And she'd warmed to him, liking his sincerity, his simple truth. *Oh, let him live! Let someone answer. Don't let Alastair have to risk going out on that wild sea!*

'Not a cheep. Completely dead,' Alastair replaced the phone.

So, where's your blessing, Catriona? It couldn't save you from the emigrant ship, couldn't bring life back to your child. We need help here; there's nothing, only silence...

'Right,' Alastair said decisively, 'the boat. It's only fifteen minutes round the headland...'

'Yes,' said Morag, 'it's the only way... And we'll need to see if there's anything we can do for that poor man over the cliff. I'll do what I can for Donald, now we've got him home...'

Alastair nodded, pulled his wallet out of the pocket of the quilted jacket Kate had worn round her shoulders her very first day, put it carefully on a shelf, Kate noticed with a pang, then ran out towards the cliff road. Kate sprinted beside him, 'Must you take the boat right out to the Point?' she panted. 'In this? It's not safe.'

'I'll be careful.'

'Let me come with you.'

He paused. Put out a restraining hand. 'I wouldn't dream of risking your life.'

'But you'd risk your own? And I'm going to have to let you go . . . Because you're right. It'd be mad for two of us to weigh down the boat. Oh Alastair, be careful, won't you?'

He bent down, started to edge one leg over the cliff. Kate tugged at his arm. 'No, Alastair. Let me. You must get help for your Dad. It's probably too late . . .' she gestured downwards. 'I'll climb down. See what's happened.'

He looked at her. 'It won't be a pretty sight—and you're not dressed for rough scrambling . . .'

'Nor are you. So much for Sunday best.' Kate said, promptly kicking off her sandals, and to his amazement, tugging her floaty dress over her head. 'Pretend I'm in a bikini,' she said, a bit embarrassed, emerging from folds of material.

'Oh, Kate, what a woman you are!' He was smiling in spite of himself. 'You'll get cut to ribbons . . . freeze.'

'I'll be all right,' she promised, shoved her dress and shoes under a rock and started to manoeuvre down the sheer slope. Loose scree scattered from under her. She clutched desperately at roots and clumps of grass, dreading the thought of what she'd find below.

He hesitated, but he had to leave her . . . He ran on down towards the sea.

Kate slithered, scraped her legs, felt sharp rock cut her bare feet. Nearly there. Glass everywhere. She had to be careful where she put fingers and toes.

And the van driver. No, he couldn't have survived. He was lying face down, his arms spreadeagled, head smashed. Blood spattered rocks and turf, seeped in pools into the boggy ground. Kate drew back, sickened; didn't attempt to touch him, turn him over, feel for his pulse. It was too obvious he was dead. She ought to cover him up, though. She should have thought about that. She'd have to go back, put on her track suit, fetch a blanket to spread over that battered body.

That much she could do. And meantime, how was Donald? *Oh God, please let him be all right*. Better go back and see. Being this far down, it would be easier to go along the shore, and from there head back up to Morag's cottage. She started to scramble down the next part of her slip-slide descent. The wind whipped her bare flesh. What would Ninian think: his house gone! There he was, lunching with the minister—and there was no way they could contact him . . . And Alastair . . . Was that an engine she could hear out at sea—already? Rocks and scrub cut off her view of the sea. Now she had boulders and rocks to edge among, hurting her feet.

It was rough going, but she made it, emerging on soft sand, the wonder of those wild waves soaking her with spray. She hugged her arms about her and ran up over the grass towards Morag's house—to see the look of astonishment on her great-aunt's face as she approached in this state of undress.

'Alastair's gone off in the boat. I climbed down the cliffs. But it was stupid, without blankets or anything. I had to take off my dress. I didn't want to tear it—or get caught. How is . . .? Is he . . .?'

'His pulse is still thready. I wish we could get the doctor to him. The first hour's vital.'

Kate nodded, put her bare arm round her aunt's shoulders. 'He's in good hands. You're wonderful, Aunt Morag.'

Morag's eyes filled with tears. She patted Kate's hand.

Kate kissed her, too strung up to say any more. She rushed upstairs for her tracksuit, trying not to make a noise as she passed the front room where Donald's life hung in the balance. She looked out of her windows at the sea. And thought she could make out a small boat tossing among the foaming white crests, the wind-whipped sea . . . *It's like a whirlpool out there. Please keep him safe* . . .

*

The boat dipped and tossed on waves which battled against him: an army of charging horses; bulls ready to toss

197

the intruder who'd strayed imprudently into this wild arena.

About two hundred and fifty yards inland three or four cottages clustered around a small jetty, a single inlet between sheer rocks. *Not far now!* Alastair thought, fighting to keep a steady path through the Atlantic's wild crescendo. Huge waves foamed ahead. The reef. He'd have to make a detour to avoid it. He set his course out towards the open sea. The wind battered against him, tugging the boat off course.

The wind—or was it currents, eddying, swirling, defying the steersman, whose knuckles were white on the rudder, whose face was tense and set.

The boat lifted high out of the water, seemed to waver in the wind, and smacked back into the sea.

He fought for control. And now ... 'God help me! The reef!'

A wave reared twenty feet above him, a huge sea monster from some long ago nightmare, come from fathomless depths to remind him of his place in the scale of things, show him his powerlessness.

A wall of water crashed about him. He was tossed like ballast out of the overturned boat. Choking, blinded and struggling, his brain replayed like a litany: 'We wrestle against principalities, against powers ...'

The current dragged him. He fought against it, blessing the life-jacket which kept him buoyant—maybe his quilted jacket helped too; but the current kept pulling him back, back into the vortex, the vicious embrace of that reef, lifting high for another onslaught. Alastair felt something smack against his head: the density of water ... Like a twig flung into a river, he was carried helpless into the undertow.

And, lungs filled to bursting with sea water, he felt himself giving in. His brain no longer functioned. Salt water bloated his gut. Deafened, choking, blinded ... *Oh, God, oh, God is this drowning? Kate, oh Kate* ... Something sharp stunned him. He was flung against the flailing propeller of the outboard. Darkness overwhelmed him. He was tossed like jetsam in the water, and now he saw nothing clearly.

Still he fought the current, the undertow, struggling to keep afloat. *Is this it, then: the sea sucking me into its hostile maw? Kenneth, is this your revenge?* The thought seemed like a blasphemy, choked him. *I couldn't save you, cut off in your young manhood . . . I deserve to die the same way . . .* But, thank God, against all the odds, he was still feeling the tide carry him forward—though his arms dragged like lead and the cold sea was taking his strength away.

*

'Will you manage back down to the poor laddie with a blanket?' Morag asked. 'I wouldn't want hoodies to get him. Or any beasts. But I had a coffee when you were at the shore. You must be hungry, Kate.'

Hungry, yes, and her mouth was dry, but worry churned at her. 'Alastair should be back. It's ages since he went.'

Morag shot a look at her, tried to cheer her up. 'He'll likely be on his way back here by road with Sandy, having phoned the doctor,' she said comfortably. 'Now, there's a good pot of lentil soup we'll soon heat up for you,' she said in the same brisk voice.

To please Aunt Morag, Kate took the soup, and it warmed and sustained her.

Then she went outside again.

White crests foamed across an angry sea. Shallow water was whipped to a sandy brown. Seaweed tangled the edges. Gulls swooped low. A small creature surfaced and dived again. Too small for a seal . . . An otter, perhaps? There was no sign of a boat. Kate tried to keep calm. She clambered down over the cliff and laid a blanket over the blood-stained, battered body covered with sand and mud, smelling of tobacco, whisky, body waste, an acrid stench of death.

She hurried back, pausing to snatch her dress and sandals from the rocks where she'd left them, to find Morag filling a hot-water bottle. 'Oh, Kate, you look shattered.'

'I'm so worried! What's taking so long? Only fifteen

minutes, he said, out to the headland, and then—all right, he had to get ashore, find a phone, make all the calls, negotiate a lift.'

'It all takes time,' her aunt agreed.

'But he should be back. I'll go out again and see.'

'I'll sit with Donald,' said Morag. Her voice shook. 'I think we're losing him.' Kate put her hand on her aunt's arm. She felt lonely, bereft. It was the nearness of death. Highland women had to be strong, she recalled, but her MacDonald tenacity seemed to have deserted her. Death . . . She barely remembered the death of her Coroskirr grandfather. Her grandmother had been cremated—a plastic ceremony, instant ritual, meaningless platitudes voiced by a clergyman hired for the occasion, and meaningless platitudes voiced by relatives whose conviviality had to be muted.

And my babies, my little daughters. Was my refusal to face death the reason why I couldn't hold you? I wish so much I'd held you!

'Kate, Kate, are you all right?'

'Just being silly.'

'No wonder—you've been through too much. The fire, that poor young man . . . Would you like to lie down?'

'Do you know, I think I'll go out to the burn. I can watch for Alastair from there.'

And she was glad to escape from the house. Was it her imagination or had the nearness of death already spread a sweetish odour from the front room where Morag was now willing Donald to stay alive?

She went to Cnoc-na-cille, to the tumbling water of the burn. Tried to calm her thoughts, remember the blessing uttered as Catriona had buried her child here. She would have had no money to buy a shroud, no spare rags, unless perhaps those linens Lady Peggy had given her. No, the bare earth would have been shroud for her starveling child—earth which a monk's unshod feet had once trodden; and Catriona would have sung her death croon, with larksong and burn song to hymn her child, her tears for prayers, her beautiful

200

blessing for a memorial.

The wind seemed to be dropping, bringing a smirr of rain. The sea was calmer. Kate's eyes scanned its grey surface. Of course he'd be safely arrived at the harbour whose cottages clung to the distant headland. She shouldn't have left the cottage, for he'd be coming back any minute now, given a lift for certain.

There'd be heavy official enquiries . . .

But now on the shoulder of Cnoc-na-cille Kate was keeping watch like generations of women before her—keeping watch for a man who had said that he loved her.

Her thoughts went back to that hostile, sandy-haired young man whom Donald had seemed to know, seemed to want to speak to. He was dead, his worldly goods scattered around him—that picture of Coroskirr, a well-worn ruck-sack—little enough to show for a life so suddenly ended.

'I'm sure he died instantly,' Morag had kept saying.

Disfigured, battered—lying there among shattered glass.

Shatter of glass: Kate couldn't know what it had meant in Jimmy's life—the sound which too often punctuated Rab's homecoming after drinking bouts. Knives or long slivers of glass had lacerated the face Jimmy bathed that last time he'd ever seen Rab before the police had come, before he'd been made gang chief . . .

Morag had wanted his body wrapped, lest hoodie crows peck it or beasts gnaw it—as they'd gnawn the heart of the man who had forced Ninian off the road, vandalized his house. Beasts of malice and envy, a paranoia which could not look beyond revenge.

Why? She recalled the poems in the exercise book. Primitive rhythms, yet a reaching out for beauty. And at the last, malicious though his attacks had been, the 'young McCann' had delayed his escape to shout a warning, had wanted to save their lives. Was he evil—or simply one of life's losers, as Ninian had said. She heard his voice in her mind, the cool hauteur: *D'you think I'm capable of this crap?* Alastair had defended her . . . Alastair. *Where was he?*

Kate listened to lamb bleat and curlew. The storm had died. From somewhere among the rocks, a cuckoo called: from time immemorial the herald of spring, mocking lovers and their vows of eternal faithfulness ...

There are apples of constancy on this hillside where that unwed mother buried her child. Where death has struck. Where two men should be returning: Ninian to find his ruined house; Alastair ... Two men with their needs are too many ...

This place of loss. The Prince so many had died for had never come back. She remembered words from Ninian's papers. Perhaps he'd used them already in his Jacobite music. 'God keep Tearlach our darling; bring Scotland her Prince. Many eyes watch for you, mourning and longing. Return and restore us, royal stag of the hilltop, king of beasts crowned with wide-spreading antlers.'

And what about the lost ones who'd sailed beyond Bernera and Barra, beyond Coll and Jura, westwards to the wastes of Canada, southwards across wide waters? Even if they had found fame or fortune, they were lost for ever to their homeland, their language was lost with them; and yet the blessing left here had never quite been forgotten. As a token that she remembered, that she would try to keep faith, Kate bent to the burn and scooped up handfuls of sweet water, rinsing palms, fingers and mouth.

The rain was beginning again in earnest. Kate turned back towards her great aunt's sad house.

*

Would he last out? Cold and weariness numbed him. The life-jacket kept him afloat. He'd kicked off his shoes, his sodden clothing dragged at him ...

About a hundred yards now, perhaps, but would he make it? The tide here, he remembered from childhood summers, ran deep, the bay shelving steeply. You'd have to be right at the edge before a grown man could find his feet.

He had to keep going, he'd got to ...

The expanse of water seemed endless. Waves broke over him. Salt water rasped like vomit in his lungs. He gagged. He was giving up, giving up. One last effort, he urged himself, but he had no strength left.

And yet he kept going. Something stronger than himself seemed to be carrying him. *The tide*, his brain told him dully. *Thank God it's still coming in.*

No, it wasn't the tide which dragged him forward, enabled him not to give in, not to let go. Willpower, perhaps, some desperate resistance to dying propelled him forward.

Or kindly unseen angels? So folk would have said long ago, telling the tale at hearthsides lit by the cruisies' glow.

Telling how a man was washed ashore, bleeding and stunned, stirring back into consciousness as he lay on wet shingle.

Telling how Sandy McPherson, setting out by chance to lift creels (quietly, for it was the Sabbath), saw the man and revived him, his wife bringing rugs to warm him little by little. And sitting him down in the house—but not too close to the fire—dressing him in Sandy's pyjamas, socks, an old sweater, wanting to call for the ambulance to cover sixty miles and then take him back over the same road for observation and treatment. You could die of exposure in that sea.

But all he could talk about was, 'An ambulance for Dad; a doctor . . . There's a young guy dead . . . The police..'

Sandy got on the phone and organized all three.

15

Kate came back from the burn to find Morag at the window, pulling the curtains shut. 'He's passed on. Donald's away.'

'Donald . . . Oh, Aunt Morag, no! And Alastair . . . He'll be devastated.'

'Aye . . . it will be a blow. His father was all he had left . . . I've washed him . . . I can't lay him out until the doctor comes. Do you want to see him, Kate?'

And no, she didn't, but felt she should. She followed Morag hesitantly into the shaded room and wondered what response to make. Did one kneel down? Say a prayer? She stood, looking at the settee with Donald lying so still. The fire glowing behind. *And I look at death a second time today. But this isn't the Donald I knew* . . . How selfish, she reproved herself, tiptoeing out into the kitchen where Aunt Morag immediately started filling the kettle.

'You must be exhausted,' Kate said. 'Let me make the tea.'

'It helps to keep busy. I'm not much good sitting around doing nothing,' Morag said, reaching for the tea caddy. 'It was peaceful,' she went on. 'He didn't suffer. I'm sure of that.'

Kate bit her lips. 'This was to have been his great day . . . Coming back to Coroskirr, to Port-na-Tuinne. That place has brought him nothing but harm. Is there a curse, do you think?'

'No, no, Kate, don't say things like that. This *is* his great day. He's home. Home to Coroskirr, after all these years. And home to his eternal rest. He was at peace. He told me so. He couldn't speak. But I knew. He'd given you something, too. A picture, wasn't it?'

'Poor Alastair,' Kate said absent-mindedly. 'I'm sorry, I was listening, but I'm so worried about him. Where can he be—and to come home and find . . . Yes, the picture . . .' And, while Morag poured the tea, Kate unwrapped paper stained with damp and age, and pulled out the painting.

'Christ the crofter,' said Morag. 'That was a treasured possession.'

'Yes,' Kate agreed. 'He met the artist in the cave, he said— his eyes were haunted with visions of hell. Donald remembered that—even after all those years. He told me how he'd chosen city streets the artist warned him never to go to . . .'

'He met Margaret there . . .' Morag reminded her.

'And barefoot street kids . . . He never forgot them, either. And now he's gone, with all his stories. A whole way of life has gone with him, a fund of knowledge too.'

Morag nodded, her face full of sorrow, her eyes looking into the past. 'Aye, he's away . . .' In the silence Kate heard her aunt's clock ticking, heard seagulls circle and cry, heard a car, men's voices, half started up. But her aunt needed to go on talking. ' . . . into the nearer Presence, looking at last upon the One you see in that picture. But what's this?'

A voice hallooed at the back door. It opened, and a man in his mid-fifties appeared. Sandy McPherson, wearing water-proofs and a woolly hat, a polythene bag stuffed with dripping clothes in one hand, ushered Alastair in—clad in a sweater, old pyjamas, a tartan blanket wrapped like a plaid about his shoulders.

Kate jumped up. Morag too. 'Alastair! How are you? What . . .'

'You capsized?' That was Morag, stating the fact calmly. But then agitation in her voice: 'You're safe, thank God you're safe . . .'

'The doctor's on his way. So are the police, and an

ambulance. Sandy's seen to it all. I'm fine. Sandy fished me out of the sea and warmed me up. How's Dad?'

'Oh, Alastair . . .'

He could see the news written in their faces . . . He sat down heavily. 'Oh . . .'

'Half an hour ago,' said Morag. 'It was very peaceful.'

Sandy bared his head. 'He was a good man . . .'

'Yes, indeed he was,' said Morag with a sigh. 'One of the best.' Silence held them for a long moment. Morag was the first to speak. 'You'll be needing tea.'

'I'll not say no,' Sandy said, sitting down.

'Nothing for me, thanks,' Alastair said. He looked drawn and shaken. 'I'd like to see Dad, be alone with him for a bit.'

'And rightly so!' Morag shepherded him formally into the front room.

'A terrible business!' said Sandy. 'We heard the explosions . . . thought they were to do with the blasting the Council are planning. You must be Morag's great-niece.'

Kate nodded, refilling Sandy's cup. 'We've been so worried . . . Do you know what happened?'

'The reef caught him . . . Seemingly he'd been in the water quite a while. I happened to go along the shore and I saw him lying. Conscious, but only just . . . The wife thought he should have an ambulance to the infirmary, but he wanted back here. Your phone's out of order, it seems,' Sandy continued. 'I'll away up the gully and look at the cables,' he added, setting down his cup.

There was a knock at the front door. Kate ran to open it, but Morag was already there. It was the doctor, and hard behind them came the minister's car. Ninian . . .

Kate ran out. 'Ninian, Ninian . . .'

The minister pulled up. Ninian wound down his window. 'What is it, Kate? Is something wrong? You're so pale.'

She burst into tears. '*Seaview*'s burnt down,' she choked. 'The dosser . . . He's dead . . . And Donald too . . .'

John MacFarlane, the minister, was leaning across, trying to catch what was going on. 'Are you going to *Seaview*?' Kate went on. 'I'll come with you... And Alastair. He almost drowned trying to get help. It's all too much,' she choked, getting into the car, and telling her story as they drove slowly on.

Smoke from *Seaview* was visible as soon as they approached Cnoc-na-Cille.

'Good God!' Ninian exclaimed.

John MacFarlane glanced round at that. 'You're in for a fearful shock,' Kate's voice shook, but then she added, 'At least all your papers are safe. You had your music in your patchwork jacket, didn't you?'

'Yes, thank God. But down there... Look. The van. Oh, my God!' Ninian tugged at the door handle. Mr MacFarlane stopped. Ninian jumped out of the car. Kate and the minister came and stood beside him, looking over the cliff road. The hills of Rhum rose against the sky, more lovely than Kate had ever seen them. Ahead were the dismal ruins of *Seaview*, the fire still smouldering, and below them—death: Jimmy's body lying under the blanket.

'A terrible sight,' the minister said slowly.

'I couldn't touch him,' said Kate. 'I just spread that blanket over him.'

'*You* did?' Ninian slipped an arm around her shoulders. 'No wonder you looked so shaken.'

Kate nodded. 'It's terrible,' she said.

'Aye... God help him,' Ninian said, making the sign of the cross over the wreckage below. '*Requiescat in pace*,' he said softly.

'Oh, Ninian...' Kate put her hand over his.

'It'll be a sad job, getting him back up the road,' John MacFarlane said. 'Bad news for his family... You've had a time of it too,' he added, turning to Kate.

She bit her lip. 'Yes. We were walking right past the house, you see, when it happened. He tried to warn us. Almost as though he wanted to come and speak to Donald. Who seemed to recognize him...' Kate stumbled out her story. 'Then everything blew up. Aunt Morag's car was gutted. So

Alastair took the boat. I climbed down the cliff...'

'Some climb!' said Ninian. 'And you in that beautiful floating dress, I recall.'

'I took it off,' she said, and had to smile at the look on his face.

'Wish I'd been there!'

'Shsh!' she whispered, half teasing, half upset by the inappropriateness of this. She turned to the minister, breaking free from Ninian's encircling arm. 'You'll be used to death, Mr MacFarlane. But, Donald. I can't believe it's happened. I was just getting to know him.'

'Aye, he was a good man,' the minister said, holding the car door open for Kate. Ninian got in too. 'You know,' he said as they drove slowly on towards *Seaview*, 'there's a terrible justice here.'

'You don't mean that poor guy deserved to be killed like that!' Kate's voice was horrified.

'No. No, not that!' But Ninian's voice was dry. 'Look, oh, look. It's all gone. There's nothing. A shell. Gutted out.'

'But you've got your music in your pocket, you said,' Kate said. And again he said, 'Thank God!'

'Aye indeed,' John MacFarlane said. 'Just think if you'd been there, Ninian. Maybe our lunch date was providential.' He laid a hand on Ninian's arm.

'Come back for some tea,' Kate said. 'I'm sure Aunt Morag will want to see you, Mr MacFarlane.'

'Thank you.' He turned the car. The hills of Rhum came back into view. Kate leant forward and touched Ninian's arm. 'Guarded by hilltops and islands, remember? The Well at the World's End...'

'I know. It's still there.'

'So what did you mean about justice?' she queried.

'A hundred and fifty years ago this place was full of smoke—and it wasn't the laird's house that was burning,' he said.

And again Kate saw Mr MacFarlane look quizzically at Ninian as he went on, 'The landlords set fire to the crofters' poor hovels. Smoked them out. Don't you think it's justice that *Seaview* should burn?'

'But you're not a harsh, repressive landlord . . .'

'I turned that guy away, mocked him too. You read his poems. I was pretty dismissive of you, then, I recall,' He glanced back at her with that ready recognition of his faults. 'You were the one who saw danger—and saw his need.'

'But what could you have done for him?' Kate asked, as they pulled up outside Morag's cottage. 'There's the police car already. Now there'll be hassle, questions. I hope Alastair's up to it . . . Thanks for the lift, Mr MacFarlane,' she added.

'Aye, indeed,' said Ninian, getting out and opening Kate's door. 'Done for him?' he repeated. 'I don't know. Given him a job. Let him stay.'

'Really, Ninian? But . . . Your music. You wanted to work, not get involved with people's problems.'

'That's just it.' His face cleared. 'You're right, Kate. I'm a musician, not a bloody philanthropist.'

She laughed in spite of herself, opened the front door. 'Come in, both of you.'

They found Morag sitting at the kitchen table with two police officers. 'Come away in. Nice of you to call, John. Have a wee seat.' She pulled a couple of chairs forward for Ninian and the minister. The sergeant shifted up to make room. 'Alastair's lying down,' Morag told Kate. 'He's exhausted. I've put a camp bed upstairs on the landing for him.'

'On the landing? Thanks, Ninian,' Kate added, sitting on the chair Ninian drew out for her. 'He could have had my room, Aunt Morag.'

'Or mine. But he wouldn't hear of it. He wanted to go back to his own house. I told him he must stay here. He needs a bit of tender loving care,' said Morag with a smile.

'He'll certainly get that . . .!' Kate said warmly, and saw Ninian flash her a look which made her colour rise, as he formally shook Morag's hand, giving her his condolences.

'Thank you,' she said, and turned to the minister. 'Now,

will we go through to see Donald?' And while she ushered John MacFarlane into the front room, there were police enquiries for Kate and Ninian... James or Jimmy McCann—Kate learnt the man's name. Seemed to have had some sort of distant connection with Coroskirr... Yes, it was probably significant that the only thing he'd actually stolen from *Seaview* was that seascape. And it was significant too, Ninian and Kate tried to stress, that malicious though McCann's attacks on Ninian had been, he had stopped to shout a warning.

'There must have been a gentler side to him,' Kate said. 'He wrote poems...' Her voice trailed away. It was plain the police officers were unconvinced.

'Our main investigation will be carried out by detectives from Glasgow. We'll take a look at your house, Mr Bruce. Will you come with us, sir?'

As Ninian and the police were leaving, Sandy looked in. 'Your wires were cut. And was I hearing that the laird's car's stranded somewhere on the road to Achnacrois? I'll stop on the road home and see if I can get it fixed. And I'll get on to the telephone people too, to sort those wires.' Morag was seeing the minister away. 'That's very good of you, Sandy,' she said. 'I'll settle with you as soon as I can.'

Sandy shook his head. 'Not at all, there's no need for that. I couldn't be leaving you stuck at such a time. Donald Cameron was a fine man. There'll be a big funeral.'

Kate stared at him. A funeral... The obsequies of death were perhaps easier to bear for someone who had not been afraid to die. But what about Jimmy McCann? Who would mourn for him?

*

Alec McCann. He was stunned when two policemen came to the door with news of his brother's death. 'Jimmy? Deid? We hevnae seen him in years. Coroskirr? Aye, we had a photograph of Coroskirr in the room at home. Our folks were

frae there, but that was way back. You could say there was a
connection, like. No, we werenae that close. I joined the
Merchant Navy cadets when I was sixteen tae get awa' frae
the gangs an' that. Jimmy wisnae sae lucky... So Jimmy's
deid? That's bad news... It's a guid thing my Ma didnae live
tae hear this. Of course we'll gie him a funeral.'

*

Soon cars began to pull up outside Morag's house as word
got round Achnacrois, and folk came to offer help and
condolences.

One of the visitors was Ninian. He came to the back door
and Kate went outside to speak to him. 'I'm leaving. Give my
condolences to your aunt again... No, I'm all right. Don't
worry.' His supple hands reached out towards her. She took
them. 'Ninian... *Seaview*—gutted. Where will you go?'

'I'm getting a lift with the police. My folks live in Argyll.
Hopefully my car will be okay, but they'll drive me there if
not. I'll spend a few days with them, recover a bit.'

'You'll need to,' Kate said with feeling.

Ninian released her hands. 'How's Alastair?'

'He's asleep. I've a feeling Aunt Morag slipped him some
sort of sedative.'

'I wouldn't put it past her,' he said, with a hint of his usual
chuckle. 'Your aunt's pretty cool.'

'She's a Coroskirr MacDonald,' Kate told him with a hint
of pride. 'Listen, those old papers. Don't go without them.'

Ninian smiled. 'Thank you for guarding them. They'd
have gone up in smoke otherwise.'

'Oh, don't,' she shuddered, hurrying in to fetch them. 'I
hope all the music writing goes well,' she said, handing him
the polythene bag. 'You say you're getting a lift with the
police?'

'Aye, they've pulled into the lay-by beside the phone
box—I mustn't keep them. So, it's goodbye?'

Kate nodded. 'Thank you for sharing the Well at the

211

World's End, Ninian. And—that thing about justice . . . That was generous.'

He tilted her chin. 'You're the generous one, Kate. "Ae fond kiss"?' he queried, and kissed her mouth gently. ' "Ho ro, my nut brown maiden . . ." ' You had quite an effect on me! But I think Alastair Cameron's stolen your heart. I can feel the electricity between you. No, don't tell me I'm mistaken! I don't wear salmon-skin round my middle for nothing!' he added, half turning away.

She laughed then. 'Dear Ninian, I hope things go well between you and Jane. I'll keep an eye out for the performance of *Sad King* . . .'

'Do—in fact, I'll send you an invite to the first performance . . .' he called. 'God bless, Kate . . .' He hurried away.

Kate watched his tall figure swing away towards the waiting police car. '*I think Alastair Cameron's stolen your heart* . . .' *Oh, Ninian, Ninian, I just don't know* . . .

She turned back into the house. Morag was busy with her visitors. Kate went upstairs. Alastair lay huddled under blankets on a rickety sort of put-u-up at the top of the stairs. Kate edged softly past him into the bathroom, emerging to see him stir, sit up.

She dropped to her knees beside him. A shaft of sunlight shone through the skylight above his bed.

'How are you? You look a lot better.'

'I feel it . . . How about you, Kate?'

'A bit shell-shocked . . . Ninian's just gone,' she blurted out. Alastair looked at her quizzically, and Kate felt her colour rise for the second time that day. 'No, I didn't mean it like that.' She stood up. 'Aunt Morag's busy with all the visitors.' Her gaze went to the sunlight which shone through the open door of her room. 'Look, the sun's out. Would you like to come into my room? It's so cramped here on the landing.'

'You're sure?'

'Of course . . .' She swept scattered clothes into a drawer, heard him go into the bathroom. She brushed her hair, remembering how she'd snipped at her curls that morning, cutting a keepsake for Alastair ... And hearing Ninian's teasing voice again: *'Alastair Cameron's stolen your heart ... I can feel the electricity between you ...'*

A tap at the open door, and Alastair stood there, smiling.

'Come in ...' Kate sat on the bed, patting the place beside her. He sat down. 'What a day!'

'You can say that again!' Kate sighed, shuddering. 'We never guessed it would turn out like this. Your poor father ...'

His hand slipped round her shoulders. His voice sounded husky. 'We were reconciled at the last. *You* gave us that ...'

She turned towards him. 'I love you, Kate,' he said.

Tears filled her eyes. 'I thought I'd lost you ...'

'I thought I'd lost you too,' he said. 'When I saw that wave—a wall of water ... I thought that was it ... I said your name in my deepest being.'

'I was praying for you ...'

She felt his hand tighten its hold. 'Your prayers saved me,' he assured her. 'I'm convinced of that. I felt strength coming I didn't know was there.'

'I'm glad, oh, Alastair ... I love you too. I didn't realize before, but now I know ...' She seized his hands, buried her face in them. He felt her kisses on his fingers, felt her tears, raised her gently, drawing her back into his arms, murmuring her name, stroking her hair.

'Can this be true?' he said, shakily.

She looked up at him, saw his eyes full of emotion. 'It is, Alastair, I'm quite sure. I love you,' she repeated, and now his lips met hers, and she offered her kisses to him. He held her close, but Kate's eyes filled with sadness. 'Your poor father ... He came back, said sorry—you've had no time to live in your new relationship ...'

He nodded. 'Perhaps it just was not to be. One grace was given, and that has to be enough. And another life was lost.'

'I know, poor Jimmy McCann. Trying to warn us ... He didn't deserve to die like that ... Do you know what Ninian said?' she confided. 'That it was justice. The lairds drove the people away, so it was only right that *Seaview* should burn. And that he should have helped Jimmy . . .'

'He's a many-facetted character, isn't he?' Alastair said thoughtfully. 'And now he's away . . .'

'His parents live in Argyll. He's going to stay with them.' Kate touched Alastair's cheek. 'He said something else too,' she said with a smile. 'He said that Alastair Cameron had stolen my heart . . .'

'Stolen your heart? Did he really say that?' He looked at her in astonishment, then he bent his head, lifted her hand to his lips. 'You've stolen his, that's for sure.'

There were voices outside. Car doors shut. Engines purred. Kate looked out to the westering sky. The last of Morag's visitors were leaving, heading back home to Achnacrois.

'My poor aunt—she'll be shattered.'

'Let's go and see her,' Alastair said, and Kate nodded, went towards the half-open door, noticed an old woollen dressing gown. She held it out for Alastair. 'Would you like this?—it's better than that blanket you had. We don't want you getting cold after your ordeal.' He took it, smiling, and followed her out of the room.

Morag looked up from her seat at the kitchen table. Unwashed cups and plates were piled around her, but for once her hands lay still, resting on the nylon overall she'd put on over her Sunday suit.

'You're up,' she said.

'Up, and rested,' Alastair smiled. 'You've been hard at it, Morag. We'll sort these for you.'

Kate, reaching across the table for the dishes, brushed her cheek against her aunt's, and Morag saw from her great-niece's eyes that loss had flowered into love: the day of sorrow had brought joy.

16

Ninian headed along the single-track road which dipped and curved around Loch Sunart. A sharp left turn would have taken him past St Fillan's overgrown isle with its ruined chapel and ancient silver bell, sweet-tongued as the sweet-tasting water of Loch Shiel, sweet too as the May sunshine which had shone for Ninian as he'd driven west three short days before.

Ninian, however, took the right fork alongside the waters of Loch Linnhe, across the ferry, running on Sundays because British Summer Time had begun and holiday traffic was beginning to flow over the empty roads of the West. Rain drove a shower of silver spears over the windscreen. He tasted the bitter juices of loss; for had he not been driven from lonely shores with wellsprings of healing, where an unvisited Christ-carving weathered on ancient stone?

Yet the man who had wished him ill had done one good thing at the last, trying to warn that old man whose talk Ninian had listened to with delight, for his voice made the simplest sentence music.

The evening sun gleamed in his driving-mirror. A rainbow arched over hillsides from which the clouds were lifting to plunge into leaden loch water.

What a day! They'd discovered Catriona's blessing. He'd walked through the rain to church, and at lunch he'd sat in the

Manse, its windows overlooking the sea, whose stormy music had surged through Ninian. He'd scribbled notes on an envelope:

Savage the wind, ravening the sea's silver weft. Shall I cast myself on your cold breast, mother of fish and seal; nourisher, destroyer of peasant and prince?

Irish monks come to the hill: their torn robes stiff with salt and sweat. They tell of an isle of holiness, Hy of Colum-cille, dove-warrior, slayer of princes, whose Christ comes like light in midwinter darkness.

For the sake of this High King of heaven shall I travel from home tonight? Instead of fame choose a cell of silence, psalms for the praises of poets; lie without covering of feather or down; leave the hearth, the high table, the smooth hands of Breeta, brightest of girls; embrace the pilgrim's white martyrdom?

Yes, there was music here; and his mind had been full of it as John MacFarlane had driven him back to Coroskirr—to discover Kate, pale, distraught, the ruins of his burnt-out home, the battered body of the man known as Jimmy McCann.

It had shaken him more than he knew. Was that why he'd taken leave of Kate, perhaps too quickly? *Another one bites the dust* ... What on earth had made him say that to her about Alastair Cameron? Was it because he'd seen Alastair look at Kate with his lean face lit with such utter devotion—devotion which Ninian knew he could never give. *You're too charitable for your own good,* he chided himself, knowing too that he'd never really stopped thinking of Jane.

His road took him through Appin country, past Castle Stalker, awash in evening sunlight, marooned on its tidal island. How gentle the countryside seemed here, after the lonely hillsides of Coroskirr! He missed those shores with their view of hilltops and islands, barren in everything but music: and music for sure he'd garnered. But he would never

216

rebuild *Seaview*. Instead, if this music did well, he'd give Coroskirr to the nation. *Too bloody charitable, as usual.* Land, like music, needs nurture; and its landlords had proved worse than Viking raiders, who'd desecrated holy places, carried away wealth and women, smoked out whole populations.

His gift would be a kind of atonement, just as he hoped absolution would flow from his music.

These thoughts eased his anguish. He pulled up outside his parents' stone villa—to be rewarded by Jane herself! She flowed from the front porch to greet him. 'How good to see you, Ninian! Don't look so surprised! I'm dog-minding for your people. They've gone off for a couple of days. By the way, a man from BBC Scotland has been trying to reach you. Sounds quite exciting. But, listen, Ninian: I want to apologize. I treated you very coolly... Your going made me realize... But let's go inside...'

She drew him in to the house. He noted the log fire his mother loved, the soft armchairs, and felt bone weary. He sank into the fireside chair and dropped his head into his hands...

*

Morag and Alastair kept vigil beside Donald's body. Morag dozed in the armchair beside the fire, her Bible sliding off her knee. Alastair sat on an upright chair, watching a second night.

'We'll have to have Psalm 121,' Morag had whispered before she'd dozed off. 'Your father loved that psalm...'

And the words, in their metrical version, sang in Alastair's tired mind. 'I to the hills will lift mine eyes, from whence doth come mine aid.' The hope of the Scottish Church breathed in those words, the faith of women and men on both sides of the religious divide, doomed for the death by drowning or for the hangman's rope—families driven into the hills, folk eking a meagre living from barren soil—for them all, that psalm pulsed with affirmation.

217

Guarded by hilltops and islands . . . guarded by God. Try as he might to focus on Scripture, his mind kept wandering to Kate. Only half daring to dream, he let his thoughts turn to marriage, living not in the old Manse at Achnacrois, rambling and full of damp, but in his own cottage in Coroskirr, modernized and extended. And then sorrow flooded him, that he could not share his dreams with the old man for whom he kept this vigil.

The Bible fell to the floor with a thump, and he jerked upright. *Must have been dozing.* His mouth felt furred, his brain seemed slow, but words came to his mind: words he himself had quoted earlier. And Kate had liked them too. 'He delighteth to take up fallen bairns and mend broken brows.' To that there was only one response, and Alastair made it, slipping to his knees on the floor. He remained there a long time, rising stiff and cramped to put on the kettle, make up the fire, and watch the first light of day dapple the sky dove grey.

*

What do the dead leave? Names in the kirkyard. Tears on the sea. Babies bequeath a drift of dreams. Emigrants: loss, a land emptied of people. And the elderly shed memories, a whirlwind of leaves, thought Kate, as she sat beside Morag in Achnacrois Parish Church for Donald Cameron's funeral. Alastair sat alone in the front row.

Ninian had sent a handsome wreath and a note of condolence to Alastair. There was a letter too for Kate: ' . . . May days in Coroskirr: a sweet interlude. You inspired new music. I'm putting the finishing touches to *Well-Blessing*, adding a new piece which came to me the day of the storm. It seems quite promising. By the way, Jane's here in Argyll. I wish you well, darling Kate. May there be doves of peace for you this season of Pentecost.'

For a moment she had thought of Ninian, his long supple fingers, his teasing eyes, salmon-skin belt. *Such good vibes, but no, we'd soon have clashed*, she told herself. *The fast lane's not for me!* Now, as a full-throated congregation out-sang the wheezy harmonium, Kate recalled Ninian's words with a smile, knowing herself to be at peace . . .

And knew that there are doves in the death of a man full of years, who, because he had taken upon himself the yoke of those who are counted as little, possessed a simplicity many who are wealthy might envy.

The minister was reading now from the high pulpit to which he had climbed in honour of the solemn occasion: 'Out of the depths have I cried to thee . . . My soul waiteth for the Lord more than they that watch for the morning.'

So Alastair had kept watch on the shore, hearing the waves of Port-na-Tuinne foam in the purple glimmer of May midnight. So, on the sea, he had cried, and felt a force beyond himself pulling him shorewards.

He had gone back to his own cottage to await the funeral. (John MacFarlane had phoned Alastair's school to ask for an extension of leave.) And during those days Kate and Alastair experienced quiet, a gentle comfort; perhaps the doves of peace which Ninian wished for her brooded upon Coroskirr this season of Pentecost.

Their peace might have been disturbed by reporters, but Morag warded off the worst of the onslaught, and, tight-lipped, gave little away. Even so the *Aberdeen Press and Journal* carried a headline:

INFERNO DESTROYS NORTH-EAST-EDUCATED COMPOSER'S HIGHLAND HIDE-OUT

Award-winning Scots composer Ninian Bruce, educated at Rothiesholm Academy and Aberdeen University, was the victim of sinister attacks by Glasgow-born James McCann, wanted in connection with the suspected murder of a security guard . . .

The coffin was carried by Alastair, Sandy MacPherson and two other men out to the graveyard, where newly-turned earth awaited the husband of Margaret and father of Kenneth, to whom Donald had at last gone home.

Later that evening, when they were at last alone, they sat quietly in Morag's living-room. Morag, who always got up early, soon went to bed, and Alastair took Kate into his arms beside the dying fire.

'I have to go tomorrow—how can I bear it?' he said.

Kate, looking at him, saw his eyes, so often wistful, lit up with the love he had denied himself the right to assert, recalled his tenderness, and felt a tugging at her heart.

'Kate,' he said. 'Will you marry me?'

And Kate answered, 'Yes.'

*

Kate and Alastair were married in October, when gales screamed around the squat stone church at Achnacrois, and high seas lashed the shore.

Kate came into the church hand-in-hand with Alastair, for a service of blessing. Ninian was there, and Jane. They sang Catriona's Coroskirr blessing together, set to Ninian's music.

But for Kate the final blessing came in a Highland hospital, with Alastair beside her, one early February day, when they watched a computer etch on a flickering screen a tiny pulsing heart-beat—the little new being their love had begun.

'It's only one,' sorrowed Kate. 'Not two, not twins ...'

And now Alastair was holding her close and she was crying, mourning her daughters who would never see waves crash over rocks or leave their footprints on Coroskirr's white sand.

'It's all right,' she said at last, leaning against him. 'I'm saying goodbye. The little baby inside me is claiming all the love I would have had for them. I've let them go.'

He pressed her hand. 'Those two wee souls! They're safe,

Kate. It's all meant something, you know.'

'I know, oh, I know.' And she drew him towards her, to touch the gentle curve of new life within her.

*

Kate's pregnancy bloomed with lengthening light, the cry of new lambs, cuckoo and curlew... At last, in a city centre hospital overlooking the River Clyde, with Alastair beside her, their daughter Catriona was born.

A month later, on a mellow autumn evening when the westering sun slanted low into the sea, Alastair arrived home from visits around his far-flung parish to find Kate nursing Catriona, the television on, and Ninian's music filling the room where an old painting of Christ the crofter hung above the stone fireplace and a coal fire burnt low.

'I've just caught a repeat performance of Ninian's Festival première. They've played *Sad King*. Now it's *Well-Blessing*. He's caught Coroskirr all right, hasn't he? Listen: there's the burn running over Cnoc-na-cille, larks and lambs, the tide bringing monks in their coracles; and now it's the sea carrying people away.'

'But it brought you to me,' said Alastair, as the music faded. He kissed her, bending over to touch their baby who lay suckled to a milky sleep.

'Let's take her out into this lovely world,' suggested Kate.

Carrying Catriona in her sling they walked along the dunes to watch the waves of Port-na-Tuinne foam and break upon a shore awash with light.

OLD PHOTOGRAPHS

Elizabeth Gibson

Christmas 1962: Bedford, Massachusetts.
Margaret with Ellie and her brother Don.
The first photograph . . .

From that moment Maggie loved him. From that moment too
she was bound to the McEnroe family:
    Ellie—beautiful, outrageous, self-destructive;
    Don—independent, stubborn, wedded to farming;
    and Julius, their lawyer father—wealthy, powerful,
    manipulative.

For Maggie, the decade of Woodstock and Vietnam marks the
start of a search for reality and the meaning of love. Only the old
photographs keep hope alive as she waits with single-minded
loyalty for the only man she will ever love.

ISBN 0 7459 1855 7

PARALLEL LIVES

Elizabeth Gibson

It was a game Clare had played all her life. *What if? What if?*

Now, in the shimmering tarmacadam heat of a midsummer afternoon, inching her red Fiat forward in the endless line of motorway traffic, she played it again. She was approaching the divide. Which way should she go? Direct to London, and risk the jam? Or peel off to Bristol?

But what if she could do both? What then?

Parallel Lives, Elizabeth Gibson's fourth novel, following her award-winning *Old Photographs*, is a deeply satisfying story of family, relationships, love . . . The fascination of this double-stranded story lies in the fact that the main character, impulsive journalist Clare Hogarth, has both her choices.

ISBN 0 7459 2243 0

A selection of top titles from LION PUBLISHING